SHOGGOTH

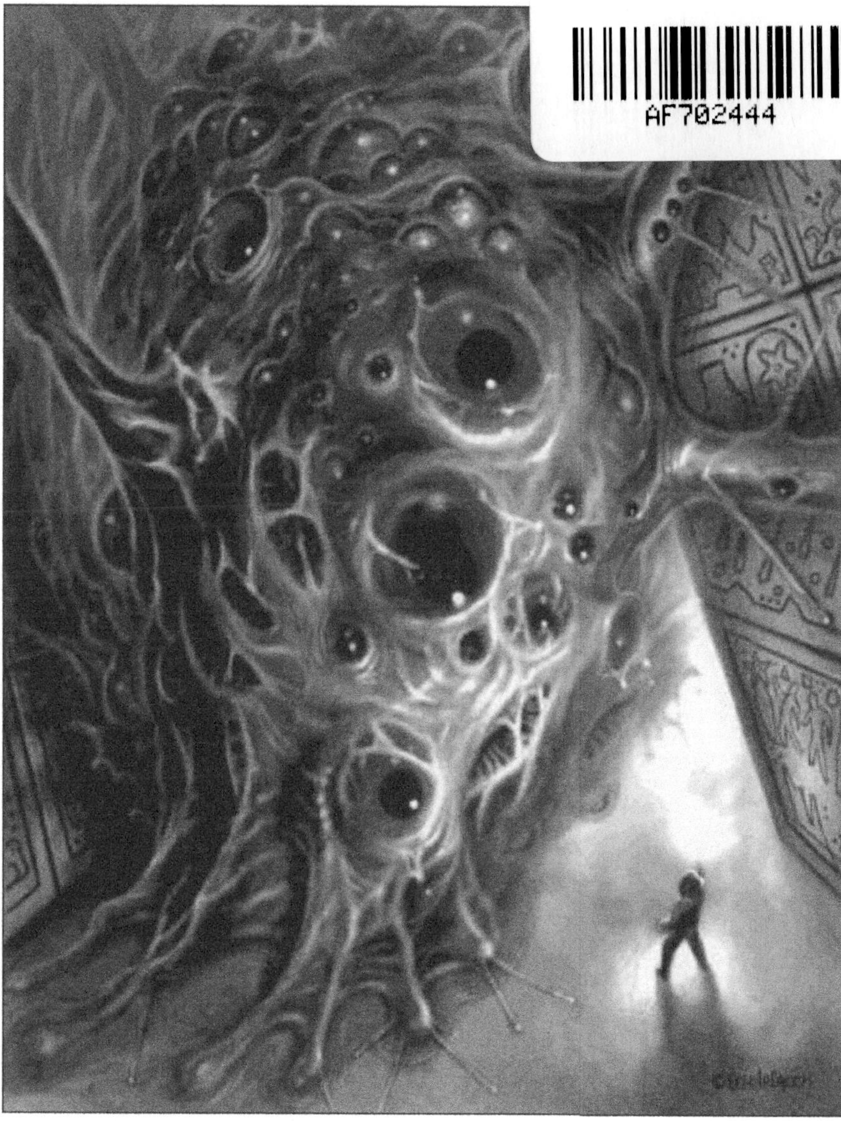

BYRON CRAFT

SHOGGOTH

This is a work of fiction. Names, characters, places, and incidents are the product of the author's imagination. Any resemblance to actual persons, living or dead, events or locales is entirely coincidental.

www.ByronCraftBooks.com

Artwork by Eric Lofgren; www.ericlofgren.net

ISBN-13: 978-1533451309
ISBN-10: 1533451303

DEDICATION

To my lovely wife, Marcia, and my devoted dog Sherlock for putting up with me during my days of seclusion while writing this book.

CHAPTERS

CHAPTER 1
CONSCRIPTION

Trihl's long green tendril inched along the shelf. The slender appendage wormed its way past stacks of bulky file drawers. After carefully selecting the correct bio-number in one stack, a stud moved, and a ready light winked. The lower lobe of Trihl's third brain projected the combination, and the fluid lock in one of the drawers gurgled briefly, raising and lowering the levels in its five chambers to their prescribed heights. Within the span of a few seconds, a shiny metal box slid out of a narrow recess, unlatched, and noiselessly swung its top open.

Trihl would have smiled if Trihl had something to smile with, but the wooden expression on the big Kroog's face was indigenous to their race. While Kroogs had an advanced level of multiple brains, colossal size and strength, unparalleled dexterity of tentacles, tendrils, and antennae, they lacked any facial muscles. Nevertheless, there was a warmth inside the huge conical body that radiated joy because Trihl was about to come full circle.

Trihl had completed the Kroog conscription that all of their species must commit to, and now the journey of millenniums lies ahead.

Excitement shot through Trihl like a bolt of electricity. It was doubly exciting because not only was Trihl now free to travel through time, visiting the lives of future ages, but Trihl's contribution to the Kroogian race had been equally as magnificent.

Trihl had spent three-fifths of a pentad developing the new life form, and Trihl knew that the outcome of this discovery would radically change the lives of all Kroogs in the galaxy; this was Trihl's conscription.

Trihl placed the fifteen sealed tubes of proto-cells in the box where they would be preserved, if need be, for centuries. If ever there was a need to call up any of these original formulas, they would be here, safe in stasis.

Enthusiastic about the adventure that lay ahead, Trihl quickly gave the locking command. The lid snapped shut from a heavy, invisible force and the stasis box slammed back into its recess. The noise echoed within the library chamber and down the granite hallway. That echo, Trihl thought, with a touch of cosmic irony, may reach farther than my travels; only time will tell.

CHAPTER 2
FEEDING TIME

Isaac looked around the damp room; it was almost time. Charlie Youngblood will be here soon. That Narraganset had an uncanny sense of time. Although he never carried a watch, he can tell you the time of day within a couple of minutes of accuracy.

Isaac was nervous. He allowed his mind to wander, anything rather than to think of feeding that thing behind the door. More and more, its ingesting of its food became repulsive to him.

He recalled when he first came to the area. The desolation was unbearable. It still was. It took almost eleven months to travel the distance by wagon train, and he had nearly died that first year of influenza. Another year followed in which they located tunnels, and he could build his house over the site.

Isaac's eyes followed the hieroglyphics along the curved walls of the subterranean room. And here I have been these past seven years; he brooded, painfully deciphering the history of a lost age.

Isaac forced his attention to a ledger on the writing desk, dipping a feather-quill pen in an ink well; he made an entry on page fifty-seven. Printed across the top of the page in bold letters was the word

LIVESTOCK. Below, written in longhand, were the words: 6 cows, 2 sheep. Below this, Isaac wrote, "the amount of food needed increases with each feeding."

It would not be so bad if it ate like any one of God's creatures, but it did not. It—absorbed its food, he decided. It drank its painfully mewling prey slowly, savoring each moment of the animal's agony.

Isaac was sure the thing savored its food. He had a sickening feeling in his stomach. He always felt that way when it neared feeding time. Isaac remembered when they first started to feed it. It was small then.

Isaac used to observe the terrible process with a mixture of horror and scientific curiosity. Then it started to grow, it got bigger, and its needs grew along with it. It would only feed on living things; nothing else would satisfy its lust. Small game was enough at first; jackrabbits, squirrels, prairie dogs, even lizards, and mice. It did not discriminate as long as its dinner was alive.

Soon its needs outgrew prairie dogs and mice. It ate much larger animals now, mainly cattle and sheep, occasionally an old Mustang if one could be caught, and on one occasion, a pig. Isaac cursed God for that day. The agonized ululations emanating from that pig were blood curdling and unforgettable.

He had bought it that morning from a Yuma Indian on the outskirts of Darwin. He had paid an exorbitant price for the two-hundred-fifty-pound sow, but livestock was scarce that spring. The previous year's early and harsh winter had delayed the cattle drives from west Texas and New Mexico, and the surrounding desert offered very little. He could have purchased a dairy cow from one of the locals, but they were beginning to get suspicious.

Charlie Youngblood had told Isaac that he had heard talk in Darwin centering on the abnormal amounts of livestock they required for a household that consisted of only Isaac and two servants. The last thing Isaac needed was a group of superstitious and excitable townspeople bursting in on his studies.

He had done his best to keep a low profile, staying at home as much as possible, only venturing out when it was necessary. When he did go into town, he was always cordial to everyone he met but never lingered. If asked, he said he was an archeologist studying the Indian artifacts and petroglyphs found in and around the Coso Range.

He had also done his best to keep the noise down when it was hungry. At these times, they would blanket the door to the tunnel with bags filled with sand to muffle the sounds it made, followed by a careful search above ground for any fissures or old volcanic vents that may have opened on the desert floor with the shifting of sand. If opened into one of the tunnels below, a vent could allow the noise to be heard for miles.

He was afraid that they would be discovered when the pig started to squeal; that was, he recalled with a shudder, the worst day of his life. The poor animal uttered a sharp, shrill, prolonged cry when the thing latched on to it. The sow did not see the creature at first. It grabbed the pig from behind and pulled her squealing and screaming into its jelly-like mass. The beast made sucking, slurping sounds. It was quick, deadly quick. The sow was stuck fast, rooted in the flesh of the thing.

Inside the dark, gelatinous layers of flesh, Isaac noticed something glowing with golden light, and parts of the thing briefly became translucent. He had seen this before when it fed. It would happen to lesser or greater degrees depending on the size of the animal it was devouring. He wondered if it was the spark of life that ignited that golden light. Perhaps the spirit of the animal it absorbed?

The female pig was still conscious after several minutes. Her squealing rose in volume until it became an ear-splitting shriek. The creature held the tortured animal off the floor of the cave. The sow's legs kicked, her body wriggled, and squirmed, only to be drawn deeper into the thing.

Isaac had never been more repulsed at feeding time than he was at that moment. For the first time, he questioned the morality of his studies. It was worse than being in a slaughterhouse. His stomach knotted, and his skin crawled in tight folds along the back of his neck.

Within the dark, cavernous vault, the torturous murder of this poor, dumb animal seemed to Isaac, the work of the devil. The deadliest of sins, a sacrifice made deep in the bowels of hell.

Isaac abruptly turned from the squealing horror and ordered Charlie and his brother, John, to stop it.

"Stop it," he shouted. "Kill it now!"

Charlie and his brother, mesmerized by the spectacle, jumped when Isaac issued the command. Charlie was the first to regain his composure.

Stepping forward, he dutifully cocked the hammer on his Springfield. John Youngblood was close behind, imitating his brother. The sound of the two muzzleloaders firing was deafening, but not as ear-splitting, thought Isaac, as the cries of that sow. The small section of the tunnel filled with smoke and the smell of burnt sulfur.

Isaac saw the lead balls from the two Springfield rifles strike the gelatin side of the thing. It reminded him of stones hitting the surface of water. The two projectiles penetrated its flesh, causing mild turbulences within, a rippling effect.

The creature, unaffected by the two bullet wounds, continued with its feeding. Isaac watched helplessly as the sow, already three-quarters enveloped in a gooey slime, strained her vocal cords to their limits. He saw the flesh on her back and one side slowly blister, then melt.

The pig's prolonged cry faltered and broke into a shrill staccato echoing off the tunnel walls like maniacal laughter.

Isaac stepped forward and moved to draw his pistol. It kept screaming, he thought; it no longer sounded like the squeal of a tortured animal; it was more human. The sow looked past Isaac with eyes that gazed into another world.

He meant to put the poor creature out of its misery, but he stopped before he had his gun half drawn from his belt. He knew what the outcome would be. It would be simple to put a musket ball in the sow's head, silencing her forever, but then they would have to cope with "it." He was confident that if he had killed the sow, the creature would have nothing to do with her. It only fed on living things. Then, they would be plagued by its cries of hunger again.

Aching inside, Isaac realized that the cries of the tortured sow, no matter how heart-wrenching and murderous they were, were not as bad as the shrieks of hunger from this creature of the tunnels.

As if in answer to Isaac's decision to do nothing, the pig gagged suddenly, followed by a rattling in her throat and the tunnel gave way to an eerie silence. The sow's eyes were glassy. Blood and white foam oozed from her snout. Her sides heaved in and out with the force of labored breathing. Respiration is still functioning, as always, he reminded himself. She was still alive, just unconscious. He was familiar with the entire grotesque procedure by then. She'll stay that way for weeks while it draws on her, feeds on her, until there is nothing left but a dried-out husk.

Isaac remembered the sickening details that followed with painful clarity. He ran from the tunnel's end to his house above, staggered through the parlor, out the front door, and into the desert. The sizzling heat of mid-day slapped his face. Isaac's knees gave out, and he fell, face forward, into the sand only a few steps from his front porch; raising himself to his knees, he began to vomit. He kept vomiting until his sides hurt, and there was nothing left in him but air.

The memory of that afternoon always haunted him when it neared feeding time. He was glad that the creature only craved sustenance every three or four weeks. If he had to provide for it daily, he would have gone mad a long time ago. Isaac leaned back in his chair and rubbed his eyes with closed fists. He was pale, and there were dark circles under his eyes. Isaac hadn't washed his black, scraggly beard and hair in weeks. He had increased his study schedule, continually working during the day and through most of the night, only breaking from the routine for a late supper. After eating, he would crawl, exhausted, to a cot he kept alongside his writing desk where he would sleep until a little before dawn when Charlie Youngblood would come and wake him, and the process would begin all over again.

After years of research, he began to decipher the hieroglyphics that adorned the circular room's walls. They had also discovered what he had guessed to be a library of records consisting of over a thousand scrolls.

The scrolls were of a thin and surprisingly flexible metallic substance. They had discovered them in an adjoining tunnel only a month after they had uncovered the underground passage. The scrolls yielded the same strange writing.

Bit by bit, he had unlocked pieces of the past, unfurling the history of a forgotten age. Isaac learned some things about a once-great race, something about their accomplishments, things about their dreams, while the creature of the tunnels remained a mystery.

He was confident that he had discovered its origin. But, what it was and what purpose it served in the ecological scheme of that ancient civilization had yet to be answered.

The creature had grown considerably since that afternoon when they had fed it the sow, and it started to change its shape. It was becoming elongated, and it looked as if it was growing a flattened head or face at one end. The results, although repulsive and alien, were somehow familiar to Isaac.

What it reminded him of, he could not recall. However, as he witnessed its daily growth and change, something knocked and clawed at his subconscious with frightening familiarity.

That was why he had stepped up his research. His desire to leave was greater than ever. Although he had no idea what the result of the creature's change might be, he felt more comfortable learning about it from his translations rather than witnessing the metamorphosis.

If he pushed himself, he would have the answers he needed to this age-old puzzle before the next feeding interval. A few weeks, he hoped. No more than a month. Just this one last time, just enough to quiet it so he would not have to listen to its constant wailing. Just long enough to keep his sanity intact and his will alive so he could gather up the evidence he had accumulated over the years and deliver it to those on the East Coast who once scoffed at his theory.

Isaac signed and dated the bottom page of the ledger. The feather-quill pen made a scratching noise across the paper. He heard footsteps approaching and looked up.

Charlie Youngblood stood quietly in front of the desk. His white cotton shirt looking yellow from the pale cast of his lantern. A long, thin scar down the left side of his face combined with the red bandanna wrapped tightly across the top of his skull gave him a menacing appearance.

"Is it time?" Isaac asked in a solemn tone.

Charlie nodded, and Isaac stood up, closing the ledger. Grabbing a lamp off the desk, he followed the Indian servant out of the room through a maze of connecting tunnels.

How many times, he wondered, have I walked these passages over the years? Looking up, Isaac noticed, for what he guessed to be at least the hundredth time, the shattered and mangled remains of chandeliers. The branch supports, spaced at even intervals, hung from the tunnel ceiling. Every tunnel they had explored in the past seven years had these fixtures hanging from above. All were severely damaged.

Charlie's brother, John, toward the end of their sixth year, had found one in which half of the lamp's mechanism was still intact. After careful examination, Isaac could not detect anywhere within the broken shell that could have contained a wick or lamp oil. Nor could he find anything that resembled the standard valve and piping familiar with gaslighting. The one thing he found were fragments of what appeared to be fine brown colored wires.

Isaac had read about experiments conducted in New Jersey with electricity. Maybe these ancient lamps, he theorized, had once been fired by electricity. But, when magnified, they turned out to be thin, hollow tubing, not wires at all. Like the creature of the tunnels, the chandeliers would have to remain a mystery unless a solution could be found in the hieroglyphics.

After crossing an immense cavern, they rounded a corner into a narrow passage. The tunnel was abruptly terminated about thirty feet in where a wooden door stood like a giant sentinel.

The tunnel, like all the other arteries Isaac, Charlie, and John had explored over the years, had at one time, opened into the immense cavern. Isaac, Charlie, and John had also constructed the door out of yellow pine timbers, one-foot-thick, using cast iron pegs and strapping to tie all the pieces together into one solid barrier. Building a frame for the door and making it fit the tunnel's unusual shape was a more significant task than making the door. Isaac knew that the door, no matter how solid they built it, would only be as strong as the frame that held it. He had Charlie and John fasten timbers the size of railroad ties into the tunnel walls and ceiling by driving heavy wrought iron rods through them into the surrounding masonry and deep into the outer bedrock.

Only when the door was secured on the frame could Isaac, Charlie, and John sleep easy again. All three of them had been uneasy about the creature since they had first discovered it. With it successfully contained in a tunnel section, Isaac felt confident that it was no longer a threat. In those early days, he felt exhilarated about their captive, a survivor from untold ages. A specimen he could safely study and learn from while he deciphered its origin and the tunnel builders' history.

But it was so much smaller then. The three would not have recognized the danger it presented if they had not wandered upon it while it was feeding. It was their first encounter with the creature. The color of bone marrow and no bigger than a prairie dog, it had wrapped itself around a sand lizard.

The two Indians and Isaac gaped in astonishment as it surmounted and then engulfed its prey with its ooze. The lizard, every bit alive, wriggled and kicked while its outer hide slowly melted. In a final attempt to protect itself, the lizard curled into a ball resembling a grotesque parody of a fetus in the womb.

They trapped the thing in a packing crate, and later, as its appetite increased, along with its size, the Youngbloods built a larger box to contain it.

Less than one year later, when the box was no longer large enough to their amazement, they closed up a section of the tunnel with the massive door imprisoning the creature in an unexplored subterranean region.

Many an evening before retiring to bed, Isaac would go into the tunnel and stand at its prison door to listen through the latch hole. During its off days of feeding, the creature's furtive movements were always the same monotonous route traveling back and forth from its imprisoned end of the tunnel to an unknown location, never varying morning, noon or night.

This mystery of the tunnels continued its trek. Rather than searching for something, the creature's movements seemed predetermined as if meant to follow an ancient pattern.

Isaac no longer witnessed its feedings since the afternoon of the sow. It was no longer necessary to observe the process. It never varied its habit; only its appetite increased, so he just looked on while Charlie and John led an old dairy cow through the opened door. Her productive days of milk giving long passed, the tired Guernsey coaxed easily. They could have prodded her to go in by herself, but the Youngbloods preferred to watch.

Isaac never asked them why. He assumed that they derived some grotesque pleasure seeing it devour its prey. Isaac suspected that the pair thought less of him for staying behind. He was also sure that the old dairy cow would not be enough to quiet the thing. Tomorrow they would have to feed it a goat or maybe even another cow, anything to satisfy its hunger.

Isaac held the massive door open with his right hand and hefted his revolver's weight in his left. He knew it was useless against the thing. Still, it gave him comfort to have it nearby. He took great care in maintaining the weapon, keeping it cleaned and well oiled. An old prospector had taught him how to keep the black powder in the gun dry by sealing the openings of all six cylinders with small amounts of paraffin wax. It prevented the dampness of the tunnels from penetrating the gun's chambers and spoiling the powder. When fired, the wax would blow out of the barrel of the six-shooter ahead of the bullet.

Isaac had applied the same principle in constructing a bomb. It was his safety device. Long after they walled up, the creature in its prison, Isaac became uneasy about its increasing size. Worried that someday the door may not hold it, he planted an explosive charge above the door frame sufficient to bring the entire ceiling down, collapsing the one artery with tons of rock and earth from the desert floor above.

Knowing that dynamite is seventy-five percent nitroglycerin and that nitro becomes unstable with age, he had fashioned the bomb out of ten pounds of black powder compacted into an old meat tin. After wrapping the whole thing tightly with piano wire, he encased the metal tin, along with a detonator, in a block of paraffin several inches thick. The detonator's wires were strung along the ceiling beyond the tunnel, opening to a small niche in the main cavern. From there, he had attached the two wires to the screw terminals of a static generator.

If the creature of the tunnels did break out of its prison, one quick shove on the handle would generate enough electrical current across the wire to detonate the blasting cap embedded in the paraffin wax.

Once they were inside, Isaac closed the door on the two Narraganset Indians. The bar lock automatically fell into place. With his back up against the door, Isaac released a long, slow breath of air. The locking bar was cast iron, two inches thick. It made him nervous when the door was unlatched and open; but, it was secure now.

Shaking, he sucked in a deep breath of musty tunnel air. Through the cracks between the thick yellow pine planking, he could hear the deep bellowing of the old dairy cow. Then, unexpectedly, the mooing stopped. The Guernsey was quiet. Isaac listened to the hurried scuffing of feet on gravel approaching, coming closer. It was Charlie and John running back to the door.

Charlie yelled at him to open up. Close behind came the eerie cry of the creature cutting through the tunnel barriers penetrating Isaac to the bone with fear. The door resounded with the vibrations of heavy pounding on the other side.

Isaac flung himself away from the door and stood there staring at the latch, frozen in panic. Charlie's brother's voice rose to a shrill scream.

"It's coming! Open the door."

Something went wrong, thought Isaac, managing to get his mind working again. The creature hungered for Charlie and John.

Then madness trickled in, and he started to giggle. All he needed was another month, maybe less. Charlie and John may be enough to keep it quiet.

Charlie and John can be its food.

The sound of two rifle reports from within the creature's prison snapped Isaac back to his senses.

"No," he cried, "I can't do this; they have been with me for over seven years." The pounding stopped, and there was no more gunfire. Isaac could hear another brief shuffling of shoe leather on the gravel, then silence.

That is a good sign, he thought, as he swung the latch bar up and unlocked the door. If it had gotten Charlie and John, it would not be a peaceful death; it would be agonizingly long like the sows. There would have been a lot of noise.

The door felt heavier than he had remembered. The iron hinges groaned and complained as he slowly pulled it open. There was a faint flicker of lamplight on the other side, but Charlie and John were not there. The tunnel was still. A voice screamed inside his head to close the door, run, but he stood fast. His hands started to tremble, and the muscles in his arms began twitching, followed by weakness in his legs.

He knew he should run, but Isaac had to see, he had to know if Charlie and John were alive. He had to see if there was still a chance. He owed them that much.

Forcing himself to take the first step, he wrenched his right leg free of the fear that held him back and entered the creature's prison. He was only three steps in when he found Charlie and John.

At first, he didn't realize what he saw. It was almost comical, reminding him of the silly antics of two comedians he had once seen in a music hall. He laughed out loud. He knew he must be going mad. And then the gruesome horror of the spectacle fell in on him. All he could make out of Charlie and John were their blue dungarees flailing and kicking.

From the tops of their heads to about the waistlines, the two brothers' front halves were embedded in the thing's body. It was as if something had plunged the upper halves of their bodies into the jelly acid slime. Rising above them, extended portions of the creature's body reared up, resembling snakes ready to strike.

When one of the snakes turned in Isaac's direction, he noticed a dark opening on its end where ahead should be. It was hollow. It no longer reminded him of a snake. Instead, it looked like an elephant's trunk. From the dark opening, he heard the noise of garbled breathing.

My God, he realized, it was a breathing tube. The creature killed with an intelligence Isaac never dreamed it had.

Looking around the section of the tunnel, Isaac could quickly surmise what had happened. The dead carcass of the old dairy cow had been cast aside, a piece of spoiled meat. The two spent muskets were lying at the threshold of the door, and the lamp had been carefully set down on the gravel, not dropped.

The dairy cow had died, but not from any slow torment inflicted by the creature. Its old heart probably gave out when the thing latched on to it, and, of course, the beast of the tunnels only fed on living things.

Disappointed and hungry, it turned on its keepers. That was when he heard the gunshots. One of the brothers, Isaac guessed it was probably Charlie, the eldest, realizing his fate when Isaac hadn't opened the door and remembering the sow, intended to make his death as quick and as painless as possible. As if going for a dip at a local swimming hole, Charlie dived headfirst into the creature, hoping to drown himself in its semi-liquid flesh.

For whatever reason, John following his older brother's lead or just recognizing their impossible situation followed suit. Only death was not going to be quick for the two.

The creature possessed a devious will to survive. It was so devious that Isaac became sickened by its clever twisting and manipulating flesh that snorkeled up in elephant trunk shapes to create breathing tubes for Charlie and John Youngblood. Like the sow, they were trapped, and God knows how many other animals they had mercilessly fed the thing all these years—trapped, writhing in excruciating pain, as their flesh slowly melted, absorbing their souls.

Only Charlie and John could not cry out in pain. Any sounds that they may have been able to utter were muffled by the artificial umbilical cord's several feet.

Isaac cursed the fear that had kept him from opening the door sooner and the black thoughts he had entertained briefly. Bowing his head, he wept for his two servants and himself.

If the creature of the tunnels ever harbored any semblance of logic, it was ravaged by its enormous hunger. With no visible means of locomotion, it moved silently towards its tearful keeper.

Isaac looked up and saw its horrible mass bearing down on him. The size of a railroad locomotive, it slithered noiselessly over strewn fragments from the tunnel's wall, over the discarded body of the cow, and the two muskets and the lantern left by the Youngbloods.

Isaac turned and completed only two hurried steps toward the door when a coiled tentacle grew from the creature's body at lightning speed and entangled his legs with sticky strands.

Isaac's fleeting thoughts of reaching his safety device outside the creature's prison and activating the detonator were obliterated by searing blasts of pain when the creature's flesh seeped through the fabric of his trousers making contact with his own.

Falling face forward, he made a futile attempt to reach for the door, and his hand fell upon the leather strap that hung from the backside of the latch; gripping it tightly in his right hand, he laughed out loud once more.

The strap was used to pull the door shut from the inside. Once in and the door closed, the locking bar would automatically fall into place and could only be unlocked from the outside.

Isaac knew well that he would be sealed in this tomb forever without someone on the other side to throw back the iron bar. The tentacle yanked on his ankles and dragged him across the sharp stones. The door pulled along with him, closed halfway.

"You are killing the goose that laid the golden egg," he shouted in a mocking, half-insane voice. It yanked again, pulling Isaac and the door another foot.

From the outer tunnel, a six-inch vertical band of light poured in through the remaining opening. The inner tunnel grew darker. When knocked down, Isaac's lamp shattered and went out. The crushing weight of the creature's advancing body extinguished the Youngblood's light. It yanked, and the door stopped within an inch of the jam.

"You are biting the hand that feeds you," he screamed. "You will wither and atrophy to nothing without me."

Yank.

The door closed, and Isaac heard the muffled clang of the locking bar falling into place. Total darkness surrounded him.

"Why would anyone create you," he said, crying, "for what purpose." Realizing that it was futile to hold on any longer, Isaac let go of the leather strap.

"To eat, to grow, and to wander back and forth," he said in a low, defeated breath. He was dragged to it. The creature's slime protracted, traveling up his legs and wrapped around his waist, the lower half of his body stung with a thousand needle punctures.

Jolted by the pain, Isaac drew his gun from his belt and put the barrel to his head. He was going to have the last laugh. The creature of the tunnels was going to be hungry sooner than it had bargained. His legs twitched and kicked involuntarily from the pain.

Remembering the sow, he pulled the trigger.

CHAPTER 3
THE DREAM

It was the dream that woke Alan. He sat up with a start shivering from the experience. His eyes focused on a framed painting of a farmhouse and barn. It was one of those cheap, Wal-Mart prints that they sold by the truckload. The frame had been drilled in the corners and secured to the wall with four brass screws. What an odd way to hang a picture, he thought. Where am I?

On top of an avocado green Formica dresser was a beat-up RCA portable television. Trailing from the back of the set was a braided steel cable, the other end of which was bolted to the wall. Nothing looked familiar. Shaking his head to free the cobwebs from his brain, Alan looked around for something, anything in the room that might be familiar to him. When he saw the hotel rate card on the back of the door, he remembered where he was, the Red Mountain Inn just outside Ridgecrest.

Alan stretched, kicked his legs out from under the covers, and sighed with relief. The dream always had that effect on him. He would wake up feeling as if he had just returned from another life, followed by a brief span of amnesia.

He didn't know what was worse, the dark beckoning aspects of the dream of not being able to remember where he was or sometimes who he was upon awakening? At these moments, he felt that his lapses of temporary memory loss were more frightening than the dream. Much of the dream's detail faded from memory moments after waking. After years of reoccurring nightmares and extensive analysis that the haunting quality of the dream would remain with him during the day.

Throwing his legs over the side of the double bed, he hesitated briefly before rising, trying to recall where the bathroom was. A half-empty pint bottle of Passport Scotch rested on the bed table. A chaser of water stood alongside. He knew that it was against his doctor's orders, but it was the only thing that helped him sleep. The scotch numbed the fear of his nightmares, and for some reason, the Passport didn't leave him with a hangover.

Two doors stood off to Alan's right; both were closed. He Pulled his lanky frame up, staggered to the one he was certain led to the bathroom and opened the door. It was a closet. "Crap," he whispered and went on to the next one.

Reflected in the bathroom mirror under the harsh fluorescent light, he saw the man he recognized every morning through the muddled confusion of the past eight and one-half years. Forty-two, but looks sixty, he thought. Long, bony hands that his Aunt Betty had told him, at least fifty-times when he was a kid, were "piano fingers." A hawkish nose, a receding hairline, and a pair of close-set eyes glared back at him. "Ward," he said aloud. "Alan Parker

Ward," he followed in a voice both a bit too high and loud. "Every time," he lamented. "I do this every damn time."

Staring back at his reflected image, old feelings of apprehension crept over him. He hadn't hesitated to look in the mirror-like most mornings. He drank more than usual the night before, and he was still a little light-headed. He had forgotten to be afraid. It would take him several seconds to build up the courage to look in the mirror most mornings. His thoughts, of that time, were always clouded with dark, crawling things. Things that faded from his mind the moment he tried to concentrate on them but left him with the fear that if he gazed at his reflection, what he would see looking back at him would not be human.

CHAPTER 4
IRONWOOD

Ironwood was pissed. Scores of unutterable curses flooded his brain. Those political clowns have killed my project; a voice screamed inside his head as he knuckled his hands into fists. They want to start their own Solyndra, right here out in the middle of the Mojave. The Department of Energy has doled out millions to support the solar industry, a sector fraught with technology challenges, propped up with billions of taxpayer dollars. To date, they have spent one-hundred-fifty billion dollars on these initiatives, and yet the industry cannot survive without government giveaways. Now they are going to rob the funds from my project to further add to their fiasco, he fumed.

Professor Thomas Ironwood steadied himself in front of the conference table. I cannot let this collection of bureaucrats get the better of me, he told himself. Don't let the angst consume you again. Vice Admiral Hawkins had told him of the change in his research department as he prepared to sit down. It was just like the crafty old bloke to catch him off guard. Hawkins looked like an emotionless stone monolith. He was a giant of a man that seemed taller while sitting than some men were standing. He had delivered the deft blow to Ironwood with abstract indifference. The professor was confident that everyone around the table knew he was furious. He could feel the blood swelling in his face, and his ears began to ring. I must be as red as a beet, he speculated.

Ironwood moved away from his usual seat to the end of the table opposite of Hawkins and sat down; the spot was reserved for Captain Eastwater, but he was late. Conveniently late, Ironwood grudgingly surmised. Taking Eastwater's seat was a childishly symbolic gesture but a gesture of defiance all the same. It was also a tactical maneuver. It gave him time to think. Eastwater had been trying to control Ironwood's department ever since he had come to the Naval Weapons Center. He was the new order, young, ambitious, and an Ivy Leaguer that didn't care for the mix of civilian and military personnel at the base. If he had his way, he would run this place as if it was Conflict Resolution 101. The truth of the matter was that the number of civilians employed at the NWC outnumbered navy personnel by three to one. It became an absolute necessity in the 1970s, and '80's to bring in more people from the private sector. The Navy needed the infusion of the scientific and business communities in order to create some of the advanced weapons technology in use today. If it hadn't been for that coalition, people like Eastwater would still be trying to invent the microchip.

"Admiral," Ironwood said with the steady voice of a negotiator, "Project Sunshine is the reason I came to China Lake."

"We are aware of that, professor. Please don't think of this change as permanent. Project Sunshine has only been . . . temporarily sidetracked."

Sidetracked my ass; railroaded is more like it, he thought as he calmly returned the Admiral's gaze. Ironwood tugged at his left ear lobe and looked around the room. There were four of them in all, including himself. Only two were in uniform; Admiral Hawkins and his aide, an Ensign Turco, who never talked but was always taking notes on his smart tablet, and Congressman Neville Stream. Stream was on Ironwood's right and about halfway down the long, gray, Formica conference table. The congressman was bald except for closely cut hair at the temples and the back of his head. His face was void of any facial hair as well. The fluorescent lights in the room reflected off the top of his head.

The congressman sat up straight with his hands folded in front of him on top of the table. He wore a three-piece, blue suit, white dress shirt, and a red tie. Awfully warm clothing to wear while visiting the Mohave Desert, Ironwood thought. But then he decided that this was the congressman's uniform as well. He felt under-dressed. His tropical wool sports jacket, loosely knotted tie, blue jeans, and western work boots probably stuck out like a sore thumb. Oh, what the hell? I bet I'm the only one here that is comfortable. Ironwood was prepared for the desert, not a full dress parade.

Eastwater still hadn't shown up. Hawkins drummed his fingers on the gray Formica, and Stream just stared at the tabletop. Annoyed, Ironwood focused his attention on Ensign Turco. The young ensign was neat as a pin, short dark hair and not a button out of place. Although no one was talking at the moment, Turco never looked up from his iPad. He was a nervous little man that avoided confrontations at all costs and followed orders like a robot. He seemed to sense the tension in the room and buried himself in his notes, an ostrich poking its head in the sand. Ironwood wondered if he had a girlfriend; Ironwood doubted it. It had been a while since Ironwood had been with a woman himself, he mused, a long while, not since before Connie died. Tonight, after this was all over, it would be painfully lonely. No matter how hard he fought, he knew he would lose, and there would be no one at home to be there for him.

The absurdity of the silence got the better of Ironwood. "This is criminal!" he said out loud, and Ensign Turco looked up with a start. "I won't allow it."

"You have no choice," said Stream, feigning boredom.

Enraged, Professor Ironwood glared at the congressman. "You are taking money that doesn't belong to you, congressman. These funds were originally allocated for the Space Guard Transmitter research, not some useless outmoded technology."

"Sorry, Mr. Ironwood, you are in no position to tell the United States Government how to spend money."

Demoted from professor to mister in one breath, Ironwood quietly observed, just a subtle change in verbiage to belittle and intimidate me. He was familiar with the congressman's background. Before Neville Stream went into politics, he worked as one of the top negotiators for the Teamsters Union, a community organizer. He later spent some time as the head of the Federal Employment Security Commission. Ironwood had watched him work his magic on C-SPAN during the General Petraeus hearings. Neville Stream was not the man to cross verbal swords.

"Besides," the congressman added. "This is a pinhole in the defense budget that left unplugged could do the world a lot of good."

Minimize the issue, Ironwood's inner voice raged. Reduce it to the ridiculous or make a mountain out of a molehill, whatever the situation calls for, you political opportunist.

"Professor," Admiral Hawkins piped in. "We are not here to gang up on you. The temporary setback of Project Sunshine is needed in order to let Project Firefly continue." Hawkins pulled a cigar from his breast pocket and contemplated it for a while, turning it over and over in his hands. The admiral looked up; his expression changed from a stern, military commander to a compassionate, pleading look. "Your breakthroughs with solar pump lasers would be a shot in the arm to Firefly. This project needs your help."

What tactic is this, good cop/bad cop? Ironwood wondered. Not falling for their less than adroit maneuver, he turned on the admiral. "I am amazed at your use of the old top-secret coded project name 'Firefly.' If my memory serves me correctly, it was part of President Reagan's NATO strategy back in the early '80s and had nothing to do with failed solar policies."

Ironwood knew what the old Firefly project entailed. It was the construction and installation of missile silos in the Black Forest of Germany's hills as a deterrent to the Soviets. Of course, it couldn't be a deterrent if the Russian's didn't know about it. So, by 1982, they let the existence of the undertaking leak to the press but not the intended locations of the silos. The project was scrapped after détente and later declassified when the Soviet Union imploded. Ironwood had become involved with Firefly shortly before its demise. Either these two guys hadn't done their homework on me, he conjectured, or they think I am a fool. The re-use of a senior project name intrigued him. Could it be that by keeping the old project alive on paper, they could use the tax dollars allocated to create a new project and maybe even feather the nest with the funds from his project, and God knows what other sources? His project would render those anti-missiles obsolete and replace them with a mobile laser anti-ballistic system at a fraction of the cost.

"It's purely coincidental," said Neville Stream, looking like he had smelled a foul odor. "The name was picked at random by a computer. But you are right about one thing. It was a strategic defense research project. 'Firefly' was a nickname as well as a code name for SDI. There was this Hollywood movie producer that laid claim to the old nickname. He threatened to sue the U.S. Government if we continued to use it, but as it turns out, there are no objections to using it when it comes to renewable energy."

"That is a tough story to swallow, Mr. Stream," Ironwood snapped back. "You two gentlemen wouldn't be misappropriating government funds, now would you?"

With his fuse finally lit, the congressman stood up and leaned across the conference table in Ironwood's direction. "Because of your vast knowledge of physics, Ironwood," he said, spitting out the word 'vast' as if it was a bad taste in his mouth. "I won't reiterate all the reasons for the further development of a vital EPA renewable energy system."

"That, congressman, is a value judgment." Ironwood couldn't resist grinning. He enjoyed getting Neville Stream's goat. "At the current rate that directional boring and fracking have dramatically increased the supply of crude oil and drastically reduced its price, your solar panels will become as useless as the Spruce Goose. I can see them ten years from now, sitting out in the desert collecting dust." Inspired by his small victory, the middle-aged professor pointed toward an imaginary desert expanse. Outstretching a hand, he turned a thumb down. "Tell me, congressman, what is in this for you?"

Stream took a step backward with indignation on his face and looked about the room. "We are all aware of the precarious position we occupy as a leading world power. We have commitments to other nations to prevent global warming. It is the fabric of our global initiative."

Ironwood had had enough of his crap. Rising quickly and squaring off with the congressman, his face only inches from Stream's. "I will take this to a higher authority."

The tension evaporated from the congressman's expression giving way to a smile. "I wouldn't. The directive came from there."

"Professor," said Hawkins stepping around the table, his voice becoming firm. "Your science group is needed on this project. I imagine that by pulling a few strings, you could break your contract with the government. I wouldn't like to see that. Your people have given us valuable service in the past. But now it isn't a question of your approval. Are you working with us or not?"

Got me, Ironwood realized. He knew it would eventually come to this. He would be out of a job. He had a reputation for hard headiness and a tendency not easily to suffer fools. He had been fired from his last position, and with the state of the economy, it would be difficult to find a research center that would take him in. But what was even worse was the situation for the eleven other people on his team. He didn't have any dependents, no debts; he could always find something to do until his pension kicked in, but there were others to consider. Most of them were young—many with families. Ironwood felt like a helpless, caged animal. He glared at the admiral and the congressman, gritting his teeth in restraint of his anger, unable to reply. His ears buzzed, and he thought he was going to explode. Then he recognized the buzzing sound. It was the admiral's intercom phone at the end of the conference table.

Vice Admiral Hawkins stepped back around the table and pressed a button marked "mic."

"Yes, what is it," he snapped, irritated by the interruption.

A woman's voice rose from the speaker in the faceplate of the phone. "Admiral, Captain Eastwater is on his way, and that man is here again, and he insists on seeing you."

"What man?" replied Hawkins.

"Mr. Ward, sir," answered the voice with a quiver.

"How did he get in?"

"He has a pass from the Maturango Museum."

"Tell him I am in a conference."

The name was familiar to Ironwood. He had known a man by that name when he was the head of the physics department at Miskatonic University. It seemed like a million years ago. "Is that Alan Ward?" he asked.

Hawkins pushed the "mic" key again, muting their conversation from the outside. "Yes. Do you know him?"

Relieved to have changed the subject, for the time being, he answered, "Yes. We worked together years ago. I hear that nowadays; he has become a leading scientific authority on terrestrial phenomena."

"A crackpot is more like it," rang a voice from the back of the room. They all turned in time to see the rear conference room door close behind Captain Eastwater. The young officer marched across the room with an air of confidence equal to a war hero's and tossed his briefcase onto the conference table. "I had to run him out of here last week. He has a petition. He is trying to save a few Indian rock drawings and an old shack that is in the way of the project." Eastwater turned to face the admiral, acknowledged his superior, and then nodded with a slight bow in the congressman's direction. "Admiral, Congressman, I am sorry for being late. We were ground testing some new warheads for the A-12, and it ran over schedule." He turned to confront the professor and noticed the stress lines in his face. "I see that you have told him." Eastwater deliberately talked past Ironwood as if he were oblivious to his words. "Good. What is done is done. Now that that's over, we can get down to work."

Ironwood gave the captain a look that killed in reaction to his insulting, dismissive attitude. "I am not a thing, captain," he said, glaring at him face to face. "You'd be well off to remember who you are speaking to; the likes of you will not disregard me."

Eastwater clumsily backed away, his arrogance diminished. Ironwood's stature was that of a strong, powerful man. The admiral, visibly irritated by their confrontation, raised his voice. "Professor, I cannot have this happen on my team! You will be working for, I mean you two will be working together for some time. I need cooperation. Is that understood?"

Ironwood turned from the admiral to Eastwater once again. The young officer had a smug look on his face. "Understood," Ironwood said through clenched teeth. "For the time being," he muttered.

The intercom buzzed again, and Hawkins jabbed at the telephone. "What is it, yeoman?"

The voice from the phone answered back with the quiver of fear more pronounced this time. "It's Mr. Ward, sir. He refuses to leave. Shall I call for the Master at Arms?"

"No," he ordered. Turning from the phone and staring at Ironwood, he said, "It appears that he has a comrade in arms in here. Send him in."

"Aye, aye, sir," replied the speakerphone.

Hawkins pressed the "mic" key once more. "Gentleman, let us

try to finish the balance of this meeting with a degree of civility."

Eastwater straightened his tie and tried to remain nonchalant. When the door opened, Ironwood was pleased to see his old friend, but Alan Ward didn't appear to notice him. His clothes were laughably out of style. A madras jacket, a blue knit tie slightly frayed, and a pair of polished cotton slacks. Suddenly Ironwood felt overdressed.

Alan scanned the conference room, looked past Ironwood with a distant stare, then glanced down at Ensign Turco, who had remained seated. Turco's head snapped down, and he buried his nose in his tablet again. Turning slightly to his left, Alan brought his hawkish features to bear on the admiral. "Admiral Hawkins," he said stiffly. "I am Alan Ward," he said, extending a bony hand.

"Mr. Ward, what can we do for you this morning?" said Hawkins, taking the offered hand while putting on his best 'how are you today' voice.

It didn't look like they were shaking hands to Ironwood. Huge, stubby ropes swallowed Alan's hand. The admiral had workman's hands, thick, strong fingers that showed traces of oil and grease. Ironwood knew that his hobby was restoring old cars. He thought they were a comical contrast. The admiral several inches over six foot and as neat as an ad on a recruiting poster, while frail Alan, with grizzled hair protruding over his ears and sloppy attire, looked like he came off the rack at Goodwill.

"It is about the construction you will be starting soon in the area of the Coso Range."

"How can you know about the," interrupted the congressman, panic creeping into his voice. "project . . . the project is classified."

"I know nothing of your plans," answered Alan to the man in the blue suit. "But the intended construction of several concrete structures out there is common knowledge in town."

"Congressman," spoke up Eastwater as he placed himself between Ward and Neville Stream. "Mr. Ward here envisions himself breaking up the project."

"Captain Eastwater, I have entertained no such thoughts. For the present, I only object to the choice of the location."

"What is wrong with the locale?" continued Stream. "From an ecological standpoint, we have found nothing of danger to the environment. You aren't a naturalist, are you?"

"No sir," said Alan, trying to contain a smile. "Not exactly a naturalist."

Ironwood had to smile too. Being familiar with Alan Ward's background, he knew that calling him a naturalist was only part of the word. It was an inside joke. In Alan's days at the University, he was widely known as "the super-naturalist."

"The area south of Darwin, predominantly in the scope of the Coso Range, is of historical value."

"Bull," roared Eastwater as if he was firing the opening shot of a salvo.

Ironwood returned to his seat as group shouting ensued and leaned back in his chair. It was music to his ears. A nasty part of him enjoyed watching their world fall apart. Content to see them squabble amongst themselves. Most of all, he was able to observe a side of Neville Stream you didn't catch on C-SPAN. Was the Congressman this easily rattled?

"Admiral," Stream challenged, "You never told me that the project site had historical significance."

"It doesn't!" interrupted Captain Eastwater. "Can't you see he is making it up?"

"Captain," entreated Alan. "You have never bothered to substantiate my stories."

"And stories are just what they are," Eastwater snapped back.

"Gentlemen," implored Ironwood from his chair. "I am interested in what Professor Ward has to say."

Alan turned at the sound of Ironwood's voice and noticed him for the first time. The dawning of recognition crossed his features. His mouth dropped open and then slammed shut, resembling the wooden jaw of a marionette.

Thomas Ironwood smiled, "It's been a long time, Alan."

"Thomas," he gasped. "Are you mixed up in this?"

"Not altogether," Ironwood replied, eyeing the congressman. "Gentlemen," he said again, only louder, pleased that the tables had been turned. "Mr. Ward, here, is a Professor of English Literature at Miskatonic University in Arkham, Massachusetts and, of late, an expert on uncovering ancient civilizations . . . a long way from home, Alan."

Alan looked lost for words, possibly overcome, surprised at seeing an old friend at such an out-of-the-way place. Poor Alan, thought

Ironwood. He is trying so hard to be proper, all the while looking as if he doesn't have two nickels to rub together. He wondered if he had fallen on hard times. His appearance indeed suggested it. "Please continue," he said.

"Thank you, Professor," Alan stammered. "This base and the region comprising the Coso Range were once crossed by a roadway used by tradesmen and settlers. In 1871, during the great western push, Isaac Morley came with a pair of Narragansett Indians and built his house on the edge of this range, overlooking the desert. Morley was a curious man with a rather mysterious background." Alan's hand shook as he tried to smooth back a stubborn, outcropping of hair on the right side of his head. "Ever since the construction of his house," he continued, "life in that region has not been normal."

Eastwater yawned, and Vice Admiral Hawkins looked embarrassed. Ironwood knew his old friend was losing his audience.

"The Native-Americans have countless legends about the territory," he added.

Ironwood could see that this was difficult for Alan. He wanted to help, but this was all new to him. The shaking in Alan's hands increased. "Shoshone myth tells us of an ancient place beneath the desert where lived 'he who would never die.'"

Neville Stream made a sour face. "And this is your historical reference? I am sorry, admiral, captain, I owe both of you an apology."

"But there is more than that," pleaded Alan. "Let me continue."

"I warned you about him," Eastwater said.

"The area has always been known for its unusual happenings. I have a list." Talking too fast and moving too quickly, Alan produced an assortment of papers from his jacket pocket. Several scraps fell to the floor. Getting down on his hands and knees, he started to collect his precious notes. "They go as far back as 1883. A man named Clervi heard strange noises coming from the ground. There is one from 1934 where the people of Darwin heard the cry of a flock of birds for several hours on end, and there wasn't a feathered creature within miles of the town."

"This is ridiculous," protested Congressman Stream.

Still, on his hands and knees, Alan scooped up the last of his papers. "If you build on that site," he said in a panicked rush of words, "the results may be hazardous."

Captain Eastwater looked down at Alan Ward but directed his words at the congressman. "The only 'things' that are unusual about the area are a few faults in the earth. At this very moment, we have a geotechnical team and a detachment of Seabees out there taking seismograph readings.

Ironwood quickly recognized that it was time for Alan to leave. They had left the conference room door open, and their raised voices must have carried down the hall. A first class petty officer stood large and menacing in the open doorway. A nightstick hung from his belt, and just below his left shirt pocket was the badge and star signifying his MA rating, Master at Arms. Another petty officer appeared from behind to investigate the commotion. Alan saw them, too.

CHAPTER 5
SINKHOLE

Gwendolyn Gilhooley touched the red wire to the positive pole of the twelve-volt battery. One hundred yards in front of her, the desert floor thumped with the force of several light explosions. Pieces of the ground kicked upward into the morning sky. The heavier clumps of dirt quickly attained maximum velocity, then rained straight down while some of the lighter, finer sand particles drifted eastward before settling back to earth.

Gwen stood and slapped the sand off her NWU, otherwise known as a Navy Work Uniform. They had only been one-pound charges, six in all wired in series. They reminded her of a string of firecrackers going off on the Fourth of July. Only this fireworks display wasn't colorful, and most of the reports were muffled by three feet of Mojave sand. She enjoyed blowing things up. It was the only thing she liked about her job. She guessed that it was the unrestrained child within her that got a kick out of it. While most of the little girls she grew up with were playing with Barbie dolls, she was blasting apart Revell plastic model replicas of Messerschmitts and Zeros with well-placed cherry bombs.

Gwen smiled and looked over at Dr. Willet. Virtual arms on his seismograph's flat-screen waived back and forth, drawing tight digital lines. The video readout recorded the same shock waves onto its hard drive. Nothing would be lost.

They had been at it all morning and would more than likely, be there for the rest of the week. The afternoon sun was too hot to work under, so they put in their time from sun up until about 11:00 a.m. Gwen had spent much of her childhood growing up in Florida, where the summers are scorching and humid. There the heat grabs at you the moment you step out of doors. But in the dry Mojave summers, it sneaks up on you, and you do not realize how hot it is until you have stepped out of it and into some shade or you pass out.

For the past three days, Gwen had bored half a dozen holes at a time in the ground with a mobile drill, planted her charges, and detonated them on Willet's signal. Then Willet and his group of geologists would busy themselves collecting their data until they picked another spot.

Three weeks earlier, she had drilled Seventy-five holes twenty feet deep in the area, obtaining seventy-five separate core samples. She had then cataloged each strata formation creating a geodetic map of the site and reported the information to Captain Eastwater. Now she was back in the same desolate area with a geologist team making a seismic map of the site. She didn't know what the Navy would build out here, but she knew it must be hot. It had to be something really special, or they wouldn't have gone to all this trouble.

Gwen was bored. The placing and detonating of the charges were straightforward. It was a one-person operation. Professor Willet and his three-person crew would mark six sand areas precisely fifteen-feet apart with orange spray paint. She would then back the single axle flatbed truck with its drill tower mounted on the rear up to each spot and punch a three-foot-deep hole in the ground approximately six inches in diameter. The drill, powered by the truck's PTO (Power Take Off), was tilted up and aligned correctly. Gwen would disengage the driveshaft from the transmission, using the transfer case inside the cab, and connect it to the drilling rig using two additional gear shift levers located on the truck's floor. Once the holes were drilled, Gwen lined each one with a four-inch diameter cardboard tube. She kept a supply of these in twelve-foot lengths strapped to the side of her truck. The tubes helped them gauge and maintain each hole's size, ensuring all were at the same depth. It also kept the sand from drifting back in.

The charges came next. Gwen was accustomed to using 2-1/2, five and ten-pound charges when blasting through ledge rock or large boulders, but she used only one-pound of blasting gel per hole seismic tests. That was all they needed. Just enough to send a shock wave through the earth so Willet and his boys could detect any possible voids or faults in the earth that might spell unsuitable subsoil conditions and cause problems during construction. So far, they had turned up a big zero. After loading up each cardboard cylinder with a one-pound charge, backfilling each with a few shovels full of earth, and detonating, the ground appeared to be solid. Of course, she could have told them that. After all, she had just honeycombed the area with seventy-five soil borings.

The blasting gel was tightly encased in a heavy plastic wrap and formed into a tubular shape twisted shut at both ends and crimped in place with thin aluminum rings.

"Looks like Jimmy Dean pork sausage," observed Willet that morning while looking over her shoulder.

Gwen hadn't said anything but shot him a sarcastic frown instead. The forty-plus geologist had got the hint and shuffled back to his equipment, looking like a hurt schoolboy. Gwen felt terrible about that and decided to apologize to him later for her behavior. She was unhappy with her assignment, and she took it out on the guy with a Ph.D.

Gwen had a degree in civil engineering and still hadn't made it past petty officer second class. And, on top of everything, her CO had assigned her to geological services. She trained to design and plan for roads, parking lots, and large earth moving projects, not to be a geotechnical engineer. Most of the time, she was just a pickup and drop-off service for the Michelson Lab guys. She would run and pick up samples for them or drill for core samples, as she had done a few weeks ago. Only occasionally, she would get to blow things up.

Gwen had majored in commercial and residential infrastructure at school. Her dream was to design someday the roads, sewers, and drainage systems for housing developments and commercial projects.

Gwen was a Navy brat. Her father was a retired chief petty officer, and she was proud that she had joined up immediately after completing high school. Her parents had been simple, hardworking, blue-collar people, and Gwen had inherited their work ethic. She had hoped to gain a lot of practical field experience in the Navy, put in her twenty years, and retire from the service when she was 38. With a pension to back her up, Gwendolyn dreamed of starting an engineering firm. She had also hoped to snare herself a good man on the way. So far, at 26 years of age, neither plan was going well.

At medium height, Gwen was endowed with an excellent figure and a face to match. She wore subtle makeup, and every lock of her short, blond hair was in place. She always thought that her figure was among her best physical attribute, though. God, she thought, had given her a little extra when she had been standing in line for body parts. She had a slim, athletic body, narrow hips, and a 44-inch bust line. The combination was uncommon, but Gwen carried it well. Some of the women she went through boot camp used to kid her, saying that even though Gilhooley might not be at attention, her chest always was.

Gwen Gilhooley was miffed. She should have everything going for her, but she could not attract the right kind of guy. For some reason, mysterious to her, or maybe she knew but didn't want to admit it, she had trouble attracting men. Her career in the Navy was going nowhere. Her parents lived in San Diego now. They couldn't keep her dad away from the shipyards. With them so far away, it only added to her loneliness.

Disconnecting the red and black wires from the battery, Gwen started to roll them up overhand and elbow. Her shirt had wilted hours ago and had glued itself to the small of her back. She could feel the sweat soaking past her hips. It was getting late. The sun was high in the sky.

"How many does that make?" inquired Willet.

"What?" she said, not understanding his question at first, being lost in thought.

"How many sets have we done this morning?" he returned a bit impatiently.

He had been referring to the number of times they had bored holes and set off charges. "Six," she answered.

"All right then," he replied with the wave of a hand, "We do one more before calling it a day."

"Damn," she whispered to herself. "This shore duty sure wasn't stacking up right."

Gwen walked to the exploded area winding up the last few feet of wire. The flat terrain was white with alkaline and barren but for a few sagebrush and a stubble of creosote brush. Off in the distance, heat illusions combined with occasional dust devils. The sand felt hot through the soles of her boots. She saw Willet scratch his head and stare down at his seismograph with a puzzled look on his face. She became aware of a vibration, a rumbling sound. She scanned the horizon, expecting to see an A-10 coming in low, getting ready to buzz them. It was a common practice with the Navy flyboys; they liked to scare the hell out of the construction and engineering crews whenever they got a chance. Anticipating the sonic boom, she cupped both hands over her ears and searched the great blue bowl of sky. There was no plane insight, and the rumbling kept growing stronger. Then, suddenly she couldn't feel the sand beneath her feet anymore. She was sinking, falling.

***

Dr. Marinus Bicknell Willett looked up from the yellow contour lines that raced across the seismograph screen in time to see Gwendolyn Gilhooley drop out of sight beneath the tumbleweed.

CHAPTER 6
THE TUNNEL

Ironwood watched from his window seat as the blades of the Sikorsky helicopter sliced noisily at the afternoon sky, kicking up the sand and setting them down softly on the ground.

Moments after touching down, Turco jumped up from his seat, slid back the big side door with a heavy clang, and stood at attention alongside the opening. A blast of desert heat and sand pelted the interior of the helicopter. Ironwood felt as if they had landed on an alien world.

Eastwater hadn't wasted any time either. He was out of his seat, only seconds later taking his place beside Turco.

Hawkins and Stream marched down the aisle and past Ironwood. From his seat, Ironwood had a good view of the open door. As the rotors slowed, Hawkins sat himself down on the door sill and swung out his legs. A seaman, wearing a paper breather mask and goggles, ran under the whirling vanes and helped him down. The admiral struggled to keep his hat in place, ducked low, and allowed himself to be escorted from the aircraft. Squinting hard against the flurry of sand, the congressman and Eastwater slipped over the edge of the sill aided by two more men with insect faces and followed Hawkins.

Ironwood wasn't in the mood to eat sand. He waited until the vanes of the helicopter stopped turning and the artificial sandstorm subsided. The Professor stole a look at Turco, observing that the young ensign had stayed behind as well. He still stood at attention, holding the door, only back a few steps from the opening, shielding himself from the gale-force wind and sand. Ironwood winked at him and was surprised to see a grin disrupt his wooden features.

The blades of the Sikorsky slowed to a halt. Outside it indeed became the calm after a storm. The last granules of sand settled to earth, and from his window, Ironwood could discern the circular pattern they had left in the sand. The desert floor beneath and around them had been wiped clean and flat. The sand had drifted up some to form a slight berm that surrounded their landing site with perfect symmetry about fifty feet away. If someone discovered this area after they left, he wondered, would they think that a UFO had once landed here? It made him think of those farms in England where large uniform circles had been found mysteriously cut into the wheat fields. He was sure there was a logical explanation for them as there would be for the mystified and hypothetical discoverer of the Sikorsky helicopter markings.

Ironwood unfastened his seat belt and went to the exit. No one came to his assistance. There wasn't anyone in sight from that side of the aircraft. Ironwood planted his backside firmly on the door sill, looked up, and to his right at the wooden Turco. "No help from below," Ironwood said, more to the air than to the ensign. "I guess that's reserved for the top brass. We must be nonessential personnel."

Turco wasn't smiling anymore. He stared expressionlessly at the desert expanse. With a shrug, the professor jumped down the remaining three feet and landed softly on the sand.

The helicopter loomed over him. He half expected the armor plating on the fuselage to ripple with life and the thing, imbued with a supernatural spirit, to gobble him up as if it were a dragonfly and he a tiny mosquito.

Ironwood looked over his shoulder. A light breeze dusted the deck of the aircraft with a fine spray of sand. Turco looked down from the belly of the flying machine but made no move to leave. Evidently, it was the Ensign's job to stay with the ship.

The sun felt hot on the back of his neck. As he walked away from the metal dragonfly, it made him feel stranger still that his were the only footprints leading away. The churning of the desert floor had already erased the prints of the others. He never ceased to marvel at the power and technology that humans created, but the true marvel was that the next whim of nature would also obliterate the large circular footprint of the Sikorsky. A simple dust storm in the evening and all traces would be gone by morning.

Standing on the outer edge of the Sikorsky footprint, beyond the reach of the blades, he picked up the trail of Hawkins, Eastwater, Stream and their attendants heading south to where four vehicles stood parked in a circle. A large Ford diesel truck with a drilling rig mounted on the back, a six-wheel-drive troop transport, a Dodge van, and a small, lightweight Dodge pickup truck. All painted the standard white bearing the Naval Weapons Center's logo on their doors except the transport. It was gray, Navy gray. There was ample military here, Ironwood noted. Around the other side of the transport was a fifth vehicle, a blue Ford Taurus with rental plates.

The Dodge van's rear doors stood open, and a canvas awning was stretched overhead with the back portion fastened to the rear end of a roof-mounted luggage rack and the other to two metal poles stuck in the sand. Underneath, shielded from the fierce rays of the afternoon sun, was an assortment of bulky electronic equipment stacked on top of each other. One piece, observed Ironwood, the one on top, looked like a seismograph. The canvas awning flapped in the breeze accompanied by the similar sound made by the canvas sides and roof of the transport. The troop carrier, resembling a modern-day Conestoga covered wagon, tugged at Ironwood's fondness for old westerns. The brief bit of magic was interrupted by the sound of static. A young man, tall and handsome and wearing a lieutenant's insignia, stood outside the transport, leaning against the driver's side door, talking on a field radio. The young officer was too far away for Ironwood to make out what he was saying.

At first, Ironwood thought that they had placed the trucks and car in a circle in hopes of blocking the wind and creating some shade, but then his attention was drawn to something metallic gleaming in the sun within the center of the circle.

He wasn't the only one attracted to it. Eastwater and Stream stood near its center, staring down at the object. The two seamen, out of their goggles and filter masks, stood alongside.

They all had been hustled onto the Sikorsky shortly after Vice Admiral Hawkins had received a hand-delivered message and not more than an hour and a half after Alan had been hustled off the base by the two petty officers. Ironwood had been asked to come along, but there was something in Hawkins' voice that had cautioned him not to refuse.

"Come on along," Hawkins said. "You will find this interesting." The admiral didn't volunteer the contents of the message, let alone the whereabouts of their destination. Still, when the chopper eventually landed, Ironwood had the feeling that he was overlooking the future site of his "project."

Walking ankle deep in the bermed-up sand, the professor came into earshot of the lieutenant on the radio, "Roger," he said after keying the microphone. "That's a good idea, Mingo. Better make it two 1500 foot runs of cable but not the small generator; I want the Detroit Diesel, and send those big lights we used last month when we did the nighttime paving."

"Roger lieutenant," a voice with a Spanish accent mixed with static answered back, "Anything else, sir?"

"Yes, bring yourself along with that equipment as well as Dexter and Rinaldi. I am going to need a lot of workforces."

"What's it like there?" Mingo squawked back.

"Picture Death Valley at its worst."

"Very funny."

"Make it on the double chief; the orders come from the old man."

"Aye, aye, sir," crackled the reply sounding disappointed.

Ironwood thought the young man had been talking on a portable radio but walking nearer, he noticed a curlicue-shaped wire trailing through the side window. It was an old-style low-ban radio. Probably a dash mount. Sometimes it surprised him that in certain areas, the NWC is very state of the art when it comes to their equipment, while in others, they still cling to vacuum tube technology. Ironwood's right hand reached instinctively for his belt, and he fingered the vinyl holster on his hip. The snap-down flap was still secure. He was concerned about it coming undone and spilling his iPhone into the sand. Bluetooth, GPS, cell, text, and the capability to run any app on the planet; made Ironwood feel like a technological giant next to the young Lieutenant's Tinker Toy radio. All of the research heads at the Michelson Lab had iPhones. It was the twenty-first century way to keep in touch with his people on the project.

Coming within the vehicles' circle, he made out a dark spot surrounding the shiny metal object on the ground, and there was movement. The sun's glare made it difficult to see clearly. It was an irregular black area with a silvery post sticking out of it at an angle, no two posts with a piece of beige linen flapping between them. Ironwood fumbled in his top pocket, pulled out a pair of clip-on sunglasses, and attached them to his spectacles. It cut the glare in half. The two silver posts became aluminum, and they projected up a couple of feet out of a hole in the ground. It was a ladder, and wrapped around the rungs, were empty sandbags, probably put there to keep from burning your hands on the sunbaked aluminum. The Mojave summers could be brutal. One of the scientists from Ironwood's team had gotten a nasty burn on his hand when he leaned on the hood of a car that had been parked all day in the direct sun.

The Professor stopped abruptly in front of the ladder and peered into the opening. It was no more than four feet across. It was dark inside the hole, and while his eyes adjusted to the gloom, it appeared bottomless. Cool air drifted up from below. It was stale, but when he inhaled it, it had a sweet, musty quality that reached inside his head and whispered, "I am old. . . So very old."

"Watch out, Ironwood," snapped Eastwater. The professor turned sharply to see the captain marching his way.

"We don't know if it's safe yet. I wouldn't get too close. I'm having some of the men shore up the ceiling around the hole just in case."

"Ceiling?" mumbled the professor, momentarily confused. Had he been dreaming a second ago? Collecting his thoughts, he faced Eastwater. "What do you mean, ceiling? I don't understand."

"I am afraid we don't at the moment either," he replied, indicating Hawkins and Stream on his right. "We, of course, just got here as well."

Ironwood hated his smugness. He wished they were alone so he could knock him on his arrogant ass.

". . . but," Eastwater continued, "it seems that one of our EA's has found herself a pretty big sinkhole."

"EA?" Ironwood puzzled out loud, almost afraid to ask.

"An Engineering Aid Professor," interrupted the admiral, apparently recognizing the tension once again building up between his two project heads. They were all sweating profusely as the summer desert sun cooked them. Their tempers could quickly boil along with the rise in body heat. "Her name is Gilhooley. She was out here with some of our geologists taking seismograph readings when she fell in."

"Excuse me, admiral," pleaded a voice from behind Hawkins. It was the young man that had been talking on the truck's radio. Ironwood noticed for the first time the Seabee insignia over his shirt pocket. He also noticed that he was wearing a sidearm. A peculiar piece of hardware for an engineer. "Lieutenant Riggs, sir, First Division Seabees. Request permission to speak, sir?"

"Go ahead," ordered Hawkins putting on a friendly face in response to the young officer's nervous tension and looking grateful for the interruption. "Please be at ease."

"Aye, aye, sir. Well, it is the hole, sir. It's kind of strange. You see, it is not a hole in the conventional sense of a sinkhole or a ground fault disturbance. Nor was it caused by water erosion from some ancient stream or riverbed that may have existed here a long time ago."

"Well, what is it then?" piped in Eastwater.

"It's a tunnel, sir," he said, hesitating shifting his weight from his right foot to his left, "and it doesn't look like it was naturally formed."

"You mean man-made, lieutenant?" asked Hawkins.

"Yes, admiral, I guess so."

"Well, that isn't so unusual, Riggs," snapped Eastwater. "These hills around here are honeycombed with caves and mine shafts from the old mining days. Some of them go back over a hundred years."

"Yes, captain, I know. But like you said, those mines were dug into the side of mountain faces. This cave is beneath a flat land area, and besides, the walls inside of those old mines are jagged rock from all of the blasting and chiseling that went on to dig them. The walls in this one are smooth."

"Smooth?" interjected Ironwood, his curiosity peaking.

"Yes, sir," replied Riggs to the stranger in tropical wool. "Smooth like poured concrete."

There was an uncomfortable silence. The admiral cleared his throat. "Well . . . let's have a look-see, Riggs." Hawkins turned towards the jagged hole in the earth.

"It's about five meters deep, sir," volunteered Riggs. "About the same in width and runs approximately the length of a football field."

"Doesn't it lead anywhere?" asked Captain Eastwater with genuine interest. Ironwood thought he detected the hint of disappointment in his voice.

"Not that we can tell, sir. Gilhooley had already explored it from end to end by the time I got here. Besides a little rubble, there isn't much to see."

"Gilhooley?" exclaimed Hawkins. "Didn't you have her medevacked out of here?"

"Uh, no, sir," squirmed Riggs. "Her injury appears only superficial. A slight sprain, she says, to her left ankle."

"That goes against procedure, lieutenant. You are not a medical man. An officer's first duty is to the health and welfare of all of his personnel."

"Aye, aye, sir, but Gilhooley is a bit . . . well, stubborn, sir."

Eastwater bent closer to the hole and laid a hand on the ladder. "It is probably just an old sewage excavation. The Indians that once inhabited this area were pretty clever. Little Petroglyph Canyon lies only a short distance from here. There you can see hundreds of intricately detailed rock drawings made by them thousands of years ago. They're probably responsible for this."

"This is not a sewer Captain Eastwater," echoed a solemn voice unexpectedly from out of the hole.

Eastwater froze. Visibly shaken by the strange voice, he looked down at the opening. Ironwood watched as Eastwater's eyes went wide with fear.

A round metal head with goggles for eyes and protruding antenna glistened in the sunlight. A small compressed air tank hung down the back.

Eastwater backed away quickly and grabbed Riggs' right arm, "Lieutenant, your gun," he ordered in a harsh whisper.

The weird alien thing rose from the earthly cavity. The creature halted halfway out of the hole and rocked back and forth, shaking with laughter. It placed a pair of humanoid hands on top of its "skull," and the thing yanked its "head" off with a quick jerk. Alan

Ward squinted in the afternoon sun. "I didn't mean to startle you," Alan lied. "I thought you'd like to see this," he smiled, tapping the helmet.

Captain Eastwater's expression transformed into pure rage. Ironwood, suppressing a grin, moved closer and peered over his shoulder. "What's the matter, Eastwater? Did you think he was E.T.?"

"Ward," he roared but was stopped from saying anything further when Admiral Hawkins, recognizing the makings of a fight, stepped between them, his large form casting a shadow over Alan.

"Mr. Ward, what in hell's name are you doing here? This is a classified project. How did you get into the base?"

To begin with, Alan was not a tall man, but standing halfway out of a hole in the ground next to Hawkins made him look like a Munchkin. Ironwood privately bet Alan felt like he was addressing Paul Bunyan.

"The supervising civilian geologist here is a friend of mine, admiral. I got in with a pass from the Maturango Museum."

Ironwood knew that the million-plus square acres of the Naval Weapons Center surrounded a significant concentration of Indian rock drawings. Fragments of old missiles and wrecks of drone planes, evidence of over seven-decades of weapons testing, lay scattered near the basalt cliffs. Pecked on these cliffs are drawings of ancient man hunting the bighorn sheep with weapons of his time, the spear thrower or atlatl, and the bow and arrow. A survey of these sites by the local museum and amateur archaeologists has been permitted ever since the late 1960s.

The admiral removed his hat and mopped his forehead with a handkerchief. A much-needed afternoon breeze played with his gray hair. "Once again, I am faced with having to deal with you, Mr. Ward. I'll spare you just a little more time, but your reasons for being here better be sound."

"Fair enough, admiral. I believe you'll find them down here," Alan cocked his head to one side, indicating the tunnel below. "Whether this is an ancient sewer or some other relic of the past, I'm sure you will agree that it will warrant further investigation before you start black-topping the desert."

Eastwater, still angry, looked like he was going to say something but Hawkins was quicker, "Proceed, Mr. Ward; I would like to see what is holding up a four-hundred-million-dollar project, please proceed."

"Excuse me, admiral," interrupted Ironwood, "but I'd like to know something first. What is that thing, Alan?" pointing to the helmet.

"Oh," chuckled Alan, "This is AIS, Audio Infrared Scanner. You can see exceptionally well in the dark with it and this filter," he continued, pointing to the mouth area, "screens out harmful gasses and replaces them with oxygen from this tank. With a series of wireless relays, the antenna allows for radio communication at great depths beneath the earth's surface. But the icing on the cake is the locator," he continued, fidgeting with a red capsule-shaped object fastened to the base of the antennae mount. "There is a small radioactive isotope in here that, although shielded from the wearer of the helmet, can be pinpointed with the proper equipment topside. It could be a lifesaver if someone is lost or trapped underground."

Alan's mood was infectious. He was on an adrenal high from his victorious confrontation with Eastwater and Hawkins. Ironwood couldn't help from being caught up in his enthusiasm. "But all of this state-of-the-art stuff," he almost laughed, "it is so unlike you. How did you come by it?"

"Oh, it is not mine," smiled Alan. "Willett has been developing it for the miners around here. It is all his creation."

"Who's Willett?"

"Marinus Willett. He is the supervising geologist I mentioned earlier. Come on," he urged, going down the ladder. "I'll give you the ten-cent tour."

***

Ironwood started down the ladder after his old friend hesitated and then looked up. Congressman Stream, who had been quiet until then, decided to make Eastwater's and Hawkins' lives miserable. Fearing news of a "historical find" leaking to the media and disrupting the project, he started to berate the two senior officers. "We've had to put up with the EPA breathing down our necks about the sage grouse and desert tortoise, and now this!" he shouted.

The congressman's three-piece blue suit that fit him so well that morning had been soaked with perspiration and hung on him like damp rags. The desert heat was beginning to take its toll on the politician from California, and it wasn't showing well. Ironwood found it hard to feel sympathy for the congressman.

When Ironwood stepped foot on the tunnel floor, two things immediately struck him. The first was the sudden temperature change. It was cool, and his wet shirt felt like cold sheet metal against his back. The second was the floor. He had expected a gritty or gravel-strewn surface. The tunnel floor was instead smooth with a thick layer of what appeared like fine sand on top. Shuffling his feet like a child making lines in the snow, he discovered that, except for an isolated area that had become littered when the desert floor above fell in, the rest of the floor was covered with several inches of dust, not sand. The professor glanced up from his discovery and spied a man in a white lab coat with an equally white goatee, and mustache leaning against a portable specimen table chatting with Alan. Behind Alan was a pretty blonde-haired woman in NWU's. Ironwood guessed that she must be Gilhooley. He detected the faint scent of Estee' Lauder White Linen. He felt a tug at his heart. It had been his wife's favorite. He wondered how Ms. Gilhooley could work all morning in the hot sun, fall through a hole in the ground, and then go spelunking for the rest of the afternoon and still smell so good.

Across the top of the table were a battery-powered lamp, a microscope, and several rock fragments. The lamp, the only source of light the explorers had, barely illuminated beyond their circle, and made it difficult to guess the tunnel's dimensions.

"So far, every tile appears to be uniform in size," said the man in the lab coat.

"Fantastic," cheered Alan. "They'll have to sit up and take notice now. I've been waiting for this moment for a long time."

"Excuse me," Ironwood broke in. "You mentioned tiles?"

"Yes, I did," answered lab coat. "But I'm afraid I haven't had the pleasure."

"Oh, my fault, I'm sorry," interrupted Alan waving his hands as if to clear the air of smoke. "Willett, this is an old friend of mine and an ex-colleague from Miskatonic University, Thomas Ironwood. Ironwood, this is Marinus Willett."

"Doctor Willett," replied Ironwood offering a friendly hand. "Alan was showing us your handiwork. That AIS is a lot to be proud of, sir."

"Thank you, professor, but I only work on it in my spare time. The mining industry is in a big slump right now. Most of the mines around here are closed down, but they'll come full swing again. The price of ore is going up, and young men will once again risk their lives down there in those shafts. Hopefully, I'll have the bugs worked out of A.I.S. by then."

Ironwood thought Willett's reply sounded more like a speech. A bit rehearsed. Arrogance seemed to run wild in the desert.

"My true love, however, is physics. Geology is just a sideline," continued Willett.

"He's modest Thomas," added Alan. "Willett holds three degrees."

"And you professor," countered Willett feigning an air of superiority. "I believe you work at Mike Lab, don't you? Chemical lasers, isn't it?"

"Only in their application with solar lasers. I leave the rest of the field wide open to everyone else."

Willett guffawed with a laugh that seemed forced, and then apparently recalling Ironwood's original question changed the subject. "Some of the rocks don't appear to be rocks at all. Some of them seem to be wall tiles. Some," he mused, "I am not sure what they were used for."

"Used? You mean such as Native-American artifacts?" Ironwood could hear Stream grunting his way down the ladder. The whole gang would be coming up behind him soon. He did not turn around.

"No, I don't think so. They look precision made. Here, take a look for yourself." Willett adjusted the lamp to shine directly onto the tabletop. Ironwood noticed a white haired ponytail dangling halfway down Willet's back almost rendered invisible against the lab coat when he turned. One by one, Dr. Willet quickly arranged half a dozen thin flat stones the size of playing cards across the plastic surface of the table as if he were beginning a game of solitaire. But unlike playing cards, these were five-sided, notched on the bottom and a half an inch thick. "These I have picked at random from off of the floor. They must have gotten there when Ms. Gilhooley fell through."

Gwen smiled, "I am always dropping into places uninvited."

Ironwood smiled. He was glad to see someone with a sense of humor for a change. "They look identical," he said, returning his gaze to the table, "But earlier, the lieutenant said the walls were smooth. Tiles wouldn't necessarily produce a smooth surface."

"Look here, professor," interrupted Gilhooley pulling a flashlight from her hip pocket and shining it on the wall. A section of the masonry, about three feet across, had been wiped clean, probably by the young petty officer when she was exploring the tunnel. "You can barely see the joint lines between the tiles. Take a closer look."

Ironwood moved closer to the wall. The joints between the tiles were almost as thin as a human hair. It made the surface appear smooth and continuous.

"To achieve that," continued Gilhooley with authority, "they would have to be machined, which means that sophisticated engineering had to take place to keep them straight and connected." She paused to allow this to penetrate. "This was not done by any prehistoric man."

Ironwood, a bit skeptical, turned and looked at Gwen.

"Ms. Gilhooley is a civil engineer," volunteered Willett, evidently sensing Ironwood's disbelief.

"Please don't turn out to be a chauvinist Professor. You look so adorable in tweed."

Ironwood had thought that he was beyond the age of blushing, but he felt his face turn a shade of red all the same. Thankful that it wasn't visible in the dim light, he forced a smile and said, "It's tropical wool. It was a knee-jerk reaction, I am afraid, but your line of reasoning does seem flawless. You have both done a lot of detective work in the short time you have been down here."

"Not really," countered Willett. "This is just surface info. Geology 101 stuff."

"With a little basic engineering thrown in," added Gilhooley.

"What we really could use," said Willett, "is an archeologist."

Captain Eastwater's voice rang out from the other end of the tunnel. "We don't need additional personnel from the outside. We will keep this strictly Navy."

Ironwood had expected him to be at his elbow and was taken back by the distance of his voice. He turned to his right and peered beyond the reach of the dim yellow lamplight. He was attracted to movement in the shadows. One end of the tunnel erupted with the white light of an LED lantern. Momentarily blinded, he held up a hand against the glare. Eastwater adjusted the brightness. Ironwood's vision restored, only a retinal after image of the brilliance remained.

"Always be prepared, gentlemen," proclaimed Eastwater. "I learned that as a tenderfoot. Boy Scouts 101."

Ironwood remained startled but not by the light; he saw the tunnel for the first time in its entirety. Before he couldn't discern its shape and size with only the sunlight pouring in from the hole above, slightly augmented by Willett's lamp, but now he could make it out in every detail. Even after his close examination of the wall tiles, he had still maintained a subconscious mental image of a roughly square-shaped mine shaft with crudely rounded corners. He was not prepared for the five-sided, perfectly formed tunnel that stretched out in both directions. The floor was approximately ten feet wide with the walls leaning away from each other at about forty-five-degree angles, lending more width to the tunnel; then, about halfway up, the walls doubled back in on themselves to form an apex or a point at the ceiling.

"Will you look at that!" exclaimed Lieutenant Riggs with an expulsion of breath. "It looks like modern architecture."

The tiles on the wall now looked a dirty ashen color under the LED lantern's prevailing white glare. They had looked yellow before, thought Ironwood, but that was by the light of the battery-powered lamp. They would be able to tell their actual color when they took some samples above ground and examined them under normal conditions, under daylight. But he imagined that the hue he saw now was probably the correct one.

Eastwater and Stream seemed more interested in the pile of rocks and sand that terminated the tunnel's end. Pressing his left hand against a large boulder as if to test its weight, the congressman leaned to his right and whispered something into Eastwater's ear. The captain nodded.

Ironwood glanced over at Admiral Hawkins, who had been quiet all this time. His gaze was fixed on the pair at the end of the tunnel. Ironwood wondered why Hawkins had been laid back, letting

Eastwater take charge. Maybe he felt that it was the captain's project, and he was trying not to interfere. Maybe not.

Willett stepped up behind Lieutenant Riggs and laid a hand on his shoulder. "Quite a mystery, isn't it, Jason? This polygonal shape is extraordinary. Nothing like any of the tunnels or caves around these parts." Ironwood guessed that they had worked together before. The population of Ridgecrest, including the Navy base, was over 25,000. Considering how related and specialized their fields were, that made for a small town by comparison.

"I wonder who'd ever want to build something in an area like this," Riggs asked to no one in particular, not expecting an answer.

"It's probably an old Indian excavation of some kind," replied Eastwater from his end of the tunnel.

"Created for what purpose?" challenged Alan Ward. He's becoming awfully bold, thought Ironwood. Probably seeking revenge for the indignation, he suffered at the hands of Eastwater earlier that day.

"I believe I mentioned that earlier," returned the captain, his legs taut with clenched fists at his side.

"You mean a sewer?" he countered, raising his voice.

Careful Alan, careful, worried Ironwood to himself.

"Yes. . . a drainage canal of some type." Marching the length of the tunnel, he faced the frail man head-on. "It's the only conclusion that makes sense."

"I believe your thinking becomes more asinine as we go along," Alan grinned back. Ironwood was surprised that he held his ground.

Eastwater was so close to him that he probably could tell what he had for lunch.

Only microseconds elapsed before the captain's reactor went critical. "And may I remind you that you are on government-owned property under the command of the United States Navy. You are out of here, mister!"

Tiny droplets of spittle flew from the captain's mouth, but Alan Ward braved the shower and held his mark.

"It is time for you to leave, Mr. Ward," interrupted the admiral, tired of all this confrontational chatter. "You have your own transportation?"

"Yes, admiral," answered Alan politely. "I followed one of Marinus Willett's employees here."

"Then I'll arrange for you to follow one of my men off of the base."

"No need to, admiral," volunteered Willett. "It has been a long day for me. My work is done here. He can follow the survey crew and me out."

"Very well, but no side trips, Mr. Ward. Do you understand me? You will drive straight out of here without stopping or taking any detours. My security checkpoints will be keeping an eye out for you."

"Yes, admiral," looking like a schoolboy who had to stay after class.

"And one more thing, Mr. Ward. Every time you are around here, fireworks seem to go off. I can't have that on my base. There will be no more archeological passes for you at the gate from now on. I don't mean to be harsh or unfair with you, sir, but we all have a job to do here, and you are in the way."

Admiral Hawkins walked past Alan and climbed up the ladder like a young man of twenty.

Still looking the part of a disciplined schoolboy, Alan turned to Ironwood, "Well, I guess I have been dismissed."

Ironwood yawned and stretched; he felt unusually tired. Looking at his watch, he was surprised that it was only three o'clock in the afternoon. "I guess so," he answered. "I feel like calling it a day myself. Say," he said, struck with a sudden thought, "where are you staying now, Alan?"

"At the Red Mountain Inn."

"Not anymore. You are staying with me. I have a little place that will make you forget California."

"That's a generous offer," he smiled, looking grateful.

"Good," said Ironwood. "Excellent." Behind him, he heard Willett collapsing his specimen table and gathering together his equipment.

"Jason," the ponytailed scientist muttered, "could I get some help getting this topside?"

"No problem," volunteered the young lieutenant. "I'll get a rope down here right away."

Ironwood turned around in time to see Willett put a handful of small flat stones, each the size of a nickel, into a clear Tupperware bowl. His eyes caught the glint of green. "What are those fragments, professor?"

"Another mystery," he answered, opening the container he had just snapped closed, holding them out for Ironwood's close inspection.

Ironwood took one out and held it up to the light streaming in through the ceiling. It felt greasy, and he detected markings or scratches on its flat surface. For a brief instant, before returning it, he thought he saw the faint impression of a face on the stone. He had seen one of these before. A fellow he knew that was in the Miskatonic University Relocation Program, by the name of Faren Church, kept one with him at all times. He believed it to be a good luck charm.

"They're green soapstone," the old man added. "All badly chipped, I'm afraid." He stared at Ironwood for a bit, then rattled the plastic container and its contents under his nose resembling a beggar with a tin cup. Ironwood reluctantly dropped the small stone back into the bowl. Willett snapped the lid back into place and put it into a drawer in the specimen table, all with one swift movement.

Ironwood felt it was time for him to leave as well.

A perfectly immaculate blue sky dotted with puffy white cumulus clouds greeted Professor Ironwood as he climbed back up the ladder. All he could hear was the wind whispering across the sand. He walked over to the shade by the side of the transport truck and sat down on a packing crate.

On the other side of the road, Stream and Eastwater had become a coalition of two again and stood quietly talking to themselves beneath the shade of several Joshua trees. Besides the Joshuas and the military hardware, there was nothing else around him but a litter of black rock, creosote brush, and a haze of salt, a landscape that continuously fell back upon itself, one spot indistinguishable from another. The black, jagged hills of the Argus Range broke up the monotony of the Mojave's horizon, with the Maturango Peak, the highest in the range, almost 9,000 feet above sea level, reflecting the afternoon sun's glare, looking down on Ironwood like a stone sentinel. Nothing but barren rock, hot sun, and whining wind, and we find what looks like the Holland tunnel beneath all of this. It certainly was a mystery, he thought.

Alan clambered up the ladder and joined Ironwood in the shade just as a seaman started to hoist Willett's specimen case upwards on a long line of heavy nylon rope.

"I'll be by after seven if that's all right?" said Alan squinting against the sun until passing into the shade.

"That will be fine," replied Ironwood plucking a sand burr from his pants cuff. "I'll write down some directions. It's a little tricky to find."

The activity around the hole increased, followed by muffled cursing. Ironwood and Alan looked up in time to see the seaman, now joined by Lieutenant Riggs, struggle with the rope. The specimen case wouldn't fit through the hole in the tunnel's ceiling. There was a general commotion among the men above and below. After several minutes, Riggs ordered two of his men to fetch some shovels, and they started to widen the opening.

"Difficult to account for something like that," mused Alan. "How do you suppose it happened?"

"What do you mean?"

"The case," he replied, pointing to the group of struggling Seabees. "We brought it down through there earlier today. Now it won't fit through the hole."

"I don't know. This area frequently experiences earth movements. Maybe the ground has shifted minutely in the last few hours."

"Unlikely, but possible. I think I'll. . ."

Alan's voice trailed off, leaving his sentence incomplete. Ironwood noticed that he was no longer looking at the struggling Seabees. He followed Alan's gaze to the stand of Joshua trees. He knew what had distracted him. It was the same thing he had wondered earlier when he sought refuge from the sun alongside the truck. The raised but muffled voices of Eastwater and Stream filtered softly through the afternoon haze. They seemed amused by the activity around the hole. Their laughter beat against the twisted shadows of the Joshua trees; what were those two up to now?

CHAPTER 7
DARWIN

It was a "Close Encounters" kind of road, thought Alan, as he guided the rented Taurus along the white line that stretched toward the black horizon.

He had been traveling the lonely desert highway for over an hour, and streetlights had become scarce. The last one he had seen marked the turnoff to a small desert town by the name of Keeler. The light pole stood in front of an old-style one pump service station. A Jeep, painted Desert Storm brown and tan, was parked beneath its canopy. The gas station was closed for the night. All the lights inside were off. He probably would have passed it by without giving it a second look except for a flurry of activity that caught his attention outlined in the halogen glare.

Slowing almost to a stop, he watched with fascination through the car's windshield as a coyote caught and then ate moths the size of silver dollars. Hundreds of the nocturnal winged insects irresistibly drawn to the light flew around and around in circles. The coyote, the moths, and the ground around them were all painted a moon-white glow. Reaching up into the swirling flurry with a front paw, the coyote would swat one of the helpless insects driving it downward. The stricken moth would bounce and then momentarily flutter on the gravel parking lot until the hungry snout of the prairie wolf lapped it up. The coyote continued his feeding activity until Alan let up on the brake and allowed the car to creep closer. Alerted to his presence by the advancing Taurus, the coyote stepped back, disappearing amidst the shadows, and waited for him to leave. That had been several miles back, and now, beyond the range of the Taurus' headlamps was total darkness. It was Alan's first time out west. He felt like a space explorer piloting a small shuttlecraft across an alien landscape. The moonless night added to the illusion. The evening stars did little to illuminate the desert expanse that he knew lay hidden under a veil of darkness so complete that when he extinguished the Taurus' headlights, he became blind. It was a childish thing to do, he knew, but the temptation had been irresistible. The first time he did it, the car had been moving. It was foolish. Foolhardy, to be precise, but when he found himself plunged into a black emptiness, traveling over sixty miles an hour, he quickly turned the lights back on. The high beam stabbed the night, the white line down the middle of the road reacted like phosphorus, and the warm green glow of the instrument panel dispelled the current of fear that shot through him.

Had that merely been a trick played upon his eyes? Was the darkness indeed that complete? After all, his eyes hadn't had time to grow accustomed to the change. It demanded another test. Pulling the Taurus onto the road shoulder, he put the car into park and shut off the motor. He hadn't seen another car for miles. The highway had been empty in both directions. The car softly chattered as the engine cooled. Reaching towards the dashboard, he switched off the lights. Everything became black. He sat quietly in the dark, waiting for his eyes to adjust. The retinal after-image left by the extinguished headlights teased his eyes briefly and then subsided.

Nothing came into view. Modern twenty-first-century man very seldom finds himself surrounded in total darkness. There usually are streetlights or the lights from buildings and houses to mark your way. Even within the closed and shuttered existence of one's bedroom, there was normally the luminous face of an alarm clock to dispel the oppressive blackness. After a while, he thought that he detected the faint outline of the steering wheel in front of him but came up a couple of inches short when grabbing for it. He literally could not see his hand in front of his face. After several more seconds, he was able to perceive a scattering of stars.

The view offered by the windshield was narrow and limited and made him curious to see the entire starfield. Fumbling for the handle, he opened the car door and stepped outside. The illumination from the car's interior light dilated his pupils and made him squint. Alan slammed the door behind him and was plunged once again into darkness as thick as layered gauze. A glorious array of stars mapped out the heavens, but the radiation they gave off was too weak to illuminate the surrounding desert plain. Looking up and walking away from the car gave him the feeling of floating in space. The night air was still. It was warm, probably eighty-degrees or so.

There were no sounds. He was floating, afloat in his mind like someone in an isolation tank, eyes blindfolded and submerged in a lukewarm, buoyant, saltwater solution. The only thing you can hear is your breathing through a snorkel, except here he had the stars—an outstanding field of stars. Looking straight ahead where the horizon should be, he felt lost. At eye level, once again, was the black nothingness. He had walked several steps when struck by a chilling thought.

He made an about face confronting his fear only to have it confirmed. He couldn't see the car. He couldn't see the road, for that matter, although he could feel its smooth surface beneath the soles of his shoes. The Taurus, the road, and any details of the surrounding landscape hid from him. The stars didn't shed enough illumination even to see a few feet. Alan was pretty sure that he was facing in the right direction. The car should be straight ahead, and as long as he kept the blacktop underfoot, he probably wouldn't get lost. There may not be another car on the road for hours to help light his way. He felt alone. There was a prickly sensation at the back of his neck. It was the feeling he usually had when he was coming out of one of his nightmares. Immediately after he had made the mental comparison, something gray and slimy came out of the darkness. It was charging down at him. He looked over his shoulder, and watched it propel itself towards him with gray-green ropes for arms. It moved quickly—a jellied thing with the arms of an octopus and a face., a horrible face that made Alan gasp for air. He found it hard to draw a breath as if the darkness itself had begun to flow into his mouth, his lungs; he was suffocating. In that one petrifying moment, Alan realized that he was in the tunnel and was running out of air. He gasped again, ran forward, stumbled, and came upon the front bumper of the Taurus. Groping blindly, frantically, he reached the driver's side door and yanked it open. He slipped back in and had the engine started with the headlights back on before he closed and locked the door.

An empty road stretched out as far as his high beams could reach. Nothing pursued him. It had come from out of his subconscious, not the desert night. He turned the air conditioner on high and directed the vents towards his face. Sucking in the cool air, Alan swallowed hard before moving the shift lever to "D" and negotiating the car off the shoulder and back onto the road.

After a few minutes with the doors locked and the seatbelt and shoulder harness holding him snug, he felt secure. The road he was traveling was Route 190, and fifteen miles out of Keeler, he came to the Darwin turnoff. Alan reduced his speed and watched the road in front of him steadily incline upwards. After about a quarter of a mile, the road began to dip down, and he saw lights ahead. Not very many, but a few that looked like they could be street lights or lights from someone's windows. They disappeared when the Taurus climbed another hill in the asphalt. To his left, a round metal sign glared back at him under his high beams. It read, "The Blue Ridge Mining Company." Alan had done a little reading about the surrounding Panamint Range. Long ago, the great silver strikes had been in Cerro Gordo, Greenwater, Skidoo, and Darwin. Today all of these mines were shut down. The ore cost was less than the expense to get it out of the ground. No sooner had Alan started to wonder if he was following Ironwood's written directions correctly than a green and white highway sign loomed up out of the darkness. "Darwin," it read.

Alan sighed with relief. The lights from Darwin came into view again as the road leveled out. There were two streetlights. Large halogens mounted on electric poles. One was in front of a low wood and stone structure and the other farther east at the intersection of two streets. Hundreds of moths swam in the white glare like the street lamp in Keeler, only minus the coyote this time. He could make out three or four houses scattered here and there with lights in the windows off to his left. The rest were dark. Some weren't even proper houses. Quonset huts with the windows boarded up, tiny dwellings the size of fishing shanties, some with the doors missing and others that looked like they had been pieced together out of sheet-metal and old boilerplate. Two houses he noticed, as the Taurus crept along, looked like they may have been substantial in their day, but the roofs had fallen in a long time ago, and all the glass was gone from their windows. Almost unconsciously, he checked the lock on the car door next to him. He had slowed to about fifteen miles per hour by then. He had noticed the low wood and stone structure when first approaching the town was immediately on his right now. "Darwin Historical Museum," a sign hung out front read. Its windows were dark and shiny like black Visqueen.

Alan wanted to turn the Taurus around and head back to the Red

Mountain Inn. Anything was better than this. Ironwood needs to have his head examined. No one in their right mind would live here. At the lighted intersection, he saw the signpost. Ironwood had said to watch for the signpost that marked the intersection of Fulton and Main. Alan thought he was eccentric, or it was his old New England school tie showing through when he had said "signpost." People nowadays say, "street sign," but there to his right, at the edge of the pavement, was a 4 x 4 wood post approximately 6 feet high. The post had been chamfered on the top and painted white. Faintly he could make out faded black letters running vertically up two sides. "Fulton" and "Main," they spelled out.

He was on Fulton, and he turned right on Main as per Ironwood's instructions. O.K. Alan, now whose head should be examined?

Passing a collection of what had once been businesses on his left, he noted the badly weathered remains of an old bank that looked like the kind that Bonnie and Clyde would have knocked over in their day. A post office, or what had once served as a post office, looked ancient and abandoned. The low fluorescent glow of a soft-drink machine on the front porch of a desert weary general store looked out of place. The store was closed for the night. "No need for a 7-11 out this far," thought Alan.

The asphalt ran out, and he found himself driving on gravel. A little farther ahead and on his left, he saw what looked like a roof and part of a foundation rising out of the ground. The roof was flat and stood only a few feet above ground level. Alan drove the car parallel to it, saw that a section of the earth had been terraced away, and a few stone steps led to a door. He realized that most of the house was beneath the ground and that you had to step down into the front entry. He could see the foundation was fieldstone, not concrete work, and the flat roof was constructed with heavy timbers. With a raised wood panel below and a frosted glass pane above, the door shone with the lights from inside. The frosted glass was about two feet square, and it had a wildlife setting with a mountain lion, an eagle in flight, and a large Joshua tree etched into its surface. It looked warm and inviting. Mounted to the door, below the pictorial setting, was a varnished wood plaque. The word "lignum vitae" had been burned into its surface.

Alan smiled. "Lignum vitae," he said. The wood of Life strictly translated from Latin. A tropical American tree of very hard and heavy wood, also known as ironwood. He had come to the right place.

CHAPTER 8
NIGHT SHIFT

Mingo and his night crew broke through the end of the tunnel a little after midnight. It took them three hours to remove the rubble that had blocked the narrow artery and another three to get a significant portion of the rock debris through the hole in the ceiling and outside.

Chief Petty Officer Domingo Mercado sat on one of the larger basalt projections that had been too heavy to move topside and looked at his watch. He was tired but had expected his relief within an hour. Hot, sweaty, and covered with rock dust, he kept entertaining thoughts about a long, sudsy shower followed by several cold Heinekens.

He had pulled lousy duty again. His last grand tour of duty was alongside the Iraqis. There he helped construct 150 temporary latrines and two tent cities. When his tour of duty was over, he put in for reassignment. As his luck would have it, he ended up in the desert again—the Mojave Desert. Although at times like this, he felt unlucky, he never complained openly. He regarded the Seabees as his family, and with all obligations of the family, you had to take the bitter with the sweet.

If asked, he would say that he had no relatives. In reality, both his parents were alcoholics, and he had a wife that couldn't stand him. He had walked out of that life years ago and never looked back.

He glanced at his watch again, more like an hour and a half before they would get here, he corrected himself. They were just goofing off now. It was a well-deserved rest for his crew. They had worked long and hard uncovering the other section of the tunnel. Other section, hell, it looked like it went on forever. Dexter and Rinaldi were exploring some of it by flashlight. He had told them not to go far until they had strung some more lights.

When they had first brought the generator on its trailer and set it up outside, they drove steel hooks along the cave wall and strung electric cable and lights. It was as bright as day in what had now become their staging area. When they all had their second wind, they would start hanging some more lights, he decided.

Mingo dribbled some water from a five-gallon Igloo cooler into his hands and splashed his face. The palms of his hands felt like dry paper. Must be something in the soil that made them chap, he thought. They had brought enough cables, sockets, and LED bulbs to light half a mile of tunnel. The big diesel generator upstairs could power four times that if they needed it. He had no idea why the top brass required all this equipment. He didn't even know why he was here at this hour. Oh sure, he could understand their curiosity, the interest everyone had for what may lie on the other side of the cave-in. But what was the rush? Why three crews around the clock? It didn't make sense to him. Why did the brass want in there so quickly when he could have mobilized their Komatsu track hoe with a four-yard bucket. They could tear the top of this tunnel and been through to the other side in an hour. Eastwater had torpedoed him on that one. They wanted to "Keep as much of the tunnel intact as possible," he had said, concerned that there may be some historical value to this place. It would be something if this place became as famous as the pyramids in Egypt. Sure would play hell with their secret weapons testing, though, Mingo grinned. He liked the thought. Maybe he could write a book about it. "I Helped Discover the Tunnels beneath the NWC," he imagined the words spelled out in front of him and framed the title in mid-air with his two hands.

"Hey chief, come here! You gotta see this," shouted Dexter from an area just beyond the reach of their lights.

Mingo slowly got to his feet, stretched, and on legs made of rubber walked towards Dexter. He must be getting old, he thought. This assignment was wearing pretty heavy on him. It was taking longer to get the kinks out of his joints.

Dexter stood in the shadows of the recently discovered tunnel section; his flashlight directed at the ground. The little exploring that they had done, always careful to keep the staging area within view, revealed multiple passages branching off a tunnel that appeared to run perfectly straight for Lord knows how many miles?

"What's up Opie," Mingo asked?

Seaman Jonathan Dexter was from Oskaloosa, Iowa, the son of a Baptist minister and just starting his third year in the Navy. He was tall, broad-shouldered, with red hair and freckles. Chief Mercado, who enjoyed doling out nicknames, said that he looked like Opie Taylor, "all grow'd up." He referred to the fictional character who was the son of Sheriff Taylor on the old Andy Griffith television show. Dexter wasn't pleased with the comparison.

"Check this out," he replied, ostensibly ignoring the comment, and using his flashlight as a pointer.

Mingo squatted down on the smooth tunnel floor and stared at a blob of tree sap. Pine tree sap, he thought—the color of amber, about three-quarters of an inch wide and no longer than his index finger. Mingo reached out to touch it with his left hand, and it moved. The Chief Petty Officer jerked his hand back with a snap. Not because it had moved, but when he had reached for it, it had lunged towards him.

"Madre' mia," he shouted. "What in the hell is that thing?"

"I don't know, sir," said the puzzled seaman.

"We noticed it on our way back," added Rinaldi, standing to the Chief's right.

"It seems to be moving toward the light."

"It stops whenever I direct the beam of my flashlight on it," countered Dexter with incredulous eyes reflecting the light.

"Hmm, let me see. Turn off your light," ordered the Chief.

Dexter snapped off the light. A pale luminescence filtered in from the staging area. Mingo, still squatting down, was in the strange thing's path. His eyes strained against the gloom. He was between it and the staging area. The little blob, some sort of animal, he realized, moved straight toward him. Leaning closer, he could see that it glided along on a fringe of fine hair. A thousand eyelashes propelled it towards Mingo; stepping back quickly, he ordered Dexter to turn on the light.

"Maybe it's some kind of desert snail," said Rinaldi.

The little amber blob had stopped dead in its tracks, and it did leave tracks. A narrow, moist trail glistened in the beam of Dexter's light. It moved on a mucus current similar to a snail, but it didn't resemble any snail or slug that Mingo could recall.

"Wait a minute," said Dexter handing his flashlight to Rinaldi. "I'll get something to turn it over with," he announced as he ran to the staging area and returned in half a minute with one of the steel hooks they used to string the electric cable along the walls.

He knelt alongside the thing. Dexter reached out with the metal hook and gingerly touched it. Dexter screamed in pain. Mingo wasn't sure what had happened. It had moved so fast. When Dexter had prodded the slug-thing with the pointed end of the hook, his hand couldn't have been more than six inches from it. It sprung upwards the moment the steel hook made contact and flew to Dexter's right hand.

The young Seabee rolled around on the tunnel floor; his arm racked with pain. "My hand's on fire! Feels like acid."

Chief Mercado reacted quickly to the situation and wrestled the young man to a seated position holding his right arm in a steel grip around his biceps. "Bring the light over here," he shouted. The amber goo started to spread. It was growing bigger around the kid's hand. The thing was transparent, and Mingo could see red welts forming on Dexter's skin where it clung. The top layer of his flesh started to crack and shrivel as if held over an open flame. Mingo tried to pluck it off, but it stuck to the kid's skin like epoxy. The tips of the Chief's fingers burned with blistering fire, and he pulled back.

Trying to ignore the pain in his hand, Chief Mercado pulled a bone-handled pocketknife from his slacks. With a well-practiced flick of his wrist, a four-inch blade snapped open. "Hold the damn light still," he roared at Rinaldi, who was shaking badly.

Dexter was becoming hysterical, and Mingo had to firm up his grip. "Hang on, son. Let me get this thing off of you." He prayed that he could. He liked the kid, and his hand was beginning to get real ugly. Keeping his left arm tightly around Dexter's and his right hand steady, he applied the knife's sharp edge to just above the wrist. The outer skin had peeled away, and the thing was starting to work on the subcutaneous layer. It was swelling up, increasing in size a little, and a faint yellow radiance flickered beneath the goo. Mingo's hand moved swiftly, and the blade sparkled with reflected light. The slug-thing tumbled a couple of times in the air and landed in the sand. Just like whittling, he thought. Mingo had scraped or, more appropriately, shaved the slug-thing off the young man's hand with one quick movement.

Then, the oversized slug rolled only once, apparently unaffected by its fall, slithered towards the staging area. Mingo got to his feet and moved to step on the thing. Grind it under the heel of his boot. He stopped the moment he raised his foot. The thought of contact with the thing, even with the sole of his boot, was discomforting.

Dexter was recovering his calm, and Rinaldi took him back to the staging area and a first aid kit.

"How ya doing, Ole Dexter?" asked the concerned Chief Petty Officer.

"A lot better, chief," he answered, quivering.

"Rinaldi," he snapped, looking past Dexter, "call the base and sickbay and get a medic down here on the double."

"Aye, chief."

Mingo turned and grabbed a miner's pick off of a pile of tools and impaled the slug-thing to the tunnel floor with one swipe. He went to the staging area with determination in every step and quickly returned with a shovel and a camper's light.

The yellow blob had retracted itself from around the pick and remained intact. There was no hole where the pick drove through it, only in the tunnel floor.

Mingo placed the battery-powered lantern on the ground to one side of the thing. His insides shook. The old nerves of steel have turned to cardboard, he told himself. He had scored a direct hit with the pick. He hadn't taken his eyes off of it for more than thirty seconds. It should have been stuck to the ground like an insect pinned to a specimen board, but it looked unharmed. Not wanting to think about it any further, he tightened his grip on the shovel handle and brought it down on the slug severing it in two. The shovel made a "ka-chunk" sound as it penetrated the soft layer of sand coming to rest against the hard tunnel floor. The two halves of the thing bumped and groped against both sides of the shovel scoop. As if realizing the limits of their barrier, both halves darted around the metal blade and instantaneously rejoined upon touching like quicksilver.

There wasn't any blood, nor was there any fluid that could pass for blood. There wasn't even a scar where the thing had been cut in half. Mingo was transfixed. He raised the shovel again and brought it down with another hard ka-chunk. It was momentarily chopped in two again. Fueled by a growing fear, he raised and lowered his arms with mechanical precision. Ka-chunk, ka-chunk the shovel went, cutting it into four sections. He had become one of his pieces of construction equipment. Ka-chunk, ka-chunk, ka-chunk, ka-chunk went the Mingo machine. Over twenty pieces of the slug-thing skittered in momentary confusion and then came together at a common point. The entire rejoining took no more than a few seconds.

"Damn, will you look at that," said Rinaldi coming to an abrupt halt at the Chief's shoulder.

Mingo turned and stared at him. He hadn't seen him walk up. "He's one tough little son-of-a-bitch."

"I wonder," nodded Rinaldi, "how the little bugger likes fire?" Taking a disposable butane lighter from his top pocket, he cranked the tiny wheel just below the orifice to "maximum" with his thumb. "Phasers on kill, Mr. Spock," he said with a smile and bent close to the slug-thing. A three-inch flame shot out of the lighter, and the slug thing sizzled and popped. Mingo felt partially relieved. At least the thing wasn't fireproof. The end that was touched by the flame shriveled and turned black. The slug had reversed its course with lashing movements and skittered back towards the darkness. A sooty stream of black smoke curled upwards from its charred flesh. The smell reminded him of burning plastic.

Dexter joined them, holding a bandaged hand. Mingo decided that finally, some retribution was being given out for the seaman's discomfort. Mingo focused his attention on its retreat, and a cold chill crawled up his back. The thing was growing. As quickly as the lighter's flame charred and disintegrated the little creature on one end, the other end would enlarge and develop at an equal rate. It was as if the thing were meant to be a certain size and volume and wouldn't vary no matter what happened to it. If that was the case, then what was it? It certainly wasn't one of God's creatures. The thought terrified Mingo. He was an engineer of sorts. He was a Seabee, a practical man that didn't believe in ghosts, UFOs, or creatures from the bottom of the sea. If he hadn't been standing there and someone had given him an account of this, he would have dismissed it, saying that it had been done with mirrors or that they all must have been drunk. But he was there, and he believed in real things, and one thing he knew was that all things could be destroyed. Even this tough little bastard.

The fire seemed to be doing it at first, but maybe there wasn't enough. Engulf it in flames so that it can't grow out on the other end. Cook it in a bath of flaming gasoline, liquid fire, diesel fuel was better; it wasn't as dangerous. It didn't have as high a flashpoint as gasoline, a safety consideration within a confined space. Best of all, there were five-gallon cans of it topside next to the generator.

Rinaldi shut off the flow of the butane and pulled away from the thing. The lighter had become too hot to handle.

"Hold that thing in place with your flashlight," commanded Mingo. "I'll be back in two minutes."

In the few seconds, it took for Rinaldi to pick up his flashlight, the slug-thing had completely regenerated itself and started moving towards the staging area. Rinaldi switched on his incandescent light. The thing abruptly stopped as if it trapped in the beam. Before turning to leave, Mingo noticed that there wasn't a trace of a burn scar.

Running towards the ladder, Mingo could hear the soft chug-chugging of the generator through the hole above. He stopped with his right foot on the lower rung. Several coils of electrical cable rolled up next to the ladder grabbed his attention. Coiled black snakes, he thought, snakes of fire. They used twelve-gauge wire to handle 110 volts, primarily to power the LEDs and the light-duty power tools. The eight-gauge was for 220 volts; they had used that for their jackhammers to bust rock. About 220 volts should fry that little son-of-a-gun faster than a bonfire and with a lot less mess, he thought, smiling. The idea intrigued him. Mingo stepped away from the ladder. He grabbed one of the cables that strung across the floor and unplugged it from the large electrical outlet that hung through the hole in the ceiling. He disconnected the other end of the heavy-duty extension cord from a jackhammer. The chief pulled out his pocketknife and skillfully cut the receptacle end of the cable off. He stripped the copper ends bare, ensuring that the positive and negative wires were spread a safe distance apart. He returned to the area surrounding the ladder and inserted the three-pronged diagonal blade back into its outlet. The 220 receptacles hung off of a portable 1500-amp breaker box. Mingo knew that it would "pop" a breaker shutting that line down on the system the moment the wires made contact with the thing. The breakers would not tolerate an electrical short. Opening the door on the box, he taped the 220-volt breaker switch in the "On" position with two heavy pieces of duct tape.

"All systems go," he said, slamming the metal door on the box. He had effectively made a giant Taser. He practically strutted to the other end of the tunnel. The cable was long enough to reach Rinaldi and Dexter, and it played out smoothly behind Mingo without a snag.

The slug-thing was still frozen in the beam of Rinaldi's flashlight. Mingo thought it looked bigger than when he first saw it. Maybe a couple of inches longer. It didn't matter. However, it would be burnt toast in a few seconds. Dexter and Rinaldi didn't say anything. They didn't need to. You'd have to be a real jarhead not to figure out what he was going to do. Squatting down within arm's reach of the little blob, he jabbed both copper ends of the cable into the thing. They penetrated the jellied flesh with hardly any resistance and went in all the way. The lights in the staging area dimmed briefly. There was no burning. No hiss. No pop. Mingo had expected it to boil like tree sap on a burning log and then burst into flames. Instead, it glowed orange deep inside its translucent body. In the blink of an eye, Mingo watched it instantly double in length and width. It grew to almost a foot long. He tried to jerk the wires free, but they had become stuck fast. He dangled it in the air from the cable end and stared as it doubled in size once more and engulfed his hand. Not only did his hand burn like turpentine in an open wound, but he also felt the shock of 220 volts coursing through his body. Mingo wished that he had gone for the diesel fuel instead. He had pulled lousy duty once again.

CHAPTER 9
THE PARTY

Vice Admiral Hawkins didn't offer suggestions; he gave orders. Eastwater grudgingly felt that he had brought them down with him written on stone tablets. "Come to my place tonight, Clayton," he had said. "Bring the missus. I'm having a few friends over for drinks and Alice, and I would like the both of you to come." The invite was a veiled command. He'd known the old salt way too long, and he wasn't about to refuse. Why did he want me there, he puzzled? Was he trying to keep an eye on me? Did he suspect my deal with the congressman? He doubted it. He had covered his tracks too well. He didn't try to hide his friendly association with Neville Stream. The congressman and his father-in-law, Carson Stillwell, had been good friends for years. Neville Stream had married Stillwell's sister back in the 1980s. That made it easy for the both of them to associate openly. Besides, in two weeks it won't matter anymore. He'll have everything battened down by then. They'll have what they need, and he won't have to wait for his pension.

Clayton Eastwater looked over at his wife in the car seat next to him. Maggie Eastwater stared out the windshield at the winding residential street lined with cottonwoods and fan palms. The stupid broomstick doesn't even suspect the deal I'm involved in, thought the captain. A faint smile, sublimely evil, wrinkled up briefly between the corners of his mouth. There was a ten-year difference in their ages. He was thirty. She was forty. Carson Stillwell was an admiral when he married her five years ago. A good career move, at the time, until the old battlewagon had a double coronary and died. Now he was stuck with this bag of bones that can't ask for the salt without whining.

Most of his connections were severed with the death of Stillwell. It could go worse with the top brass if he divorced the daughter of a dead admiral. He was going to have to stick it out a little longer. Play his character by the book. He knew there was a danger. Immense danger if he got caught. But anything was better than just sitting around, buying cars and houses, going to the movies, and just waiting for the end. Sometimes, he thought, the game seemed more important than the money and the opportunity to escape. As it was, he felt that it was just enough to give life a hair-trigger.

Eastwater slowed for a stop sign posted at a richly landscaped intersection. Seeing no cars in the opposite direction, he continued. Admiral Hawkins lived in an upscale neighborhood in the southeast section of Ridgecrest near College Heights. His was a Mediterranean style, two-story concrete block, and stucco home with a three-car garage. The Eastwaters had a small apartment on the other side of town. Clayton was always finding things he didn't like about the admiral's home. He hated two-story houses. "All that traipsing up and downstairs." He didn't care for the architecture style either, "If he likes Mediterranean so much, why the hell doesn't he move to Italy?"

The admiral's home was at the end of a brick cul-de-sac. Captain Eastwater followed the sweeping arc of the street and parked alongside the curb. Several of the admiral's guests filled the driveway. A poppy-red 1965 Mustang convertible was parked on the right side of the drive. It belonged to Hawkins. He had just spent the last ten years restoring the car. A young woman, the wife of a Lieutenant J. G. under Eastwater's command, sat behind the wheel admiring the car's interior. "I guess I'm going to have to make a fuss over the damn thing as well," he brooded.

Eastwater got out of his car, then waited at the curb for Maggie to get out and join him. "Ain't she a beaut?" called out the young woman in the Mustang.

"The best I've ever seen," he hollered back, mustering up a smile. With Maggie at his side, he turned and surveyed the admiral's front door and welcome mat. Taking a deep breath, he marched ahead.

***

Congressman Stream dropped two ice cubes into a short glass and filled it halfway up with Scotch.

"That's a pretty stiff drink you're making, Neville," said the red-head woman young enough to be his daughter.

"Not at all, my dear. I've been cutting back. Why there was a time that I did this with one hundred and fifty proof vodka while attempting to construct a martini, as custom dictated in those days, I would then pass my glass several times beneath a painting of Antonio Carpano."

"Who is that?" she asked, genuinely interested.

"Why, the inventor of vermouth, of course."

The young woman covered her mouth with a dainty hand and giggled politely. She had been a volunteer on his re-election campaign last year, and he could tell immediately upon meeting her that her adoration for him could be put to good use. Ever since then, she had become his personal secretary and travel companion, except when it was necessary for his wife, Heather, to make public appearances with him. Today, Heather Stillwell-Stream was in Boulder, Colorado, spearheading a health care rally. The following Friday, she would be addressing the graduate class at Vassar about "Women in the Workplace." She was far away, thank God, and he was sure that she shared the same feelings about him. Theirs had been a marriage of convenience. A powerful union. It represented the two greatest elements of power: the welding together of money and politics. He had come a long way since those days as a struggling assistant district attorney. His wife's money and his contacts did more than award him a seat in the House of Representatives eventually. He had also become the head of the Ways and Means Committee, and he held that chair position for over ten years, a seat of power that had given him control of over two-fifths of the United States Treasury.

Neville Stream took a healthy sip of his drink. It had been a long day. A faint pink smudge streaked across one side of his nose. His makeup had run. He normally wouldn't be this careless if the press had been around, but there were no cameras tonight. He always tried to keep the red veins around his nose and below his eyes powdered when he was under the camera lights. Tonight, was more sociable than political, and he would let his hair down a little. If anyone said anything about it, he'd laugh it off and say it was stress lines or sunburn. And, if there were any press lurking around, he'd cut their balls off in the job market and make it impossible for them to find work in journalism again. He begrudgingly recalled the crusading journalist in Chicago that nailed him and Congressman Nathan Sells for their little escapade with a waitress after hours in a fashionable eatery. She had entitled her story, "A Waitress Sandwich." It had taken five-hundred-thousand dollars to cover that one up with several well-placed stories and with well-paid witnesses destroying the waitress's credibility and the career of the reporterette.

Congressman Stream turned in time to see Admiral Hawkins' front door open wide. He smiled when Clayton and Maggie Eastwater walked into the foyer. Stream felt relieved because he had resolved himself to spend the rest of the evening in the company of fools until then. He watched the young officer make a few obligatory handshakes around the room. Clayton Eastwater's wife stood obediently at his side while exchanging polite conversation with Mrs. Hawkins. The Admiral's wife was a sturdy woman who looked like she spent most of her time in the kitchen baking cookies. She wiped her hands on an apron, and motioned them towards the family room, mentioning something about drinks.

Clayton appeared eager to accept the offer and negotiated his way across the terra cotta floor tiles and up to the bar. Scooping up some ice with a glass, he didn't pause until he had filled it with scotch and then emptied half of its contents.

"Throwing caution to the wind Clayton?" inquired the congressman.

"You know I hate these damn things."

"I know; that's why I asked Hawkins to invite you."

"You! You son-of-a-bitch! What did you hope to gain?"

"Nothing but positive exposure. You are my nephew, after all. It wouldn't look good if I were in town for a visit, and I ignored family."

"I am not your nephew. I am married to your niece, and that's as far as it goes."

"A mere technicality," Neville Stream sighed, "a mere technicality." The congressman paused and stared straight ahead. Maggie Eastwater was tangled in Mrs. Hawkins' apron strings, and Buffy, his redheaded traveling companion, had been cornered by a drooling ensign. They were alone at the bar. "Have you got them digging out that rubble?" His voice had become stern.

"I've got three crews working around the clock. With any luck, we'll have it uncovered by morning, Eastwater answered, looking over his shoulder to make sure no one was in earshot."

"Good. And the location of the vault room?"

"That may take some time. I've mapped out a ten-square-mile area with our seismic surveys. We are currently establishing a database."

"The easiest way to obtain information, Clayton, is to steal it."

Eastwater downed the other half of his drink and almost choked on the ice. He knew what his uncle-in-law was suggesting. "Those files are top secret," he managed to blurt out, and he hoped not too loud. "I could spend the rest of my life in prison if I get caught."

"I am sure you are exaggerating, Clayton. Just a few old papers dating back to World War II that should have been declassified years ago. No one will ever miss them."

Stream could see that his "nephew" was shaken and stopped talking when a navy man in dress whites approached the bar to check on the supply of glasses and ice.

Motioning Eastwater away from the bar, he lowered his voice and asked, "Where is Hawkins?"

"Out on the front lawn showing off that Matchbox car of his."

"Excellent. Come with me."

"Where are we going?" he almost whined.

"To the admiral's study. We can talk privately there."

"I don't know. I don't think this is wise. What if someone sees us going in there?"

"I don't think they would begrudge us talking over some personal family matters, do you?" he answered, smiling smugly.

"I see a couple of my men over there. I really should go over and . . ."

The congressman took hold of the Captain's arm and led him towards the study door. "How many times do I have to tell you, Clayton? Don't get involved with people who have nothing to lose.

maybe, and his bronze tan added to his youthful appearance. "Anybody home?" he said again.

The Professor's eyes opened wide. He stared at Alan uncomprehendingly for a second or two and then burst into an apology. "Oh, Alan, I am sorry. Must have dozed off." He sat up, rubbed his eyes, and looked about the house trailer. "I was exhausted for some reason. How are you? Did you have any trouble finding the place?"

"It was an adventure," he said, recalling his experience in the dark. "But your directions were excellent." Alan went up two metal stair treads and walked inside. The trailer's interior was almost as unique as its placement for structural support to the roof. The inside had been stripped clean of its kitchen cabinets, interior walls, closets, and all traces of plumbing. In their place were bookshelves. Practically every inch of wall space, except where windows intervened, was lined with plywood shelves edged with thin strips of white pine. The shelves were full of books, of course. A gray metal desk the size of a battleship, Navy surplus he'd wager, occupied the center of the room. A couple of old Girsberger office chairs stood vacant next to the desk. The sofa, which Ironwood occupied, sat beneath a picture window with crank-out casements. The awning casements were fully open, but the surrounding curtains were still.

Through the window, he could make out a stretch of desert dotted with sagebrush and in the distance, not more than two hundred feet away, was a tall chain-link fence with several strands of barbed wire on top. He could see all of this by the light of a halogen lamp mounted on an electrical pole next to the fence. "What is that fence for?" he said, pointing out the window. "Who'd put a fence out in the middle of the desert?"

"The Navy," answered Ironwood. "You're looking at the back of their property. That's where the million-plus acres belonging to the NWC ends. In perspective, it occupies three counties; Kern, San Bernardino, and Inyo."

"Fantastic," he said after a low whistle. "I guess I never visualized how much land they occupy." It had taken Alan over an hour and a half to get to Darwin from Ridgecrest. He took Route 178 West out of town to the U.S. 395 North, then from there to State Road 190 East to the Darwin cutoff. During that travel time, he remained within arm's reach of the government property line circumnavigating the Naval Weapons Center.

Ironwood stood and stretched. "Come on. I'll help you with your things."

"That's been taken care of…" he said with a wolfish grin.

"I take it you have met Mrs. Murchison?"

"Yes," he answered, still grinning. Is she your. . .?"

"Housekeeper," he said firmly, finishing Alan's sentence. "Then, seeing you are settled in, there is only one thing left to do," he crowed, giving Alan a playful shove towards the open door. "Let's eat! I'm hungry as a bear."

CHAPTER 11
AFTER MIDNIGHT

Gwen Gilhooley sat in the dark; her skin was all gooseflesh. The hair on the back of her arms stood straight up; something had startled her. It was an invisible force that had dragged her into an upright position. The bedspread draped across her legs. Something had awakened her, but she couldn't remember what it had been. Her hands and face felt charged with static electricity.

Taking only short, shallow breaths, afraid to make a sound, she looked around the dark bedroom. What the hell was the matter with her? She probably lived in one of the safest places in the country! The security was excellent, especially at a weapons testing center where everything is top secret, including your bra size. Even though the accommodations weren't the best in the world, she preferred living on the base. She grew up on Navy bases around the globe. Being on base, to Gwen, was like being at home.

Some light from Nimitz Boulevard filtered in through her bedroom window. She knew that her "neighborhood," as she thought of it, was a bit creepy at first sight, but she had grown accustomed to it. It was like living in a ghost town. Originally there had been 13,000 civilian employees and assigned military personnel living on the base. In the 1970s, that changed when the FHA accepted a statement of permanence from the Navy, and military personnel was no longer required to occupy government quarters. As the years passed, more and more people bought houses in Ridgecrest and the surrounding area, and now the majority lived outside the gate. Family housing on base dwindled from nearly 2,700 units occupied in 1976 to just over 800 units in residence today. Gwen lived in one of these units. A two-bedroom, yellow, wood-frame with red trim and brown asphalt shingles. The architecture style was post World War II housing, and there were rows of them along Nimitz Boulevard. Unfortunately, two-thirds of them had their windows and doors covered over with plywood. While some were converted to temporary storage facilities or office space, most were unused. Gwen didn't have any next-door neighbors. The houses on either side of her were unoccupied. No one would hear her if she screamed for help.

Damn it, girl, cut it out! She scolded herself. Get a grip, gal. Gwen massaged her hands and then her face dispelling the feeling of static electricity. She was getting her calm back. She still wished she could remember what frightened her so. Could it have been a noise? There weren't any sounds right now coming from outside. Well, get up, girl, and look out the window. Maybe somebody is trying to steal your car! Although why anybody would want to rip off a 94 Dodge Neon was beyond her.

Gwen threw back the covers and started to get out of bed when she heard something that made her stiffen. The sound wasn't coming from outside. It came from somewhere within her bedroom. It was a creaking. Exceptionally low, but a dull squeaking, like the rubbing of dry leather against wood. The door to her closet was closed, but the light inside was on. She had forgotten to turn it off when she had gone to bed, she hoped. A faint pencil-thin radiance shone beneath the door. The constant abrading sound continued. Gwen cocked her head from one side and then to the other, trying to locate its source. It was in the room with her. Tuning in on the sound, she sensed that it was directly in front of her. It came from behind her closet door.

Gwen swallowed hard and slowly. Quietly she reached for her bedside table drawer and slowly slid it open. Her hand immediately fell on the loaded Glock 30. She snapped the weapon up in the dark. Her reflexes were automatic. She had practiced for many hours with the 45 caliber subcompact. Gwen could place a 5-shot group inside a 2.5-inch circle at a range of 25 yards. The clip was full, and she always kept one in the chamber. A total of ten rounds. She wasn't about to waste valuable time or give herself away in the event of danger by cocking the breach to prime the weapon. Her dad had taught her well. Her father started her target shooting when she was ten, and he had instilled in her a respect and a healthy fear of a loaded gun. She wished he were with her now.

Gwen slid noiselessly out of bed. She wasn't wearing anything. She always slept in the nude, come summer or winter, but now she felt uncomfortable about it. It made her feel vulnerable. The cool carpet fibers welled up between her toes, and cold chills ran up the backs of her legs. Gwen walked towards the closet door in a slight squat; she gripped the Glock out in front of her with both hands. Gwen was tempted to spray the closet with all ten rounds knowing that the 45 caliber slugs would turn the door into splinters, but she felt that it would be prudent to see who or what was on the other side first before firing.

The creaking friction continued. Gwen imagined the finger of a hand, gloved in leather, stroking the doorframe. She transferred the gun into her left hand, grabbed the knob with her right, and yanked the door open. The light from the 60-watt bulb made her flinch. She dropped to one knee and resumed her two-handed grip on the Glock.

***

Alan sat up in bed with a start. His vision and his mind's eye fought against one another for control of his senses. Portions of an alien city with spiraling towers in night-black masonry shimmered briefly and then folded in on itself, leaving only a faint memory of its existence. A painted wicker chest of drawers and a dressing mirror gradually filled his field of vision. "I am back," he said between gasps for breath. He knew where he was this time. The return was quicker than other trips had been. Alan was in the guest room at Ironwood's house. His entire body shivered uncontrollably even though the room was warm. His pills were at his bedside, and he slipped one under his tongue. The bone-numbing chill he was experiencing frightened him even more. He was afraid that there might be a failure in his circulatory system. He pressed two fingers against the artery just below the jawline and located a faint pulse that grew with each succeeding beat. Some warmth returned to his hands, and he relaxed against the headboard. Each dream seemed to suck him down further. Each time the dream world he occupied every night made it harder for him to return.

In his dreams, he is always in the same place. A primal city far beyond anything the human mind could comprehend. A dark city constructed with enormous blocks of stone. His first memories of these dreams included a view from a great round window overlooking titanic flat roofs and endless leagues of giant buildings stretching to the horizon. He had been dreaming about this foreign city for almost seven years, and as time went on, more details became apparent to him. He eventually realized that he never saw any steps or stairways. However, walkways were abundant in the form of elevated tubes going from building to building, while others were just simple paved sidewalks at ground level. Then there were the towers. There were thousands of them everywhere he looked. Narrow cylindrical structures shot up between the buildings into the steamy gray heavens. He didn't recall ever seeing the top of one because they all disappeared into the clouds.

Later he began to have visions about exploring the lower depths of the city. Sometimes he would wake up in the early hours of the morning with the memory of it fresh in his mind. Other times the memory of these things would fade rapidly after waking, and all he'd be left with were abstract images rolling around in his head, breeding nonsense and muddled confusion. It wasn't until after years of therapy and self-discipline that he could preserve these images within his conscious mind. It was only then that he could recall, with any relevance, the multiple levels of black vaults below and the work he did there. He remembered row upon row of charcoal metal boxes, each one engraved with curvilinear hieroglyphs. The metal boxes, or file drawers, were stacked at a great height, and each continuous row was separated by narrow tables running parallel to them. It was at one of these tables that he stood and wrote. He remembered a loneliness so painful that his writing was his only consolation. His solitude was augmented by the echo of his pen scratching across its writing surface—a surface that did not seem to be ordinary paper and a pen that did not seem to use conventional ink.

He wrote about himself. Nothing exciting. Nothing exciting ever happened to him except in his dreams. All the same, he wrote about the life history of Alan Parker Ward. He did this; he believed because he had been instructed to do so. By whom he could not recall. He did remember that one of the boxes was his, and he had vague recollections that his writings were stored there when he wasn't working on them. In the thousands they must have numbered, all of the other file boxes held dim suggestions of dark perils.

Alan had little sensation of "self" in his dreams. He wasn't disembodied; rather, he felt displaced from his physical being. He fought to try and acquire a mental picture of himself in the dream world, but it was only until recently that he could come to grips with it. For six of the seven years he spent in and out of the dream world, the image of himself eluded him until now, and it only served to heighten his fears of his nightmares.

He wasn't physically alone in his dreams either. Although he hesitated to think of his companions as "people," they treated him with great kindness. Kindness, he eventually decided, similar to the way we treat our pets. Calling up memories as transparent as smoke, he retraced several of his dream journeys below the mystery city, and in all such cases, they had followed him. One lucid moment, he retained the memory of walking or what seemed more like gliding because his movements were so fluid along a narrow tiled passageway. He had the acute sensation that he had traveled the corridor many times before. At both ends of the corridor, several of the city dwellers either waited or followed. He guessed then that his companions were probably his keepers.

The first time he saw his keepers, he woke to fits of screaming. His cries were so loud and desperate that later it took him almost ten minutes to convince his landlady not to call 911.

It was at the end of that tiled corridor, in the room housing the file drawers, that he retained his first mental picture of them. Each had a collection of bulbous eyes that never blinked, mounted on thick fleshy stalks, that turned and looked at him when he entered. The stalks were attached to immense elliptical forms. Sunken veins, with elevated spaces between, covered their bodies. A pair of bulky but limber arms protruded from the middle of their girth and terminating them were pincer-like claws. The beings used these claws in conjunction with half a dozen windpipes jutting from a raised spine comprised of pink gristle entwined with a thin twisting of muscle fibers to communicate. They did this by a series of whistles and clicks. At the base of each stalk, where a head should have been, a pulpy mass sprouted a collection of tentacles and tendrils. It was these they used to perform functions requiring tools and dexterity.

When the sight of these entities no longer frightened him into the waking world, he began to concentrate on his physical form while in the dream world. Although Alan did a lot of writing while there, he could never recall what his hands might have looked like in his dream world. As fragmented as most dreams are, he never remembered seeing any mirrors that could have reflected his image. As his deep fantasy sleeps continued over the years, Alan Ward was able to exert some measure of control. Primarily he was at his strongest while traveling the long corridor to the file room. He had often taken that journey, and many times he tried with a great force of willpower to look down at his feet. Always when his eyes would slowly move the distance towards the floor and before affording a view of his feet, he would wake up in a cold sweat.

Alan took another deep breath and decided not to try to go back to sleep but to wait for dawn instead. He didn't have the strength tonight for another drop into the mystery city. Sometimes the transition from dreams to the waking world grew more difficult because they seemed more like memories than fantasy.

***

Lieutenant Jason Riggs channel surfed for what felt like an ungodly length of time. The cable TV service available in his apartment building offered over a hundred stations, and he had zipped by them all twice. It never ceased to amaze him that there was nothing worth watching with all those channels scheduled. It was past 10:00 p.m. Pacific Time and Jimmy Fallon had signed off. He should have gone to bed hours ago, but he couldn't sleep. Jason had a full day ahead of him tomorrow. Even though he was exhausted, he couldn't shake the feelings of apprehension that haunted him about leaving Chief Mercado, Dexter, and Rinaldi down in the tunnel all night. The place gave him the creeps during the day, but it must have been suffocating down there at night. Not that there was any difference in the quality of air at night as opposed to the day. It was because Jason Riggs was claustrophobic.

He enjoyed the bright, sunny open spaces the Mohave provided. He didn't even mind that it was hotter than blazes in the summertime and as cold as the North Pole at night in the winter. He enjoyed the duty, as well as the open-air benefits it gave him. His career in the Seabees, so far, had primarily dealt with road building and earth moving. But now, he had to deal with that narrow space beneath the ground. The thought made his mouth go dry. Not all close spaces bothered him. Elevators, for one, didn't upset him because most of them had well-lit interiors. A good dose of bright lighting always helped to dispel his morbid fear of confined places. That was why he had ordered his men to string so many electrical cables in the tunnel. When lit up, he hoped it would be as bright as daylight down there.

For the third time, Jason surfed to CNN and watched a taped delay of a debate that had occurred the day before on C-Span between Neville Stream and Elliot Granger. Elliot Granger, a congressman from Iowa, opposed the recent military spending cuts and what he called "excessive base closings." It looked for a while that he might have the upper hand in the debate when he pointed out the lack of base closings in Congressman Stream's district and accused him of trading his vote on health care to save them. Stream ignored the accusation and cut Granger to ribbons for not realizing the strategic quality and high tech value of the Navy and Air Force bases in his California district. He compared them to a base that Granger fought to keep open that he said, "Guarded the shores of Lake Michigan against Indian uprisings." Jason thought that this was the spot that they should have inserted a laugh track. Neville Stream was eloquent. Each retort he delivered with off-handed cleverness that seemed a little too off-handed and a little too clever as if the whole thing had been scripted.

When Stream became dramatic and started to defend his patriotism, outlining a military record of six years in the National Guard, all six of which no enterprising reporter on CNN would bother to mention occurred during the Vietnam War. Jason surfed to another station in disgust.

The young Lieutenant's mind shifted back to Mingo and the guys. Did something else bother him about the tunnel? The whole idea that it was a leftover from some ancient civilization disturbed him even more. The confined section of the tunnel had been closed up for hundreds, probably thousands of years. If they hadn't have stumbled on to the thing, it would have remained buried forever. Like a sarcophagus, a coffin. Jason hated coffins. Especially ones made of steel. Plain metal with handles on the side and the top bolted down. His father had been shipped home from Vietnam in one of those. When his dad had left for his tour of duty in Nam, he had told seven-year-old Jason that he was the man of the house and that Jason was to take care of his mom while he was gone. When it became apparent to Jason that Dad would never be with them again, he knew he had to be strong. Dad had stepped on a land mine in Nam. The sergeant in charge of the coffin's disbursement had recommended to his mother that it not be opened. Little Jason, at the time, wanted his daddy more than anything and knew that if they had just let him out of the box, everything would be "all right again." He carried that feeling to the graveside, where he watched them lower the coffin into the cold ground.

Jason did not fear enclosed spaces right off; that all changed when his father died. He dwelled on his father locked in a box.

There was a steel dumpster at an apartment complex next to their property. The rusty thing was a good six feet tall. One afternoon in August, when he saw thunderheads collecting in the east, he climbed over the side of the giant trash receptacle and closed the lid after him. Earlier that day, they emptied the dumpster, but it still smelled of garbage.

When the storm rolled in, he was squatting in the bottom of the container, trying to shield his nose from the stench. But his child's mind imagined that the odor was that of rotting flesh. He also imagined dark crawling things inching their way towards him. He held onto his father's words to bolster his courage. Just as he thought he heard claws scurrying across the metal floor of the tomb he now occupied, several loud thunderclaps rocked the dumpster. A furious outpouring of rain fell, the lid of the dumpster leaked in several places, pouring streams of chilling water over his head. Some of it ran down the back of his neck, feeling like cold squirmy things crawling down his back. He held on steadfast in his determination to ride the storm out and his fear of the closed space. It was all over in fifteen minutes, and he had received a good drenching.

He thought he would catch hell from his mother when he returned home soaking wet. Annie Riggs surprised him when she greeted him at the door with a warm towel and a dry change of clothes that day. She was abnormally quiet and had never asked him where he had been. After he had changed, she brought him into the kitchen and served him a steaming bowl of tomato soup. The hot soup warmed his insides and dispelled the chill. When the soup was nearly gone, she casually asked him if he felt better. He nodded the affirmative, realizing the full depth of her question. A half a dozen cherry and apple pies, for their church bazaar, were cooling on a wooden sideboard. Annie Riggs had been baking pies all day, and she would have had a clear view of the dumpster from their kitchen window. Jason loved his mother more that day than ever before.

She had been a young bride when his father had married her, but she was wise beyond her years. It was probably for that reason that he always felt comfortable coming to her for advice for years to come.

Looking back now, he knew that he was lucky that the dumpster wasn't struck by lightning. Likewise, he knew that he had also received a genuine lesson in facing his fears besides a drenching. Or so he thought until his fifteenth birthday. Ever since his standoff with the dumpster and the thunderstorm, he felt free of his phobia about dark, closed-in spaces. But his victory over his phobia became short-lived. As he grew closer to manhood, it gradually became a morbid fear, almost a premonition that something horrible would come for him if confined in any one place for any length of time. When Jason was older, he would learn more about phobias. Simply that facing one's fear may dispel a particular aversion for a time, but it may not eliminate its roots. The cause or origin of that phobia may exist deep in the subconscious and could manifest itself later.

So, it was by the time Jason turned fifteen, his annoying little fear of cramped, dark places had grown into full-blown claustrophobia. The final trigger to that mechanism became activated by high school rivals on the football team. It was an innocent prank, like dousing the coach in Gator Aid or de-panting a guy in front of the cheerleaders, only in this case something went wrong, and it became ugly. After practice, three of the team's biggest kids decided to lay and wait behind parked cars as Jason crossed the parking lot on his way to the bus stop. Not one of them tipped the scales at less than two-hundred-pounds, and Kaczynski, the biggest, easily weighed two-forty. Kaczynski was the first-string halfback. The other two were linebackers. On the other hand, Jason was still trying to make second string and barely weighed one-hundred-fifty pounds.

Kaczynski and his two superstar wanna-be's were out for revenge. During the scrimmage, the halfback and his pals were on the blue team. Jason was on the white team. The upset came when Jason tackled Kaczynski. He was clowning around pretending to dance around his opponents when Jason hit him low and caused him to fumble the ball. The outcome was humiliating for the first-stringer. His screw-up gave the white team the ball and the winning edge they needed. Kaczynski had lost to a second-stringer, a runt. The coach had called him and the blue team "girls."

The big halfback planned his revenge carefully. He had thought of all the usual pranks: stealing Jason's clothes, snapping the runt with wet towels, or just beating the crap out of him, but none of it felt good until he saw the coach's car keys lying on his desk. He knew the coach always stayed late until all the equipment was put away. Besides, he'd return the keys to his desk before he would miss them.

When Jason stepped around a rusty Buick, the three giants leaped on him. He was quickly overpowered. Kaczynski deftly produced the ring of keys with one hand and popped open the trunk. Jason suddenly became difficult to control. He lashed out with his arms and legs in a screaming fit. He landed a hard right into Kaczynski's jaw and broke one of his front teeth in half. Carl Toth, one of the linemen, nose exploded in a shower of blood when the heel of

Jason's left sneaker slammed into his face. Wounded and bloody, the three of them tossed Jason forcibly into the trunk, and Kaczynski swung the lid closed with a metallic bang.

They hadn't expected him to turn into a wild animal. Kaczynski held his mouth and cursed while Toth cried like a baby. Jason's screams of terror and his pleading to be let out would have usually delighted the boys, but their wounds took all the fun out of it for them.

Jason's terror, however, was absolute. Despite the grace of God and Coach Harlson's quick thinking, his time in the trunk wasn't short enough. No more than ten minutes elapsed between the time Coach Harlson caught Kaczynski returning his keys to his desk than when he unlocked the screaming Jason from his trunk.

The ten minutes of terror slowed to hours for young Jason. It dragged on with excruciating agony. A second became a minute; a minute turned into an hour. The only thing that moved at a fast pace was his heart. Fueled by anxiety-based fear, he clawed and kicked at the trunk lid, but the old Buick was as solid as boilerplate. Jason let up on his pounding, swallowed hard, and took several deep breaths to keep from hyperventilating.

Inside, the trunk smelled of mildew—mildew, and death. Something was in the trunk with him. He turned his head and listened. He heard it move. It was something old and rotten, something dead, but it moved. He had to push those thoughts from his head. It won't be much longer. They'll have to come and get him out. It whispered his name. Not once but several times over and over. "Jason. . . Jason," it said slowly in a faint whisper of a voice. It went deep inside his head; it moved closer. Jason kicked and kicked and kicked the underside of the trunk lid until his feet became numb with pain. He collapsed back against what felt like the spare tire and gasped for breath. The smell became foul. He knew now that it wasn't mildew. It was that odor of rotting flesh again. Then something cold and clammy touched his neck. Jason broke into a fit of uncontrollable screaming and crying.

The sight of Jason Riggs, overcome by total hysteria, drove slivers of fear up Coach Harlson's spine when he opened the trunk.

Jason recovered quickly that day. After a few minutes in the open parking lot and he began to breathe easier. A small crowd of some of his classmates had formed, and his fears soon gave way to embarrassment. He had met his fear face to face again, only this time he had caved. He had lost the fight. The shame had been pure hell for a fifteen-year-old. He decided from then on to conceal his phobia at all costs. Kaczynski knew about his claustrophobia. He had let it be known to the big halfback years earlier when they were both in Boy Scouts together. At the time, they were the best of friends sharing deep dark secrets about one another. In the future, Jason resolved, he wouldn't reveal his weakness to anyone.

All of a sudden, Jason realized that he had been staring at a satellite view of California for the past ten minutes. The weather channel predicted clear skies and soaring temperatures over the Mohave Desert. Big deal. He pushed the channel selector again, on the remote, and switched to Fox News. The financial crisis in France was worsening; the Middle East was still beating itself back to the Stone Age, and popping up on the screen, presented as "Breaking News," was a picture of the President grinning and swinging a golf club. Jason pushed the "Power" button, and the screen went blank. His apartment felt empty, along with the dark T.V. screen.

He knew he had done well down in the tunnel today. It had become a lot more comfortable when Eastwater had fired up the powerful LED lamp. Gilhooley had helped as well. He had to be strong for her. Gwen was like a rock when it came to strength. He liked her a lot. He wondered what she was doing.

***

Gwen sighted along the barrel of her Glock 30 into the empty closet. Well, almost empty. Besides a dozen pairs of dress shoes, a pair of combat boots, work boots, two pairs of Nike's, six complete sets of NWU's, her dress whites and her blues, several dresses and an assortment of jeans and tops, the closet was empty. Or, more accurately, it was devoid of any living thing. The rubbing sound had ceased as well. She had been holding her breath up until then and exhaled explosively. Slowly rising from a squat, she entered the closet, still holding the 45-caliber weapon out in front of her. "No boogie man here, girl," she said out loud. She couldn't help from smiling. She didn't know whether it was out of relief or because she felt a bit foolish. All she knew was it felt good to smile. After inspecting some suspicious-looking folds in a couple of her dresses and looking behind a winter coat, she declared the situation all clear.

Reaching for the pull chain on the ceiling light, Gwen stopped and looked down at her feet. A faint current of air blew up her bare legs. There was a hole in one of the floorboards. "What the?" she puzzled. She didn't remember seeing this before. Gwen left the closet momentarily, returned with a flashlight that she kept on her bed table, and got down on her hands and knees. The floor of the old house was sheathed with tongue and grooved Douglas-fir boards. A knot the size of a quarter had fallen through, leaving a small hole. Shining the light down on it, she heard a brief scuttling noise beneath the house, then silence. The hole was too small to see anything, and the light was of no help. She thought she detected the faint odor of honeysuckle for a fleeting instant, but the sensation disappeared as quickly as it came.

Turning off the flashlight, she stood up and dragged a cardboard box filled with old magazines to the middle of the closet floor, covering up the hole. The houses in her neighborhood were built on crawl spaces. She imagined that it wouldn't be difficult for an animal of some kind to get under there. The notion of rats under her house made her skin crawl. She'd make it a point tomorrow morning to call base housing and report it. She closed the closet door and returned to bed.

CHAPTER 12
THE CYCLIST

Alan had no sooner stepped out of Ironwood's front door when a great cloud of dust embedded with tumbleweeds swept across Main Street, transforming his shiny black wingtips into chalk.

It was a little after 7:00 a.m., and he was looking for Ironwood. Shortly after showering and shaving, he had knocked on his friend's bedroom door, only to discover that Thomas had already risen. He found coffee brewing in the kitchen, poured himself a cup, and then searched all the other rooms in the house with no success. Even Ironwood's house trailer/study was unoccupied. That was when he headed for the front door.

Alan looked down at the cup of coffee in his hand. A thin layer of dust and sand floated on its surface. Frowning, he turned the cup upside down and watched the spilled coffee pool up like mercury on the dusty limestone road.

Further up Main Street, where it intersected with Fulton, there was still some asphalt left on the road. Darwin looked as lifeless by day as it did at night. There was virtually no activity. Except for a young man he spied riding a bicycle along the north end of Fulton, the town appeared deserted. Ironwood had told him that the population of Darwin was about forty-five people. Right now, it seemed to be less than that.

They didn't talk much last night. Both were exhausted, and Alan had been hungrier than he had imagined. Downing several helpings of dinner had occupied most of their conversation time. Before leaving for the evening, Mrs. Murchison had served up broiled chicken breasts, steamed broccoli, wild rice, and a spinach salad. Alan ate without pause until he felt like he would burst. He was usually a light eater. To him, Eating was something you did out of necessity, and last night left his body a starved engine that needed fueling. He guessed it resulted from all the excitement that day, plus faced with a home-cooked meal. Alan typically existed on fast food. Ironwood was an excellent host; he smiled gratefully.

The old mining community that stretched out before him looked more like a junkyard than it did a town. Straight ahead, about five-hundred feet away, stood four house trailers with their paint sandblasted off. On the other side of Main Street, to his right, was a red Quonset hut with two pickup trucks and a 1955 Studebaker out front. All three of the vehicles were severely rusted. An incredibly old Austin Healey sat out in the middle of the scrub wood with its tires and engine missing. To the northwest stood several rows of ten by twelve one-room shacks, all abandoned and crumbling by the weight of the harsh Mojave seasons. Decades ago, they had once been simple dwellings of the transient miners that came with hopes of striking it rich. Many of the larger homes, if still livable, were wood framed with green asphalt shingles on the roofs and tar paper on their sides. Surprisingly enough, dotted here and there, were a few new homes constructed of rough sawn plywood siding, dark brown and tan shingles, all with satellite dishes on their roofs. Still, the only sign of life was the young man on the bike. He must be peddling hard; Alan observed because he created a small dust storm in his wake.

Alan scanned the horizon, his gaze fixed on one of the many mine shafts that dotted the surrounding hills. He wasn't looking at it; rather, he became focused in thought on the tunnel they had found beneath the NWC. Intuition told him that the tunnel held the key that would not only unlock the secret of his dreams but would restore a missing chunk of his past. There was something hauntingly familiar about that tunnel. It did not remind him of the narrow corridor in his dreams, the one that led to the file room. That would be too easy. Or was it? Maybe it was the five-sided shape? He couldn't remember the exact shape of the dream corridor, only that it was narrower and constructed of cobblestones or tiles. He had been pressing his memory ever since he went down there.

The young man applied strong force to the peddles of the mountain bike and increased his speed. He shot up Fulton and turned right on Main Street in the direction of Alan. With the sun to the cycler's back, he appeared as a blackened silhouette. He let go of the handlebar with his right hand and waved. Alan returned the polite gesture.

He had to get down in that tunnel again, he brooded. Now that he was thrown off the base, Alan needed Ironwood's help more than ever. Ironwood had been a gentleman last night, only keeping to lighthearted conversation, never pressing him once with questions that Alan knew must have been on his mind. He wondered how much he should confide in his old friend.

Alan's jaw dropped dramatically when the cyclist came to a skidding stop in front of him. Ironwood sat straight up in the seat; his body dripping sweat. His old friend did not look his years. His sinewy body looked like it belonged to a twenty-year-old. Clad in only a pair of Nike's and blue spandex shorts, Alan guessed that he had to be less than ten percent body fat.

"Good morning," said Ironwood, barely winded. "I see you've already had your coffee," pointing to the empty cup in Alan's hand. "Then we have both got our start in the morning. Give me a few minutes to shower, and I'll meet you in the study."

The rear tire of the bike made a brief grating noise on the gravel as he headed around the back of the house. Alan stood dumbfounded for a few seconds more and then headed indoors to wash out his cup.

***

"So, Alan, what in the hell are you doing way out here?" Ironwood decided on the direct approach. It had the effect he had hoped for; Alan fidgeted in his chair, leaned forward, and appeared to be carefully choosing his words.

Ironwood didn't derive pleasure from making his old friend

uncomfortable, but he was confident that there was more to his presence here than the mere study of Indian artifacts. Massachusetts was a good distance off. Ironwood quietly stared at Alan Ward. After asking an essential question at this stage of the game, the first one that talks is the loser.

Alan cleared his throat. “For several years now, I have been studying an ancient belief that before the dawn of man, our planet had been inhabited by another race of beings. A sort of pre-civilization theory.”

Thomas Ironwood was familiar with similar theories. Consequently, Alan’s statement did not arouse his inner skeptic. He had worked at Miskatonic University at one time, in the physics department, along with Alan Ward, who was in the English department. One department at Miskatonic known throughout Arkham and parts of Massachusetts as a research center on the paranormal, more informed than even Duke University. The “Mythos Department,” as it came to be known, was comprised of members from the various science departments. Ironwood was certain of this because he had been a member himself years ago. On the other hand, Alan was from the English Department and, to Ironwood’s recollection, was never part of that unusual academic group.

Alan swallowed hard. He was perspiring heavily. Ironwood glanced at the thermostat. It was seventy-two degrees inside. An old GE air conditioner blew frosty air at them. Around 8:00 a.m., it had started to get warm outside, and Ironwood had closed the place up and turned on the window unit. Without holding off the approaching heat of the day, the Airstream trailer would have been an oven inside by late morning. Alan bent over and picked up a thick leather brief he had brought with him and set it on Ironwood's battleship gray desk. "What is that, Alan?" Ironwood asked.

"A book and some papers from the university." Alan slid the brief to the middle of the desk. The leather was old and cracked, and the zipper was broken because it was secured around the middle with a black vinyl strap held tightly in place by a brass buckle. The professor noticed that the strap was a belt trimmed down to fit with new holes crudely punched in it. The papers it contained must have numbered over a thousand pages because the thing was as thick as the Los Angeles telephone directory. Fingering the vinyl strap, Alan added, "This is the main reason Miskatonic sent me here."

"How's that?"

"You are familiar with the rock drawings that are found here in the Petroglyph Canyon?"

"Some," Thomas replied. "Crude drawings carved in stone of men hunting sheep. What of it?"

"Well," Alan continued cautiously. "Occasionally, other images have been found pecked into the flat rocks, except these images aren't so recognizable. They're primarily geometric and don't bear any resemblance to man or animals. They would have easily been written off as mere artistic designs, except that the same images were discovered in Nevada, Arizona, and Peru."

"Yes. Dry, barren places that have been left untouched for

centuries. I've heard that it is believed that some of these rock drawings are over ten thousand years old, but that is more guess-work than it is the results of any evidence gathering."

"Exactly," Alan replied enthusiastically. "Rock drawings are almost impossible to date. The Shoshone Indians won't lay claim to them. They believe that they were created by a race of people that lived here before their time. A new theory has developed, though, among some of my colleagues, linking this region and several points around the globe. I picked up the ball and worked out a deal with the Science Department. They helped me acquire a small grant from the Nathaniel Derby Pickman Foundation to finance my trip here. It was both to their benefit and mine."

Ironwood wondered what the benefit was for Alan.

"I'm going to try and establish a factual basis to substantiate their theories," Alan concluded.

"And what theories might those be?"

"The idea has evolved among the heads in the Mythos Department that this may have been an outpost for a small colony . . . possibly a stop-over point for an ancient civilization."

There, he said it, thought Ironwood. He mentioned the Mythos Department. "What civilization?" he pressed on.

"That's the mystery," responded Alan. "It's still pretty vague. All we know for sure is that they were pre-Inca. Until I'm allowed to examine certain areas surrounding Little Petroglyph Canyon before your friends bulldoze it under, I won't have a clue."

"And that's what you were trying to explain to Eastwater and the rest of them yesterday?"

"Precisely," he said, looking a bit embarrassed. ". . . only I'm afraid I did a bad job of it."

"I wouldn't brood over it. Eastwater pushed for a fast track on this project, and he doesn't want anything to get in his way."

"I am sorry, Ironwood, but I can't stand your colleague.

"Colleague?"

"Eastwater. He's the type of man that I loathe on sight."

"No need to apologize, he's hardly a friend or a colleague, and there is no love lost between us. Unfortunately, he came with the project like the mold that came with the penicillin."

"What is this project you are involved with?"

"I'm sorry, but it's classified top secret."

"You were researching chemical lasers before you left the university. Is it connected with that?"

"If something's classified, I can't talk about it," Ironwood said definitely.

"Sorry," Alan said, fidgeting in his seat once again.

Professor Ironwood altered course and brought the conversation back to the beginning. "How much time do you need to examine the area?"

"Two weeks, three at the most."

"That sounds reasonable," Ironwood said, scratching his chin. "I wonder why they wouldn't accommodate your request. They work closely with the local museum here on their digs. Why wouldn't they do the same for you?"

"I don't know," said Alan sheepishly. "All I ever got were doors slammed in my face."

"What reason did Vice Admiral Hawkins give you for their refusal?"

"None. I met him for the first time yesterday. All my requests before then went through Eastwater."

Eastwater's role in this was almost conspiratorial; Ironwood reflected becoming absorbed in the puzzle. Or was he, Thomas thought, as paranoid as a conspiracy theorist? Most of Eastwater's actions could be explained away as someone who was overzealous at their job. Couple that with his apparent dislike for civilians on the base, and voila, you have a logical explanation. Except, his surreptitious behavior around Congressman Stream did look suspicious; this was developing into a docudrama. Eastwater and the congressman were not the only suspicious characters in the play, however. Ironwood stared at Alan. The fortyish English professor, somehow turned archaeologist, unconsciously fussed, and fidgeted his hands together, making a cat's cradle out of his fingers.

"Alan," he said in a raised voice. "You have been talking in circles. We are old friends. My father knew your father. Level with me."

Alan's eyes became moist, and he stopped squirming in his chair. "A lot happened after you left."

"Enough to turn an English professor into an expert on lost civilizations? It's been over ten years since the university booted me out, but your reputation has continued to grow within the Mythos

Department."

"How did you know? I mean, you've been away."

"I have friends at Miskatonic U. I keep in touch. They tell me that you went through some startling personality changes several years ago."

"I was ill for a while."

"I know." Ironwood knew what most of their senior associates knew about Alan Parker Ward. He had collapsed during one of his morning lectures to his English Lit class. He remained unconscious, in a coma for two days, at St. Mary's Hospital. When he awoke, he had almost total memory loss. "You had amnesia," he said, gently prodding.

"Retrograde amnesia is what it is called. Mine was a severe case. It made the textbooks," he added, forcing a smile. "Of course, I don't have any recollection of the time, but my doctors told me that I displayed all the signs of a stroke, but the symptoms vanished after I regained consciousness."

"But you still had amnesia?"

"Yes," Alan answered back, staring blankly at the wall of books behind Ironwood. "They told me that in cases of severe memory loss, specific areas of the brain show pathological changes. In my case, there were none. I was perfectly healthy when I came to, except my speech was awkward, like a foreigner unfamiliar with the language. Even though my strength returned at once, I still required a tremendous amount of physical therapy. There hadn't been any muscle atrophy, fortunately. Instead, it seemed that I needed reeducation in the use of my hands and legs.

"The resident psychiatrist at the hospital, years later, told me that I had first tried to conceal my memory loss, but when that failed, I became eager for information. My chief efforts were in history, science, and very obscure folklore."

"Your pre-civilization theory?"

"Yes."

"So, your studies eventually brought you to the Mythos Department at the university?"

"Yes," he replied again, paused, and then reluctantly added, "I wasn't very cooperative back then. An old friend of mine told me that I was reclusive in my research and very unwilling to share any of my findings during those days. Something in my aspect and speech seemed to incite vague fears and suspicions amongst my colleagues. They felt that I was becoming removed more and more from normalcy as time went on. One ugly story circulated about my supposed association with occultist groups."

"What about Jennifer and your son? Where were they during all of this?"

"My wife left me, got a divorce. She has re-married since then. I haven't heard from my son in several years."

Alan had painfully blurted out the last two sentences. Ironwood sensed a heavy sadness in his old friend's life. "I am sorry," he said. "I didn't know."

"You see, I was another person back then," he answered, his eyes welling up with tears. "By the time I regained my memory, my life, as

I had known it, had been irreparably torn apart."

"How long did you suffer from this memory loss?"

"Five years," he almost moaned.

"Good lord, Alan. I had no idea. In all this time, did you ever have any recollection of these events?"

"None," he replied in a low voice.

"But you seem normal now. What happened?"

"I woke up one morning, only I was five years older than I remembered last. You can't imagine how painful and difficult the process was re-entering into normal life. The loss of five years creates more complications than can be imagined. I was astonished and so disturbed when I learned of my actions during the lapse that I had to go under extensive therapy and counseling."

"I'm sorry," said Ironwood knowing it sounded stupid to repeat it. Alan had turned his face away from him towards the opposite wall. After a moment, Ironwood cleared his throat. "So, it was the studies and actions of your 'other self' that lead you back to the Mythos Department to develop this theory of yours?"

Alan turned and looked at Ironwood with anger in his face, anger not directed at him, instead of rage against a cruel and alien destiny. "I don't have any theory," he said, baring his teeth. "I am not a scientist; you know that. There are things that I remember. Things that may have a connection with those rock drawings out in the desert."

"But you said you didn't remember anything."

"I don't," he snapped back. "I don't remember any of my actions during those five years.

"Then I don't understand. What is it that you do recall?"

Alan turned his gaze towards the ceiling and squeezed his eyes shut. Tears streamed down the side of his face. "The only memory I have is in my dreams." He took a deep breath and let it out slowly as if a tremendous weight had just been removed from his shoulders. He spoke calmly, "They are vague dreams, but they are reoccurring. When I dream, my ability to distinguish between reality and the dream is distorted. I sometimes form fanciful notions about living in one era and casting my mind over another. In all cases, I always end up in an alien-looking city, unlike anything I have ever read in books or seen on film. At one point in my dream, I am always standing at the opening to an underground passageway. Next to it, there is this symbol carved into the dark masonry. It has always stood out plain in my memory. I believe I see it every night in my sleep. I was shocked when I found it last year reproduced on a page in the Necronomicon."

The Necronomicon was an old book. The mention of it stung Ironwood sharply in the soft tissues of his brain. It was possibly, the oldest book in the world. It was undoubtedly the vilest. The library at Miskatonic kept one of the few remaining copies of it under lock and key. It was a complicated diatribe, more complicated than the Book of Revelations and more challenging to translate than the Dead Sea Scrolls. The book alluded to other worlds, alien beings, and Armageddon. It was also the focal point for most of the studies in the Mythos Department at Miskatonic University.

Alan ran his hand over the leather brief. "Since. . . my return, I have made it my life's work."

Ironwood became momentarily startled and looked down at the thick bundle wrapped in leather. "Alan, you didn't steal it from the university, did you?"

"No," he smiled. He quickly unbuckled the strap with the dexterity of a practiced hand and let the leather brief flop open. "I Xeroxed it."

Ironwood had to laugh as he rose to his feet and bent over the book. Alan flipped hurriedly through several pristine white copies of the ancient text. The chemical smell of newly copied paper filled his nostrils. Ironwood had expected the odor of an aged document. The many pages became anachronistic, the new white paper reflecting the image of an ancient parchment containing long-forgotten writings, thousands of years old.

"Remember me mentioning Isaac Morley when I interrupted your staff meeting yesterday?"

"Yes."

"He came here in 1873 on a similar quest. Originally from England, he traveled to Arkham and then to the Mojave. He came to this area searching for the same symbol and built his house overlooking its ancient message. Ah! Here it is," he announced, jabbing an open page with his index finger.

Ironwood walked around the other side of the big gray desk for a better view.

"This is the symbol that has haunted my dreams and sent Isaac

Morley over 3,000 miles to find."

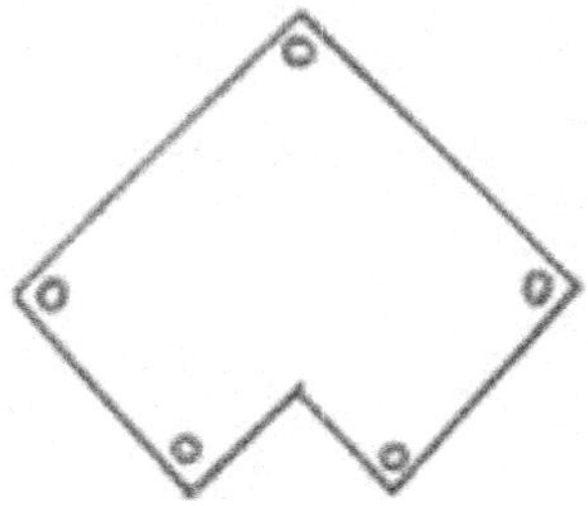

CHAPTER 13
THE MORLEY HOUSE

Ironwood stared at the five-sided design etched into the dark basalt rock. It was identical to the drawing photocopied from the old book he saw earlier in the day. To his right, a winding canyon of fractured volcanic rock meandered endlessly toward the south. It was a deep and jagged cut into the landscape as if carved by an impatient god with a dull knife. Centuries of wind, rain, heat, and bacteria had conspired to darken the once pale rocks' surface to hues of brown, blue, and black, creating canvases of stone. The rock art was what the Coso's ancient humans had chipped through the darkened surfaces and exposed the lighter rock. Thousands upon thousands of designs covered the rocks like prehistoric graffiti. Some designs were indecipherable. Others were as familiar today as they were thousands of years ago; bighorn sheep, a dog, a mountain lion, quail, deer, lizards, and man as the hunter.

The surrounding area was once a land of volcanoes, hot springs, forests, lakes, rivers, and the ancient ones. Now it had been laid barren by low moisture and intense winters and summers. The climate had made this desolate country almost uninhabitable, with only the smallest and heartiest of God's creatures surviving. The Shoshone knew the desert mountain range that looked upland as the "Mountains of Fire."

The ancient ones of Native-American mythology have vanished now. The designs, immune to time, have remained clear and distinct upon the rocks, while the meaning of the images, like the people who had conceived them, had faded entirely.

The Coso Range's rock drawings had on many occasions become the topic of conversation during off-hours and on breaks on the base and in the Michelson lab. None of Ironwood's friends or colleagues were archaeologists. Still, it wasn't uncommon to see a physicist or an A-10 pilot on their days off together sharing a common interest when it came to the mystery of the petroglyphs—the question of why these images carved in stone had become an enigma. The age of the designs is also a mystery. All attempts to date them have proved futile. Each one had weathered the passage of time differently. Each one's physical appearance reflected its past through a short story or medicine signs. Most of these abbreviated tales were told by roughly drawn pictures of ancient man hunting—most, except the one that Thomas Ironwood was examining. The five-sided image was a good four feet across and stood alone on a solitary projection of black rock. The majority of the rock drawings were spread along the canyon walls. This solo piece, the results of some volcanic upheaval centuries ago, endured outside the canyon near its mouth. The drawing in itself was not surprising because its broad and almost perfectly smooth surface would have presented an irresistible offering to any prehistoric artist. Instead, it was the precision in which the design had been rendered. The other petroglyphs in the canyon were pecked through the dark varnish that had formed on the basalt rocks exposing its natural light beige color. They accomplished drawings using stone chisels and hammers, and it showed. Even though the petroglyphs were fascinating, they were at best crude stick figures by virtue of their existence and their sheer numbers.

They were probably a form of symbolic, sympathetic magic used to ensure a plentiful hunting season. The lone hunter, waiting in a stone-blind for a bighorn sheep or a deer to come to the river edge for a drink, passes away the time by chiseling the image of his imagined prey into a nearby rock. The river has long since dried up; only centuries of these crude rock drawings remain.

Ironwood ran his hand down the geometric design. All five sides of the drawing were surprisingly straight and regular. The engraved lines didn't look like they had been pecked or chiseled into the surface. They had the appearance of being machine grooved.

"The designs are all that remains of them," said Alan coming up from behind."

Ironwood jumped, forgetting that his friend was nearby. The pointed end of the engraved symbol reminded him of a directional arrow. "It . . . almost seems to be pointing to something."

"Isaac Morley felt the same way. The last word we have of him is in a letter he sent an associate in Arkham, shortly after discovering this drawing. He shared the same sentiments with him."

"Where is Morley's house?" Ironwood asked.

"Straight ahead." Alan swung an outstretched arm resembling a sharpshooter aiming.

Ironwood's eyes followed the direction indicated to a sandy knoll just on the horizon. The outline of a large wood-frame house looked black against the white-hot sky.

***

Alan and Thomas drove along an old mining trail in the direction of the Morley house. "More bumpy lime rock roads," shouted Alan over the roar of the car's motor. His tailbone was sore from all the bouncing, and the thin upholstery on the seats of the old Willys convertible didn't offer much padding for comfort. It amazed him how such a flat, dry, treeless country could be so bumpy to travel over. "Haven't they heard of blacktop yet in the old West?" he exclaimed, forcing himself to be cheerful.

Ironwood smiled and navigated the car around a large rock in the road.

Alan was amazed when they first went to use Ironwood's car. The 1950 Willys Overland Jeepster convertible had been parked on the roof of Ironwood's house when they first fetched it. The roof was supported by the same massive wood beams extending beyond the house's rear and over the patio. Unlike the open patio area, it had been sheathed with two-inch-thick tongue and grooved roof boards and then coated with heavy layers of tar, tar paper, and gravel. With three-quarters of the house being below grade, it had been a simple architectural feat to cantilever a portion of the roof at an angle to meet the road's grade. It was, to say the least, eccentric.

Nevertheless, he had to admit that the effect was impressive as well as practical. The street that ran in front of Ironwood's house was narrow; it didn't afford much room for a car to park and still allow another to pass. Thus, the roof made an excellent parking lot.

The old Willys had been a surprise as well. At first glance, the sixty-year-old ancestor of the American Jeep looked wholly restored. While driving, Thomas explained to Alan that the yellow and tan sports vehicle had its original four-cylinder engine and three-speed standard transmission upgraded to the 4.0-liter six-cylinder engine and five-speed transmission found in today's Wranglers and Cherokees. Combined with a reinforced suspension to handle the package, these refinements allowed the little Jeepster to fly across the desert faster than the Road Runner pursued by Wile E. Coyote.

Mid-morning temperatures had risen sharply, and Alan thought he was going to melt. Mounted beneath the dashboard was an after-market air conditioner. There were no roll-up windows in the little convertible, but plastic side and rear curtains were lying on the back seat. "I put those on," said Ironwood pointing to the back seat, "and use the AC when it really gets hot."

Ironwood had bought the Willys from Vice Admiral Hawkins. It had been the admiral's labor of love. "Hawkins had become obsessed with the 1965 Mustang," he said as he backed the car off the roof and onto Fulton Street. "He was fairly willing to part with the Jeepster when I came along and made him an offer."

trouble."

"Trouble? Yes," he said with a laugh. "A lot? No. I am classified as a GS-15 civilian. What are they going to do? Demote me? Besides, my project is too important to them."

Alan was about to take advantage of the opportunity and started to ask him once again what his project was about, but Ironwood waved the question down with his right hand. At the exact moment, the car lurched through the opened gate, pressing Alan against the seat.

"Security patrols tend to concentrate on the parameter," he said, rapidly shifting into second. "They use SH-2 Sea Sprites, standard Navy helicopters to cover the area. The quicker we can get near the Coso Peaks, the easier it will be for us to elude them."

Alan watched with admiration as Ironwood put the little car through its paces. After several minutes of traveling through a low sandy wash and then across the hard rocky ground, he decided that the modified Willys Overland could handle any terrain.

Off to his left, Alan spied a yellow and black sign that read, DANGER, TOXIC GAS. "What's that all about," he said, raising his voice above the wind and motor noises.

"It's an old mine shaft," Ironwood hollered back. "It's cautioning to be alert for carbon dioxide. Some of the magma from volcanic vents can open cracks in the earth, and especially with holes in the ground like this one, allowing large amounts of trapped CO2 gas to leak upward along fault lines."

"Is it deadly?"

"Breathing air with more than thirty-percent CO2 can very quickly cause unconsciousness and death. Last year we had two navy personnel die of asphyxiation while digging a deep ditch for a storm sewer."

Scattered occasionally amongst the thorny bushes and patches of scrub grass were other metal signs rusted and vibrating in the wind advising against unauthorized entry. It wasn't until they had reached Petroglyph Canyon that Alan breathed easily again. At least he was on familiar ground.

When they eventually left the Petroglyphs and started for Isaac Morley's house, he realized that he owed his old friend a debt that he may never be able to repay. He felt deeply grateful to Ironwood for risking so much to bring him to the Petroglyphs and the Morley house. He had been to both locales twice before by way of field trips through the local museum. On both of those occasions, he had felt close to unlocking that part of his past kept from him all these years. Only a little more time was all he needed. When his Maturango Museum pass into the NWC was taken away, he fell into deep mourning for that part of his life that he thought rendered impossible to reclaim. Now that hope had returned, and he had even found it possible to smile again.

As they approached the old house, the ground had flattened out, and the ride became smooth again. Alan leaned back in his seat and relaxed his sore muscles.

***

Ironwood turned off the car's engine and put on the parking brake. They both stared at the crumbled remains of Isaac Morley's front porch. The morning breeze had subsided, and the air was unnaturally quiet. "How old is the house?" Ironwood asked, realizing after he said that his voice had been almost a whisper.

"One hundred and thirty-seven years come next spring."

At one time, the large two-story wood frame had been impressive. Italianate towers at each corner and a slate roof must have looked like a castle to the locals back in the gold rush days. Now the old mansion bore the scars of extreme wear. Sand pitted and opened to the wind; it was a wonder that it still held together.

Ironwood took a flashlight he kept in his glove compartment and switched it on and off to ensure that the batteries were still good. They both got out of the Jeepster simultaneously, as if on cue, and approached the house.

"The last owner hastily vacated a little over one hundred years ago," Alan added. "Very few people go near it. The Shoshone believed evil spirits inhabited it. I have been over it from top to bottom in hopes of finding some vestige of Morley's work. It's pretty barren."

"This should be interesting," Ironwood said. The front door to the house had nearly become unhinged. It was wide open and tilted at a thirty-degree angle. Ironwood noticed that only one screw remained to hold the top hinge in place, and it was severely rusted. A gentle shove would probably be all that it would take to bring it down. "What a desolate place to build a house," commented Ironwood looking at the rubble that had once been the front porch. "He must have had one hell of a reason?"

"Oh. . . I wouldn't go that far. I know a physics professor that lives like a hermit out here in the desert."

"No comparison," Ironwood briskly pointed out. "I live in a town with forty to fifty other people, I have a car that allows me quick access to civilization, I have a cell phone, and I have DirecTV. No," he added, shaking his head, "Morley was truly isolated. His reasons to live out here must have been very compelling."

Alan shrugged his shoulders and smiled.

Inside, Ironwood discovered each room to be as disappointingly empty as the next. The house was wood lathe and plaster construction instead of drywall; in places, the lathe showed through like brittle bones between rents of dead flesh. In some of the rooms on the second floor, they waded ankle-deep in the lathe and plaster that had fallen from the ceiling. Shafts of Mojave sunlight streamed through large holes in the roof. Alan discouraged exploring the earthen floor cellar because it was as vacant and barren as the desert except for a pair of concrete wash tubs that stood in one corner. The desert had invaded every room that they explored, piling little heaps of sand in each corner as a calling card.

"Except for Morley," said Alan as they returned to what had once been the foyer, "there has been only one other principal owner. That was in 1897, a Phillip Clervey. His stay lasted exactly a fortnight."

"What happened to him?"

"He vanished."

"Vanished?"

"Just disappeared. The only thing anyone knew of his whereabouts is that Clervey had been seen that last evening running through the town of Darwin screaming unintelligible things—never heard from again."

"You've done a lot of research."

"Some," Alan said, mopping his forehead with his sleeve. "Copies of the Darwin Sun are on microfilm at the public library in Ridgecrest. The rest is common gossip. The people in the surrounding territory back in those days kept close scrutiny on Morley's habits. They even kept a record of the amounts of food he consumed."

"What on earth for?"

"It seems that Morley used an abnormally large number of livestock for a household of that size."

"Whatever happened to Morley?"

"He disappeared as well."

"What do you mean, disappeared?" Ironwood frowned.

"Just that. One night he and the servants just up and vanished. Not a trace. Oh, there have been stories of noises from. . ." Alan abruptly stopped talking and cocked his head slightly as if he listening for something. A slight metallic grating noise became apparent and sounded like it was coming from the next room.

Ironwood and Alan exchanged glances and then quietly approached what had once been the living room. They rounded the doorway, and a loud metallic clang caused the two of them to turn with a start. A sand lizard, a good twelve inches long, stood poised like a porcelain statue on top of a termite-riddled fireplace mantel. On the floor was an old coffee can, rocking to and fro, apparently just toppled from its place on the mantel shelf. Ironwood leaned against the door frame and sighed. "A lizard," he said with the expulsion of breath.

The sand lizard made a spastic jerk to its right and disappeared through a hole in the wall just above the mantel shelf. Ironwood stepped rapidly to the fireplace and shined his flashlight after it. "It seems that the lowly reptiles are the only ones who dare to live here anymore," he said, peering into the hole. When Alan didn't reply, he turned around to see that his friend had his back to him. His right hand was up towards his face, and Ironwood had the impression that he swallowed something. A second later, he heard the snap of a lid being closed, and he watched as Alan quickly concealed a small pillbox in his right jacket pocket.

"Alan, are you all right?"

Ward did an about-face and, with a smile that looked forced, said, "Yes, I'm fine. Just a little startled, that's all."

Ironwood thought he looked pale. "Are you ill?" he asked.

"No, I'm perfectly well. So," Alan said, pointing to the fireplace and faking good humor again, "did our host go and leave us?"

"Yes," he answered, also faking a smile. What was wrong with him? We have been out in the sun for two hours, and he looks as pale as a ghost. "He was very rude," he added. "Left without saying goodbye."

Ironwood breached the awkward silence that followed when he remembered where their conversation had left off when the lizard had intervened. "Alan, you mentioned something about noises being heard?"

"Oh, yes," he said, delighted to talk about something else. "Most of it the usual haunted house stuff, although one report was quite specific. Shortly after Clervey was given up for lost, a group of people from Darwin heard a chorus of strange sounds coming from the house."

"What kind of sounds?"

"They said it sounded like a flock of birds."

"Birds?" Ironwood sounded incredulous.

"Yes. Seagulls."

Seagulls were uncommon in the Mojave. Although they were prevalent on the west coast, they very seldom came this far. That was a strange thing to hear, Ironwood decided.

"The Darwin Sun reported on these sounds on three separate occasions. The reporter of the piece wrote that they grew fainter each time that they heard them. One conflicting report, though, has me troubled ever since the Seabees uncovered that tunnel."

"What was it?"

"The mayor and two of the town council back then swore that the sounds, although emanating from Isaac Morley's property, did not come from the house. They said they came from beneath the ground."

Even though the temperature inside the old Morley house was in the nineties, Ironwood felt a faint chill. The house had an uncomfortable feeling about it, and he longed for the sun's direct rays. Stepping out onto the rickety front steps, he looked up at the blazing noonday sun. Peering at it through squinted eyelids, he swore he could see flames dancing on its surface. He heard Alan's steps behind him. "The name `Coso' comes from a Shoshone word for fire. It probably referred to the abundant volcanic vents that send out hot vapors. Before the navy closed this area down to the public, the hot springs were popular among Indians as well as whites. These escaping gases could have caused your strange noises."

"Could be," said Alan, but he sounded unconvinced. After a long pause, he pointed off toward the horizon. "The Navy plans to build a supply road right down through here."

"And take the house with it, I suppose?"

"Not only that, they're going to blacktop over half of the area."

Ironwood contemplated the dancing flames on the sun and felt sweat trickling down the back of his neck. "Alan, how would you like a partner in your venture?"

"Really?"

"We share a common ground. We both have work to do out here, and we both share a mutual distrust of Clayton Eastwater. As you know, I cannot tell you what my project consists of; I'm sworn to a secrecy oath that I don't take lightly. But I can tell you this. As far as my Navy project is concerned, there is no reason you shouldn't be allowed your few precious weeks of exploring. This area will be swarming with civilian construction workers for the next six months building several concrete block structures along with the roads and parking lots. After they are done, some of us from Mike Lab will move in, and that's when the secrecy starts. Until then, you should be allowed to play archeologist and Spelunker all you want, if it was up to me, that is. Through all of this, Eastwater has been behaving suspiciously. It gives me an uneasy feeling. Of course, he has always been a fly in the ointment to you, blocking your entry into the base. I'll try to help in any way I can to speed up your research, and if you find anything that might involve Eastwater in all of this, I would appreciate it if you would pass it along."

"Deal," said Alan with marked enthusiasm. "I admire your strength Thomas, and if it is any consolation, you had me when you said, partner.'"

The cell phone on Ironwood's hip started to play "The Star-Spangled Banner." Surprised, Alan asked, "Your phone works all the way out here?"

"The Navy installed a series of one-hundred-sixty-foot cell towers on the base property a few years ago, so they were always connected." Grabbing the phone, he touched the "Answer" icon on the glass faceplate and pressed it to the right side of his face. "Ironwood," he said.

"Lieutenant Riggs here, professor," said the voice on the other end. "There has been an accident at the tunnel."

"Any casualties?" Ironwood, alarmed, responded brusquely. The statement caused Alan to look at him questioningly.

"We don't know, sir. Will you come right away?"

The question, thought Ironwood, was awkwardly phrased coming from an officer used to giving orders. "Certainly," he said into the mouthpiece. "I have one thing to take care of, and I'll be there in roughly an hour."

Ironwood heard the young officer clear his throat. "Captain Eastwater has ordered me to tell you that he wants you to drop whatever you are doing and come here immediately."

"In that case, Lieutenant, tell Eastwater that I'll be there in two hours." He touched the faceplate once again and returned the phone to the holster on his belt. He knew that the lieutenant would not relay his message, but it gave him satisfaction, nonetheless. What he should do, he thought, was bring Ward along. The unwanted baggage would really set Eastwater off. He wouldn't do it though, he wouldn't be responsible for what would happen to his old friend, and now colleague in the crossfire of rage that he knew would ensue. "Come on, Alan," he said. "It's time to go home."

They turned and walked back towards the Willys. Ironwood could tell that Alan was full of questions. He looked like he would burst at the seams.

CHAPTER 14
TUNNELS

Ironwood drove the Willys quickly up to the tunnel site. He had dropped Alan off at his house in Darwin and returned to the NWC by way of his back door route. The round trip took a little over two hours. The Willys roared to a sand spewing halt, and Ironwood jumped out, still dressed in jeans and a cowboy hat. At arm's length from the steering wheel, he pressed on the center hub. The Jeep's horn blared with a quavering ululation. The result had its desired effect. Before he had walked halfway to the hole in the ground, he saw Lieutenant Riggs pop-up partially out of the cavity and signal him to come along.

Ironwood grabbed the ladder with both hands and noticed that the opening had been widened by several feet and reinforced with four-inch by twelve-inch oak framing.

Lieutenant Riggs noticed the professor's interest and volunteered, "We've had problems with it closing on us. I guess the earth shifts a lot in this area."

A couple of yards away stood a sizeable trailer-mounted diesel generator spewing carbon monoxide into the open air. Several heavy-duty electrical cables ran away from the generator leading down into the hole that Ironwood was descending.

Dropping down the last two rungs of the ladder to the tunnel floor Professor Thomas Ironwood was astonished by what he saw. The interior of the tunnel was brightly lit. The short section that he had examined the day before appeared to stretch on forever. Electrical cables strung along the top of the tiled walls followed his line of sight. Spliced into the cables every thirty feet or so were sockets that held high-lumen LED bulbs brightly illuminating the passageway.

Jason Riggs tapped Ironwood on the shoulder. He was wearing cotton work gloves. "Welcome aboard, professor. I'm glad you could make it on such short notice."

"What is all this, lieutenant?" He said, amazed by his surroundings.

"We have been working in shifts, 24/7, and have uncovered a lot."

"But this is amazing. The debris that you encountered must have been enormous. How did you get it out of here?"

"The cave-in wasn't as extensive as we thought. It only went for a few yards. When we cleared it, we found what you see. The small amount of dirt and rock we dug out so far was taken topside by the way of a makeshift rope elevator Chief Petty Officer Domingo Mercado fashioned together," the young lieutenant pointed in front of them. With its many ropes neatly curled up was the "rope elevator," a flat bottom with three-foot-high sides constructed of thick plywood.

"Your chief petty officer needs to be congratulated. He's quite the engineer," replied Ironwood.

"I would," said Riggs, "but he's missing. We think we found him a few minutes ago."

"Missing?" answered Ironwood but decided not to press it any further when he noticed something unsettling in the lieutenant's countenance. Was it fear or just fatigue?

"Follow me, sir," he said, looking straight ahead.

Riggs led the way with Ironwood close behind. "How far does the tunnel go?" Ironwood asked.

"About a mile, sir. It makes a gradual turn to the east and then stops up against another obstruction of rubble. But there are also branching tunnels off of this artery."

"Branching tunnels?"

"Yes, sir, fifteen to be exact, we haven't had the time to explore them all yet."

***

The tunnel did seem to stretch on forever, with various sister tunnels branching off at random intersections. Ironwood walked a good quarter of a mile before encountering the subterranean anomaly. There were two, one on the right and the other on the left, both facing each other. The walls of the main artery, at each, interconnect gradually curved outward with fifteen-foot radiuses joining to the adjacent tunnels. All the regular polygon tunnels' walls and ceilings were laminated with the five-sided notched tiles he had observed the day before. The same design Alan showed him in the Necronomicon. A definite sign of advanced engineering skills, he thought.

Stopping several yards further in, they had to step over a short but passable debris field next to a much narrower artery that was entirely blocked by rubble. "What happened here?" he inquired.

"Another cave-in, sir, we're not sure; it must have happened during the night. We found one of our electric cables sticking out of the rocks. It had been ripped loose from its socket. I thought it looked as if something too large for the opening had been rammed through, but Captain Eastwater thought it was incidental in light of pushing forward. The men haven't had a chance to clean this up yet."

Advancing deeper in Ironwood couldn't help noticing that every time Lieutenant Jason Riggs came upon one of the dark connecting tunnels, he would widen his gait and hurry past it.

Ironwood stopped and stood where an intersecting tunnel was immediately on his right and another on his left. This time they were of the same width and height as the main tunnel, but the interiors were devoid of any light. The Seabees hadn't run any electric cables in them, having the color of outer space, the darkness was complete. A faint breeze blew across his face; it made a barely audible noise as if it were whispering or chirping, or was it a squawking sound? Lieutenant Riggs didn't seem to detect it. It gave Ironwood a chill to peer into the side tunnel's depths. He rolled the sleeves down on his denim shirt and buttoned the cuffs. For a brief instant, he thought he caught the faint whiff of gardenias.

"This way professor," pleaded the lieutenant.

Ironwood stayed within the main artery, ignored Lieutenant Riggs' request, and swept away years of dust and sand from the tunnel floor with the side of his boot. He squatted down and observed that the same five-sided tiles adorned the walls, except they were smooth and shiny; they looked slippery. Professor Ironwood reached out to touch the floor's frictionless surface.

"Wait, professor," implored Lieutenant Riggs. Removing an extra pair of cotton work gloves clipped to his belt, he handed them to Ironwood. "Put these on, sir."

"Why?" countered the professor.

"When touching the wall or the floor tiles, it's like frostbite," Riggs answered, pulling the glove off his left hand. The tips of three of his fingers were wrapped with Band-Aids. "I don't know why," he said, puzzling over his hand. "They're not even cold."

Ironwood did as he was told and donned the offered gloves. It's like glass, he thought, running his now protected hands over the floor tiles. "Polished glass," he said in a low voice.

"What was that, sir?" asked the lieutenant.

Ironwood stood up straight, stretched, and examined a portion of a sidewall. "The tiles on the walls, although the same size and color as the ones on the tunnel's floor, are of a different texture. The floor tiles are like polished glass. If all this dust and debris did not cover them, it would be like walking on ice." His hands still explored the walls. There was a tingling sensation that penetrated the cotton gloves. Something tugged at his sense of self. Had they stumbled upon an ancient gateway to secrets of the inner earth and vanished eons? An image flashed before his consciousness, a glimpse of giant trumpet-shaped plants reaching several stories into the sky and towering buildings made of thick elastic material. Was this a psychic image? An ancient residue left behind?

"Professor, please, we need to get going," Riggs implored again.

Suddenly aware of his surroundings, Ironwood responded with a nod and slowly started to follow. Is this some monstrous lair of elder secrets echoing for the first time, after uncounted epochs, to the tread of human feet, he theorized? He shook his head clear of the fanciful notion and walked on.

***

Another quarter of a mile in Ironwood and Riggs came across four men gathered around what appeared to be a dark bundle on the subterranean floor. He came closer and was able to see that one of the four was Captain Eastwater.

The Captain becoming aware of Ironwood's approach eyed him up and down noticing, with a look of disapproval, the cowboy hat and denim. "Ah, Ironwood, glad you could make it."

"Captain," he replied. "You wanted to see me. . ." his words trailed off. He became immediately aware of the dark thing on the floor. It was a man. Or what was left of a man. He was drawn up into an embryonic position huddled against the wall. The skin of the corpse was dark brown and stretched thinly over the skull. It reminded Ironwood of dried leather. Fine wisps of hair stood straight up on the head of the bony, skeletal remains. The dead man's features exhibited pure horrifying agony. Pinned to his shirt collar was a small gold anchor entwined in chain superimposed with the letters "USN" in silver, the Chief Petty Officer's insignia.

"Is this the missing CPO, Domingo Mercado?" Ironwood said in a somber voice.

"Most likely," Eastwater snapped back. "But it won't be official until there is an autopsy. That is the chief medical officer's duty. Until then, professor, mum's the word. Loose lips sink ships," he added with a wry smile.

"Then why in Heaven did you ask me here," Ironwood countered, not bothering to conceal his irritation.

"Oh!" the captain replied. "This isn't it. What I want you to see is further down." As he turned to march away, he said to one of the three remaining men, "Ensign, let me know when the CMO arrives." Eastwater turned to Ironwood, "Two more lads are missing, Seaman Jonathan Dexter and Petty Officer Anthony Rinaldi. I have requested additional personnel. In the morning, we will start searching the rest of these tunnels. Until then, I have issued orders to clear more rubble. We will see just how far this cavern goes.

"What do you think happened to the CPO and the other men?" asked Ironwood.

“I have no idea, professor.”

***

Ironwood walked on a good distance with the captain, passing several more intersecting tunnels until they came to a raised platform. The area was also lit by the spaghetti arrangement of electrical cables and high-wattage light bulbs. The platform didn’t disrupt the architectural flow of the tunnel. Instead, it was recessed. A large rectangular hole in the tunnel wall stood about four feet above floor level. Studying it in all directions, the Professor guessed that it was approximately thirty feet in width and at least ten feet in height. Its depth was impossible to ascertain because a considerable amount of dirt and rock at the back of the opening, most likely due to a collapse of the tunnel ceiling, obscured any further investigation.

A half a dozen men wearing patches on their shirts of a Disney-like cartoon bumblebee wielding a hammer, a wrench, and a machine gun with the words stitched below, “SEABEES CAN DO!” worked to clear the rubble. All of them wore cotton gloves. At the edge and to the center of the opening stood a solitary post with a conical base wiped clean, revealing a shiny surface. Ironwood guessed that it was made of chrome or polished stainless steel. The flared pedestal tapered upwards to become a tubular limb four feet tall. At the top of the post were the remains of a peculiar mechanism. Brown wires spewed from a smashed receptacle. The vessel's shape and size were also impossible to ascertain because one or several falling rocks from the cave-in had rendered it indistinguishable from its original form.

Still wearing his white cotton gloves, Ironwood lightly squeezed the tubular post between his thumb and index finger. The shiny non-metal substance cracked with a soft "pop." It was very brittle, only a shell. A yellow silt material poured from the crack. Touching a few of the brown wires, they crumbled and turned to powder in his gloved hand. As if all the life had been sucked out of it like the corpse of CPO Mingo, he thought. Ironwood jerked himself free of the morbid thought. "Any idea what it is, professor?" Captain Eastwater sarcastically inquired, walking up from behind.

Momentarily startled, Professor Ironwood turned and glared back at the Captain. Lieutenant Riggs stood to his right. "I will need more than thirty seconds to voice an opinion," he answered.

"What a pity. I was hoping for more from you."

Ironwood responded, "It is not my job description to satiate your needs, captain." He recognized that this was one more of Eastwater's strong-arm political ploys. For some reason, Eastwater wanted him, and probably his crew, away from his Space Guard Program as well as the mystery of the tunnels. Ironwood would not give him the satisfaction; he was not going to cave. He smiled at his double entendre and turned to closer examine the odd device. Littered around the chromium base were handfuls of greenish soapstone fragments like the ones that Marinus Willett had found. He picked one up in his left hand, Ironwood un-holstered his iPhone, and touched the "MAG LIGHT" app icon on its screen.

A bright LED light from the smartphone shone on the stone

fragment. With the magnification at 100%, Ironwood could observe it in full detail. Under the glare of the LED light, the stone looked more gray than green. It was five-sided, like a chevron, and it dawned on him that it was the same shape as the tunnel. It was also the same outline as the floor and wall tiles, minus the interlocking notch at the bottom. The stone was the size of a nickel, but it looked huge under the magnifier. Across the surface of the object was a series of five indentations, dots. The impressions were close to each corner of the five sides. It reminded Ironwood of a face. It became apparent to him, at that moment, that this was also a replica, in miniature, of the petroglyph he and Alan Ward had observed earlier that day. Touching the camera icon within the "MAG LIGHT" app screen, he sent the magnified image to his photo stream.

"I've sent for some of the boys from the Mike Lab to examine this thing. So, don't touch any more of this stuff," ordered the captain.

Rather than slugging the arrogant S.O.B., thought Ironwood, I will try to remain nonchalant. When Captain Eastwater looked the other way, he pocketed three of the green stones. Still undetected, he placed several of the brown wires and some of the yellow silt between the folds of a handkerchief and returned it to whence it came.

Alan and I need to examine the old Morley house again, Ironwood decided.

CHAPTER 15
MEANWHILE

It was 110 degrees in the shade. Zachary Taylor Harris was glad that the glass cockpit he sat in was air-conditioned. He flew the SH-2G Super Seasprite helicopter with the precision of a well-trained Navy pilot. The two computer smart displays in the cockpit kept him within the boundaries of the Naval Weapons Center. Zach held the chopper at an altitude of five hundred feet, sometimes dropping down to one hundred if an anomaly needed closer inspection.

The Seasprite was designed to house a three-person crew, two pilots, and a sensor or SENSO operator. A single pilot could also fly the flexible integrated tactical avionics guidance system. Zach didn't need tactical because his duty was to keep an eye out for interlopers.

Sitting in the additional pilot seat was Warrant Officer Biddles. Biddles was in training as a Navy chopper pilot. Zach didn't have the heart to tell him that their jobs would soon be rendered obsolete along with the Seasprite. Seasprite helicopters had been mothballed by the Navy a few years back, but the NWC kept a handful of them around for patrolling the perimeter. Like the Seasprite, its pilots would also become outmoded when drones retired them to other duties. The boundaries of the NWC, by then, would be traversed by unmanned aerial vehicles. Geeks would control the UAVs, with joysticks, in their comfy little offices sitting in front of their computer terminals—the Chairforce.

Zach Taylor looked over to where Warrant Officer Biddles was sitting. He was from Idaho and, since potatoes came from that state, naturally, the boys at the base called him "Spuds." "Another boring day at Black Rock, Spuds," grinned Zach. His face mask was unsnapped, so ground control wouldn't be able to overhear their conversation.

"Do you ever catch anyone trying to sneak onto the base, sir?"

"Nothing to email your sweetheart about, ever since 911, they've put us regular naval aviators on extra alert. I've never tagged a terrorist. The only trespassers I've spied besides dust devils and tumbleweeds were a couple of drunks hunting jackrabbits."

"Maybe today is your lucky day, sir," replied Spuds pointing down and to his right.

About five hundred feet below was a figure. It was a man walking stiff-legged. "What the hell!" exclaimed Zachary Taylor Harris. "He's walking deeper into the desert. In this heat, he must be nuts."

"Maybe he's delirious, sir, sun stroked," added Spuds Biddles.

The Seasprite passed over the stranger. Zach adjusted the chopper's controls, turned hard to the west, and brought the craft down to one hundred feet in front of the interloper. Sand mixed up with bits of tumbleweed churned around the mystery man. Ignoring the flying debris, he kept on walking. He wore the United States

Naval Mobile Construction Battalion's desert pattern camouflage utility uniform, minus hat, or helmet.

Zach set the Seasprite down fifty yards away from the man. Zach and Spuds ran towards the interloper as the blades of the chopper wound down. Approaching the advancing serviceman, they stood in his path. The man in desert tan continued his pace. He stared ahead as he walked, oblivious of the two other men. Backing up, Zach put a hand to the chest of the delirious walker. "Hey, Seabee, stop! Attention!"

The Seabee stopped and gazed intently into the afternoon sun. His uniform was soiled as if he had been crawling around in the dirt, and his sleeves were torn. There were second and third-degree burns on his face from being out in the desert sun too long. Even with the massive sunburn, he looked pale, extremely anemic. Along his neck and arms were distended welts. The red pustules made Zach think of the sucker marks that squids make on their prey. Above the right shirt pocket of the comatose derelict was the name, "Dexter."

***

Gwen Gilhooley pulled her car into the driveway. There was a small Toyota pickup truck parked alongside her house. It was painted white. The sign on its door read "License to Kill Exterminators." Below, the company's phone number ended with the last three digits, "007." Cute, she thought. She got out and lugged a laundry basket filled with wet clothes. The sound of a compressor running greeted her. It was mounted on the bed of the Toyota. A hose trailed away to under the crawl space. "Good," she said out loud and to herself. The exterminator must be under my house in hot pursuit of the bugger that kept me up last night.

She went up the front steps with her heavy load and unlocked the door. Traversing the living room in long strides, she set the laundry basket on the kitchen counter. Gwen had just returned from the base Laundromat. She never used their dryers. It cost too much. There were two clothes poles with lines strung between them in her backyard. Gwen "Save a Buck" Gilhooley, she thought, it should be part of my family crest.

While retrieving a handful of clothespins from a kitchen drawer, her cell phone buzzed. It was a familiar buzz, an annoying buzz, that could only come from her duty station. It was a text that simply read "STAT." When the job calls, it is one thing, but when they say, "Stat," it means dropping everything and report for duty. Gwen was madder than hell. She would have to leave her wet laundry unattended. They'll probably get mildewed, she fretted. Then I'll have to wash them all over again when I get back. Damn!

***

Travis shifted his position on the chaise longue. The tan on his left side was deep enough. He smeared some oil on his right side with the palm of his hand. He loved laying naked out in the sun. The hair on his lean body had been shaved clean. He wanted nothing between his flesh and the sun's rays. Beside him, in the other chaise, was Dorian. His massive muscular frame rippled in the afternoon glow. Travis kept him in steroids and human growth hormones as part of their equitable bliss.

Travis stared at Dorian. His blond hair shined like gold. He loved their lifestyle, but it had its upkeep. It was expensive. Their high-rise condo in Las Vegas wasn't cheap either. He and Dorian needed another job. He got up from the chaise and lit a Marlboro. Walking to the parapet wall that surrounded their balcony, he looked down. They were sixty-four stories up. The bumper-to-bumper traffic moved slowly below. The cars appeared too small to be even Matchbox size when you are over 650 feet in the air, he mused.

Their bankroll was starting to shrink, and they needed another contract. Travis had one in the works. He was waiting for the call. The ball was in the client's court, and all he could do was wait. He tossed his lit cigarette over the wall and hoped that it would land in some bitch's hair. If this one came through, it wouldn't be easy, but it would set him and Dorian up for quite a while. It would probably be pretty bloody, so it would have to be done quickly.

The cell phone on a tray table next to his lounge chair rang. He picked it up and answered, "Hello."

"Is John there," a voice on the other end asked.

"No, you have the wrong number," responded Travis.

"I am sorry," said the voice and terminated the call.

"Payday," Travis said with a smile. The name "John" was their "open sesame," their secret code for the person to hit; it was all done, so simple and so low tech. The client, or probably one of his stooges, calls from a payphone faking a wrong number but the correct number for Travis and Dorian. Even if the NSA were eavesdropping, they would come away with squat.

Travis walked over to the recumbent Dorian and kissed him on the forehead. "Come on, darling," he whispered. "We've got work to do."

Travis was aroused; as long as he could remember, he had always wanted to kill someone in uniform. It was anarchy at its finest.

***

Vice Admiral Jack Hawkins sliced a ball for the third time. He hated golf. It was a helluva way to spoil a good walk. He didn't know why he kept at it. Well, actually, he did. He was three years away from retirement, and his kids, kids? Hell, adults were more like it; his son would turn forty next month, they had bought him a complete set of Big Bertha clubs, and they weren't cheap. They thought that the Callaway Classic golf clubs would be a good pastime. Hawkins didn't want to disappoint them, although he'd rather be skeet shooting.

They were on the sixth hole, a par five, and Doc Farmington was down in four. Hawkins wanted to wipe the smug look off of the doctor's face. The course at the NWC was bare bones. The tee boxes and the greens were a luscious shade of emerald. Water is a precious commodity in the desert, and consequently, they were the only irrigated areas. The fairways and the roughs that surrounded them were brown with dead vegetation.

If I can get a hundred yards on this next shot, I can make it on the green with a respectable Bogey, the admiral wished. He was on the edge of the rough—a straight shot over a bunker in line with the green Hawkins gathered together every muscle within his large frame and swung a nine iron with major league force. He topped the ball and watched it bounce for fifty feet along the fairway, aggravation mounting; he walked up to where it rested and swung at the ball with frustrated abandonment. This time the golf ball traveled with a modest arc towards the green but fell short and landed in the sand trap.

Doc Farmington had parked their golf cart on the other side of the sand bunker. As Admiral Hawkins walked up, he heard his cell phone chirp. It was clipped to his golf bag in the back of the cart. Overjoyed with the interruption, he snatched it up. "Hawkins," he announced into the mouthpiece.

"Admiral," replied the voice on the other end. "It's Ironwood. I got your voice mail message."

"Yes, professor. We need to talk. See me in my office at 2 p.m. and bring your colleague.

"You mean Ward?"

"That's the one. Don't take your back way. Use the front gate. I'll have clearance there for the both of you. Don't breathe a word about this to anyone." Hawkins closed the clamshell on his flip phone without waiting for a reply. Ironwood was a civilian, and by all rights, he couldn't issue him orders, but he knew that when he "asked," the old prof would come. With a grin on his face, he shouted, "I guess this has now become a six-hole golf course. . . Duty calls!"

Before the good doctor could reply, his cell phone made the sound of bells chiming. Looking at the phone's readout, he glared back at the admiral. "You're not setting me up, are you?" he challenged.

"What do you mean, doc?"

"I just got a priority text from sickbay. It says, 'Medical Emergency.'"

Vice Admiral Jack Hawkins just smiled and shrugged.

***

Cac was his cyber name. It was an acronym for Charles Augustus Chase. He believed that, when pronounced, it sounded like a feline gagging on a hairball. He thought that the articulated nickname was funny. He insisted that everyone call him Cac. The acronym for a choking cat should also have been a metaphor for his lack of personal hygiene as well as his lack of personal appearance.

Cac was overweight, bordering on critically obese. His five-foot-six-inch frame was over two-hundred-fifty pounds. His usual attire was flip-flops dangling from dirty feet, well-worn Levis, and a tee-shirt, as a rule, soiled, which typically sported an assortment of contradictory sayings. On a Monday, for example, his shirt may read,

"NOBAMA 2012," while the following Monday, because he usually got a good week's wear for each shirt before laundering, it might read, "I'M A DEMOCRAT . . . SHOVE IT" or "MR. POLITICIAN LEAVE MY SOCIAL SECURITY ALONE!" At first glance, Cac's political affiliations could have been difficult to ascertain until it was learned that he purchased most of his wardrobe at Ridgecrest's Goodwill Store. Cac loved the ease and carefree attire associated with tee shirts providing that they were in his size, XXXL, and no more than twenty-five cents each.

***

On the morning that Professor Ironwood walked into the lab, he was fuming. He had brought Alan Ward with him, and it irritated Ironwood that they had to take the long way around to get their gate passes. The installation's main gate was located at the intersection of Inyokern Road and China Lake Boulevard in the city of Ridgecrest, a helluva distance to drive compared to his back door route. The underlying cause of his aggravation ran deeper; he was sick and tired of the interference from Captain Eastwater, infuriated that Neville Stream was co-opting his life's work, and now he has been told to report to the admiral like a kid sent to the principal's office.

Ironwood didn't know what Congressman Stream had up his sleeve, but he did know that he didn't trust him. How can a pompous ass like him get reelected term after term was genuinely amazing? He raged within himself the country, was fraught with central political control, not the rule of the "elected," and followed by a media numbed citizenry with almost zero attention span and less memory. If all the energy put into garnishing votes could be turned into useful work, we could be a great nation again. He believed that he was condemned to live in a democracy where every fool's vote is equal to a sensible man's.

When Ironwood entered the lab, he couldn't help noticing that the shirt that Cac was wearing had a drawing of a lamb on it, standing on its hind legs, holding a machine gun, and smoking a cigar. The caption below read, "TO HELL WITH DEMOCRACY." The professor smiled and then burst out laughing. The heat of his anger quickly fizzled, extinguished by the humorous irony. He recalled the famous saying of Benjamin Franklin, "Democracy is two wolves and a lamb voting on what to have for lunch. Liberty is a well-armed lamb contesting the vote," "Morning Cac," he said with a chuckle.

Cac squeaked out a reply. Cac was twenty-seven, considered by some to be a computer genius, but sounded like a twelve-year-old when he spoke. Ironwood also knew that he was more than a genius when it came to solar-pumped lasers. He was a leader in the field, and that's why Ironwood had made him the team leader on his project.

***

Alan Ward was surprised and a bit nervous. Ironwood had been firm bordering on rude when it came to revealing anything about his work. All his colleague would say was that the project was "top secret," and now he was standing in the middle of it. He could not comprehend why he had become so privileged. Alan looked around the laboratory. He was amazed at the age and condition of that portion of the Michelson Lab. Ironwood and his group had been tucked away in an older section of the building. Mid-century modern didn't quite describe its appearance. Although it was probably built during that time frame, it was far from charming; it was strictly utilitarian. Cinder block walls painted a high gloss gray and well-worn steel desks and lab tables. One bore the remains of acid burns made long ago on its black linoleum surface.

There was a large picture window at the far end of the room comprised of layers of heavy plate glass with wire netting sandwiched in between. An early version of shatterproof glass, Alan surmised. In a corner, to the left of the big window, was a control panel made out of a four-foot by eight-foot piece of plywood. The plywood was painted the same gray as the walls. It, too, had the look of something that was once serviceable many decades ago. A number of small slots and screw holes in it probably held an assortment of toggle switches and gauges once upon a time. The strangest thing about the control panel from a 1950's sci-fi movie was the automobile shift lever smack dab in the middle of the plywood. Alan gawked at the steampunk contrivance.

Charles Augustus Chase snickered, "That's an automatic transmission shift lever to a 1965 Mustang."

Alan turned with an incredulous look to Ironwood. Smiling, the professor said, "I am sorry, Alan. Cac, this is Alan Ward; Alan this is Cac." They shook hands. Cac's hand was clammy.

"I don't understand," replied Alan.

"We are developing satellite-based solar-pumped lasers," announced the professor. "This laboratory was established to create a system that would allow us to transmit energy from outer space. Cac and our crew have greatly enhanced both the collection efficiency and beam quality of present-day solar lasers."

On the other side of the room were more desks and worktables. Several PCs and laptops, probably networked together, Alan thought, and scores of electrical components all foreign to him. The old-fashioned control panel opposite was anachronistic compared to the high-tech equipment. It was out of place, like a clunky black rotary-dial telephone sitting on a desk beside a sleek new smartphone.

"This was originally used as a testing lab for Nike missiles," added Cac, getting excited and animated. "It was a vacuum tube technology back then, thus the old control panel. Outside the window there," he pointed with a shaky hand. There is a giant pair of steel doors in the pavement with an elevator below. That's where they would keep one of their anti-aircraft missiles, a Nike. And that is where we keep our Space Guard Transmitter; we call it the SGT," he added, beaming with pride.

"In the past," said Ironwood jumping in, "trying to get a power plant to the edge of the Earth's atmosphere seemed deeply unlikely, but our group has been working on a project that we believe will make such an audacious idea simple. The basic concept of the Space

Guard Program is to deploy a large platform in space near Earth, typically in a high orbit where the sun shines almost constantly, where it would harvest sunlight, convert it into electricity, and then transmit it to receivers on Earth; for use."

"It could be potentially dangerous as well, our own Death Star," Cac supplied with a horse laugh.

"It has a strong defense potential as well," Ironwood continued in a slow and deliberately lowered voice. "In today's world, and in the right hands, it could save a lot of lives."

"Yeah, just think about the potential," shouted Cac. "In the eighties and the nineties, our satellites could read a license plate of a car parked in front of the Kremlin. Today we can tell you the bra size of the driver. The targeting would be a piece of cake. Imagine the next time some terrorists attempt to decapitate school children on live TV. We would be able to pick all of them off like a world-class sniper from deep space." Cac looked from Ironwood to Alan Ward. Neither appeared to appreciate the analogy.

"You have such a space platform in orbit now?" Alan asked.

"No, Alan," said Ironwood. "Right now, we have three small satellites in low orbit for experimental purposes only. Cac likes to call them the Lithium System."

"Lithium is the element that is atomic number three on the periodic table," barked Cac from across the room, interrupting again.

Ignoring Cac, Professor Ironwood continued, "These satellites are incapable of carrying the necessary equipment to generate the power. Right now, we employ the SGT that Cac mentioned. Its solar collector beams the energy to one of the satellites whenever one is within our hemisphere, and if we have done our work correctly, the satellite will redirect that beam to a spot on earth we have chosen. Currently, this round-about way we will be using can only transmit a third of the energy that a space platform would be capable of projecting someday."

"Two Fresnel lenses focus sunlight on a parabolic mirror with an ingester juiced up by some quantum processors I developed. The term 'speed of light engagement' never sounded so sweet," Cac joined in with an almost epileptic frenzy.

"And that's the reason you chose to set this up in the desert," Alan remarked.

"One of many reasons, Alan," answered Ironwood with a smile. "Of course, there is plenty more sunshine here than on the eastern seaboard."

"Ok, but what's the Mustang shifter for?"

Cac let out another horse laugh. "It's so we can suck up to Admiral Hawkins. He's a classic car freak and a nut about old Mustangs. We will be ready for our first demo in two weeks. I could set it up, so all anyone had to do was press the 'Enter' key on my laptop, hell I could rig it to be triggered by my iPhone. After that, we would witness the elevator doors outside open and the SGT rise up to do its business and take out a target at a predetermined location. But I decided not to do that."

"Then what did you do?"

"I set the trigger mechanism to the 'D' for drive position on the shifter, and we will be giving the honors to the admiral."

***

Jonathan Dexter sat up in bed, screaming. Intravenous blood and saline drip line tubes hung from his left arm. A nurse and an orderly fought to hold him in place. Doctor Julius Farmington reviewed his chart on a tablet computer. His red blood cell count was dangerously low, and his blood pressure was through the roof. After ascertaining the seaman's blood type, they administered the transfusion and beta-blockers to manage the cardiac arrhythmia. So far, deliberated the doctor, neither was having much effect. The induction of a sedative, many times, can improve the condition of an acutely unstable patient, he observed. Doctor Farmington nodded to the attending nurse.

Still managing to control her patient, the nurse applied a syringe to the intravenous drip line with the aid of the orderly.

Jonathan Dexter slowly relaxed and fell back against his pillow. "It's growing, chief," burbled from his distorted mouth, "Jesus, your arm!"

***

Thomas Ironwood and Alan Ward sat on the opposite side of Vice Admiral Jack Hawkins' desk. It was proportionate in size to the Admiral, a giant antique monstrosity constructed of mahogany. Between Hawkins and the summoned two, along the desktop's edge, was a row of flags about six inches in height on individual tiny wood bases. Each was a flag from a different country. Hawkins had told them that every flag represented a country that he had either visited or where he had once been stationed. Ironwood counted forty-five. He also thought the flags and the huge desk presented a psychological defensive barrier between the admiral and any visitors seated opposite.

Ironwood didn't say a word. When Alan started to speak, he covertly kicked him in the shins. The professor hoped that his "first one that talks loses" strategy would be beneficial here as well.

"I am glad you could make it," said the admiral. He pushed a button on the desktop, and the door to his office closed automatically. Ironwood heard a metallic "click" as a locking mechanism latched into place. An electronic humming noise followed immediately after that. At first, Ironwood thought it might be the air conditioner kicking in, but then he realized that what he was hearing was a counter-surveillance tool used to disrupt and distort any possible listening devices.

"No one is in hot water here, gentlemen, the admiral declared. And before we go any further, I want to make it clear that I am in full support of your program, professor. As for you, Mister Ward, the FBI, ran a check on you, which is standard for all visitors to the petroglyph site from the Maturango Museum. You're harmless. I could give a rat's rear end if you went spelunking from now until doomsday. But there is one more clarification, and that is if any of you breathe a word of my declarations or the pursuant conversations in this room today, I will have you both thrown in the brig. Is that understood?"

With relief, Ironwood said, "Yes." Some weight lifted from his shoulders. It was great to have a comrade in high places. Alan, on the other hand, had the wind taken out of his sails. Ironwood kicked him again. "Yes!" he let out with a yelp.

"Good," Hawkins added. "The other night, I had a cocktail party at my home in Ridgecrest. What I am about to show you is confidential. He swept the flags on his desk aside like Moses parting the Red Sea. Turning the flat screen monitor to his personal computer around to the two visitor's vantage point, he plugged in a thumb drive. After selecting the proper icon on the screen, a Windows Media player appeared. Clicking "Play," moments later, Thomas and Alan were peering into a room. It had the appearance of a private library. "That is my study," offered the admiral.

The point of view was probably videoed from the other side of the room because a door opened at the far end, and they observed Captain Eastwater being pushed inside by a gentle but firm hand. Congressman Neville Stream followed quickly behind. Stream surreptitiously looked out the door and then closed it. The two walked towards a library table, bringing them closer to the camera view. A nice "Two Shot" thought movie buff Ironwood.

"At this stage of the game Clayton, your database of seismic surveys is crap. I want that file, and I want it now," ordered the video image of the congressman.

"What do you expect to find?' answered Eastwater, visibly

uncomfortable.

"The pot of gold at the end of the rainbow. You are in this too deep already. If you are worried about a court-martial and jail time, that will seem like a holiday compared to what I can do to you."

Stream's intimidating tactic was clearly painful and unnerving to the captain. "All right, but it will take time. I will have to find the right moment when there is the least amount of personnel on duty at the Security Management Office. The SMO has multiple protective measures for safeguarding classified national security information. I will have to obtain the appropriate security clearance."

"Make it happen now," the congressman countered with a raised voice. "I've told you before that this file dates back to the Second World War. If you get caught, just tell them that you thought it was declassified and that you were doing research on a book you were going to write on the history of the NWC."

"I could photograph them, I guess."

"Now that's my nephew," chided the congressman with a wry smile. "Thinking outside of the box is the mark of a successful man. Come on; I'll buy you another Scotch."

The two left the room and closed the door behind them. The image went black, and the word "Done" appeared in the screen's upper left-hand corner. "The camera is motion-activated," Admiral Hawkins informed his confidants. "It's a little larger than an ink pen and was concealed in the bookcase."

"That's really high-tech admiral. Did your people at the Michelson Lab make the camera?" Alan Ward asked.

"No, I bought it at RadioShack."

"What was that all about, admiral?" Ironwood interjected.

"That those two are up to no good. If I am any judge of Congressman Neville Stream, there have to be either big bucks in it for him or something of greater importance to his political aspirations."

"With all due respect, admiral," Professor Ironwood implored. "Why us? Can't you have this SMO investigate them?"

"Not on your life. Neville Stream's web of cohorts is pervasive. He probably has several moles planted on the base. I don't know who I can trust. One false step on my part, and he'd have me in front of a Congressional Oversight Committee on trumped-up charges."

"But you would be found innocent," Alan naively proposed.

"Stream has a sycophantic media on his side. They would tear me to shreds, and the truth would never get out. No gentleman, your tunnel is the source of his deception."

"Our tunnel?" exclaimed Ironwood.

"Absolutely! I need you to keep after this thing. I am asking you to keep me abreast of whatever you turn up."

"Since we are offering confessions," Ironwood responded, a bit shamefaced. "I revealed the Space Guard Program to Alan. With all the subterfuge I've witnessed between Eastwater and Stream, I thought it best if I had someone to watch my back."

"That will be your cross to bear," replied the admiral.

"Well, Alan," Professor Thomas Ironwood said, turning to his companion. "I am certain now that we need to take another look at the old Morley house."

CHAPTER 16
THE MYTHOS DEPARTMENT

"Miskatonic University, how can I direct your call?"

"Mythos Department, please."

"Whom shall I say is calling?"

"Professor Thomas Ironwood."

"One moment, please."

"Nathaniel Peaslee."

"Nate, it's Thomas Ironwood."

"Tom, you old son of a gun, how the hell are you?"

"Doing my best to survive, Nate."

"The last I heard about you, they said you were a hermit living in the desert."

"Sounds like a lame cover story. I'm out here in the Mojave working on a military project."

"Army, right?"

"Navy."

"Navy! What do they do for water for all those boats?"

"They turn on the faucet. Look, Nate, I need a favor."

"Do you want your old job back, Tom? Just say the word. The Mythos Department hasn't been the same without you. We certainly could use an old bomb-thrower like you."

"No, Nate, as long as the Millennials in administration consider the threat of the Old Ones as junior varsity, I don't want anything to do with them."

"Ok, ok, what can I do for you?"

"Alan Ward is a houseguest of mine, and I need you to check into something for me."

"Poor Alan, is he behaving strangely again? You know about his amnesia?"

"Yes, I knew. He is what I guess you could call a shell of his former self. He is the Alan Ward we use to know, only seriously diminished. He looks ill, and as far as his memory goes, he is still missing a few years of his life,"

"So, what is he doing living in the wild west?"

"That's why I called you Nate. He says he is out here on a grant from the Nathaniel Derby Pickman Foundation."

"Impossible."

"Why?"

"The Nathaniel Derby Pickman Foundation is tapped out. It's the lousy economy, Tom. Donations from the private sector are in the dumper. Even if they approved a grant for him, he'd have to wait a decade before any funding would be available."

"Nothing?"

"Nada!"

"Thanks, Nate."

"Keep in touch, prof."

When Nathaniel Peaslee disconnected the call, Ironwood heard static followed by three short beeps on his smartphone before the screen went black. Could someone have been eavesdropping, he troubled?

CHAPTER 17
RETURN TO THE MORLEY HOUSE

Inside was a black hole. White lines slashed the darkness vertically. Professor Thomas Ironwood and Alan Parker Ward shone their flashlights into a dim abyss below. Dust gently floated in the beam of their lights, making the rays stand out like broad lasers in the pitch darkness. Ironwood shivered; it was much colder here.

"Why did you derail our detailed exploration of the cellar before?" asked Ironwood, visibly annoyed.

"I didn't think it necessary. I've been over it quite a few times. It's as barren as the desert," replied Alan, a bit of an edge to his voice.

The two stood on a decrepit wood landing leading to a flight of steps. The construction of the stairs was in the same state of decomposition as the rest of the house.

"Keeping in line with modern research methods, we'll try the process of elimination," declared the professor with a touch of rare humor.

Careful of the time-worn staircase, they descended one at a time. Upon reaching the cellar floor, their search seemed baffling. Each inch of the earthen floor and stone foundation walls had such a solid nondescript aspect. The thought of anything out of the ordinary appeared ridiculous under the revealing LED glare of their flashlights. Ironwood commented, "If there are any hidden passageways or secret cubicles within these walls or the floor, they are well hidden.".

"That's what I was saying, prof," Alan returned.

Slowly they moved carefully over the entire subterranean surfaces, vertically and horizontally, considering every inch separately. An hour elapsed, and they both stood on opposite sides of a pair of cast iron washtubs, knowing little more than when they started. Earlier, they had attempted to move the tubs, but they wouldn't budge. The vessels turned out to be immovable.

"They were the only articles left behind after the house was abandoned," offered Alan. "The weight of the tubs must have been too significant to remove them, plus they are bolted to a concrete base, probably to prevent the legs of the washtubs from sinking into the earth when filled with water," he added. Alan shined his light on the crudely formed concrete base. A sand lizard scurried across the dirt floor and disappeared into a tiny orifice beneath the platform.

Ironwood shined his flashlight on Alan, and Alan shined his on Ironwood. They stared at each other. They were speechless. Ironwood set his light on the floor, stooped down, and summoned all his strength to lift the two tubs and the concrete platform. Alan, recognizing that Ironwood was unable to dislodge them, dropped his flashlight and assisted with added muscle to no avail.

Experimenting in every-which-way possible and exerting double strength on the platform, Alan and Ironwood felt a slight movement. "It slid horizontally about an inch," shouted Alan with unconcealed excitement.

"The damn thing was meant to slide," added Ironwood, joining in on the excitement. "There must be a fulcrum point."

Testing different directions to push the tubs sideways, they soon discovered a corner pivot next to the stone wall. Applying muscle power in that direction, the washtubs, concrete base, and all, slid on its corner, almost effortlessly for over five-feet. Alan and Ironwood scrambled to retrieve their flashlights.

Exposed below was another concrete surface with an iron manhole inset in its center. In the middle of the circular lid were two holes, close together, approximately one-half inch in diameter. "See those two holes," said Ironwood, pointing.

"Yes, I do," answered Alan triumphantly. "I told you I had explored this cellar several times before," he proclaimed. "And I believe I know where the key to open this concrete and iron tomb is hiding." Alan Ward jumped to his feet and focused the beam of his torch on the floor joists above. Hanging over where the washtubs once stood was a rusted metal bar. One end of the bar was bent. Alan grabbed it and almost shouted, "I observed it here before on several occasions and wondered what it was used for; I thought it was an old longshoreman's hook."

Ironwood took the metal bar from Alan and, after weaving its hook through the two holes in the utility hole, deadlifted the iron lid upwards with the ease of a man that did resistance training. A gust of stale air swept up from below. The subterranean pair aimed their LED torches like laser beams.

For a brief moment, they could distinguish nothing in the stygian hole. In the seconds that their eyes took to adjust to the bright glare, they observed a cylindrical brick wall leading downward. It was a sheer drop of about ten feet. Imbedded in the brick wall was a wrought-iron ladder, and beyond its length, the hole appeared to strike off onto a flight of stone steps. Ironwood wondered if the steps may have emerged to the earth's surface in another age.

***

The wall had been constructed with a less common type of brick, molded rectangular blocks of clay-baked stone hardened by the sun. Irregular in shape, no two bricks appeared to be of the same size. The sloppy mortar joints were as uneven as the bricks themselves. Fire ants scurried in and out of the cracks. A scorpion crawled across the knuckles of Ironwood's right hand. He noticed it and, mildly annoyed, shook his hand and watched it tumble off to the stone steps below. Professor Ironwood climbed down the wrought iron ladder. He looped the vinyl wrist strap on the end of his flashlight through a buttonhole and over a button in his shirt collar where it hung securely. The LED torch swung back and forth as he slowly descended, casting ghostly white images on the cylindrical brick cavity.

Ironwood cautiously pressed on, not waiting for Alan to follow. Hand over hand, he traveled downward, pausing momentarily, testing the strength of the ancient ladder, gradually easing his weight on one rusty iron rung after another. When ironwood looked down with each step, the stone staircase became more discernable. He could see that it had been chiseled out of one gigantic piece of solid rock. No joints or seams were visible that would have been the telltale evidence of smaller stone blocks stacked on top of one another. Looking up, he could see Alan Ward peering down at him. Ward appeared small, framed in the circle of the manhole. It was like going down into a sewer, a dark, gloomy open drain with me as the waste that's flushed, he reflected with a bit of melancholy, and then he smiled at his perverse humor. Professor Ironwood had, after all, volunteered to go down first. He insisted, in fact. He was concerned about Alan's health. Alan Ward was frail. Ironwood was at least fifty pounds heavier than his old friend, mostly muscle, so it was wise for him to test the ladder's strength. He also thought it best that he be on the firm ground initially to help Alan down off the ladder.

Ironwood set foot on the top tread of the flight of steps. It was gritty under the soles of his boots. Removing the flashlight from his shirt collar, he shined it down the stone staircase. It was a black yawning aperture. The beam of the flashlight wasn't powerful enough to penetrate its depths. It was cool, even cold, he thought. For a brief moment, he was struck with an uncontrollable shiver. "Alan," he shouted, looking up the round well shaft. "Attach your light to your collar button like I did and come on down."

Alan was far more agile than Ironwood had expected, and he made it down the ladder and to the stone staircase in half the time. "Well done, Mr. Ward, well done. You surprised me," declared the professor. "Shall we proceed?"

"Is it too late to tell you that I am afraid of the dark?" Alan exclaimed. Ironwood looked incredulous. "Come on, I'll lead the way," Alan declared with a laugh. "Follow me."

CHAPTER 18
BENEATH

"Those idiots at the tunnel, I hope they blow themselves up!" Gwen exclaimed, jamming on the parking brake. The Dodge Neon momentarily lurched forward in her driveway as if in response to her rage. She had wasted most of the day at the tunnel site politely disobeying orders. She had been ordered to the airstrip, then choppered out to the area where she had fallen into that damn hole the day before. Upon landing, she saw that her flatbed truck with its drill rig was parked nearby along with the trailer that held the blasting gel. Why it was there, she didn't know, and before she had a chance to find out, Lieutenant Jason Riggs had her by the arm and was leading her down the ladder into the earth.

She didn't mind being manhandled by Jason, but she wished it would have been done under the influence of candlelight and wine. "What's up, lieutenant," she cooed, momentarily forgetting her annoyance.

"You are needed."

"Aye, aye, sir. What did you have in mind?" They had finished their climb down, and Gwen stood facing the young lieutenant. She didn't take her eyes off of him, not even to notice the enormous tunnel works that surrounded them. They stood less than a foot apart. Riggs returned her gaze with a smile. Gwen hoped it was the right kind of smile.

"We need your explosives expertise," he answered, still smiling.

"So, this was your idea, lieutenant?"

"No petty officer, the orders came from the C.O."

"Aye, aye," she returned only sadly this time. It was then that she first noticed the extensive length of the tunnel with all the cabling and bright lights. "Wow, this certainly has grown," she exclaimed while being led through the passage. She walked with Riggs for what seemed like a mile or more. Every so often, during their trek, a Seabee would pass them by, going in the opposite direction, pushing a wheelbarrow load of dirt and rock. Then they reached the end of the cavity. More Seabees with picks, shovels, and sledgehammers worked at the dead end. A huge boulder blocked the tunnel. It was the size of the passageway itself. The men worked unsuccessfully, trying to break down the enormous stone.

There was writing on it. A funny kind of writing, Gwen thought. It looked more like hieroglyphics, but they ran vertically instead of horizontally like the ones she saw in books—intricately carved with great precision, not like the crude petroglyphs in the canyon. The inscriptions looked machined. In an instant, she realized that the glyphs were written horizontally. What she thought to be vertical writing, as in some Asian scripts, was simply parallel line after line of engraved rock that had been turned on its side. Although the meaning of the script was totally foreign to her, there was somehow an underlying meaning. It touched her inside, and she felt her skin crawl. It was the same sensation she felt the night before when something lurked beneath her house. "Something lurked?" she quaked internally; why did I think something was lying in wait last night? The mental cringe aroused her suspicions. The big stone, somehow she knew, must have been part of a greater structure that had toppled over on its side, probably thousands of years ago, crashing through the tunnel's ceiling.

Captain Eastwater was nearby observing the action. He was wearing NWU's looking like a Seabee, which he was not. Gwen came to attention. She saluted, and the captain returned it. "Petty Officer Gilhooley reporting, sir."

"Excellent," he replied. "As you can see, we have a barrier to breakthrough. I had your equipment brought here. It is topside. I want you to blast this obstruction to pieces. Is that understood, Petty Officer Gilhooley?"

"Aye, aye, sir, but I am unable to do that." She was shaking slightly but still standing at attention; Gwen was not one for disobeying orders.

"Explain," demanded her superior officer.

"My blasting skills are limited, sir. I am only experienced with light to medium charges for geodetic surveying."

"I am well aware of that, Gilhooley. Just get your nitro down here now and bust this thing to bits!"

"I respectfully decline, sir," she responded, still shaking. "I am not certified to do that kind of work."

"Petty Officer Gilhooley, that is a direct order," he shouted.

Gwen could see her cell door slowly closing, locking her into the brig, but she had no choice. "Again, with all due respect, captain, I cannot. I don't know the first thing about that type of work. It is beyond my duty scope. You will need a certified demolition expert. I could easily blow us all up along with that big rock."

The Captain issued a few more threats and promised to put her on report. Gwen still had to respectfully deny his request. Sitting in her car, later, she knew that she would soon be up in front of her C.O. and hoped the write-up she would get wouldn't be too severe. It was insubordination for a lowly petty officer to disobey direct orders from a captain a million pay grades above her; it will be an A-grade fustercluck. There was one bright spot in the lousy day, though. Jason Riggs had asked her out. He took her back to the waiting chopper, and before the pilot fired up the engine, which could drown out their conversation, he asked her to dinner. The condemned woman was granted a last meal, she cheerfully recalled.

Gwen wondered what all the rush was about. Why was Captain Eastwater in such a hurry, especially when a Bureau of Land Management archeologist should have been contacted about the big rock with all that writing on it? The captain chose to ignore that protocol. She got out of the Neon and slammed the door. Emotional conflict ensnared Gwen. She was both angry and happy. Upset about a possible black mark on her, up 'til now, spotless record and overjoyed that she and Riggs were going to be breaking bread together. She was looking forward to their date, but in contrast, she was not looking forward to a load of wet, mildewed laundry sitting on her kitchen counter.

Walking towards the front steps to her house, Gwen stopped suddenly. The pest control guy's truck was still parked alongside the house. After all this time, the compressor, fastened to the truck's bed, which enabled the service contractor to spray his repellent, was still running. Gwen went to the driver-side window of the Toyota small truck. No one was inside. She followed the hose, which trailed from the compressor terminating under the house. Gwen got down on her hands and knees and ambled on all fours into the crawl space. Cobwebs and spiders' eggs encrusted the floor joist above her head. Clambering a short distance beneath the house, Gwen noticed, to her amazement, that the compressor hose disappeared into a hole within the earthen floor. Edging closer, she could see that the opening in the ground was large enough to swallow a man or a woman. Gwen also noticed, with a shudder, that the hole was positioned directly below her bedroom. She stuck her arm into it up to the shoulder but couldn't feel the bottom. Grabbing a clump of dry soil, Gwen dropped it into the hole. The dirt ball's noise hitting bottom in less than a second told her that the nethermost area was not that far below. Oh my God, she thought. Was the pest control guy down there? Did he fall in? Maybe he had a heart attack, or he had breathed too much of his pesticide. The chemical fumes from the hole were almost unbearable. "Hey, Mister! Are you down there?" she hollered. Several times she yelled, but there was no reply.

Starting to back out the way she came, she thought she heard the sound of movement coming from the hole and stopped. Was something being dragged through the dirt? "Hey, Mister," she shouted again. Only silence followed.

Backing out from under the house, Gwen immediately knew what she had to do. Within a few seconds, she was charging through her front door, living room, hall, and spare bedroom. She could call base security for help, but there might not be enough time. If the pest control man was truly down in that hole, then seconds could be precious. It may be a matter of life or death. Flinging open the spare bedroom's closet door, she removed a large aluminum suitcase and tossed it onto a twin bed. Below, a yellow and black emblem on the case in bold letters read, "Bio Hazmat Suit." Gwen was attached to the Bio Hazzard Unit on the base. They created the "Unit" shortly after the Ebola outbreak in the states. She had trained extensively with the suit in various simulations and situations. It was a flash spun high-density polyethylene encapsulated suit that would keep out every deadly microbe known to man as well as toxic gases and radiation. It wasn't the Cadillac; it was the Rolls Royce of protection, also equipped with a Dark-Light Cowl for night vision.

Gwen flicked the catches on the case to "Open," breaking its air-tight seal. The aluminum case hissed as the self-actuating vacuum protection was disabled. Her training had been thorough. Gwen could get into the hazmat suit and sealed up in less than five minutes. Before donning the suit, she decided to leave a note.

***

Residential landscape irrigation was strictly verboten ever since the enforcement of California's water restrictions, so when Gwen walked across what was left of her parched lawn in the yellow protection gear, she felt like she was trekking the surface of Mars. The Hazmat suit had a built-in air supply adequate for thirty minutes, providing she didn't over-exert herself. With each step, Gwen could hear her breathing magnified within the suit's helmet.

Gwen detoured briefly from her destination and obtained a length of tow rope from the trunk of her car. She approached the foundation of her home. It took her longer to wriggle into the crawlspace than it did for her to don the hazmat suit. Due to the suit's bulk, she had to be cautious about catching it on any protruding nails from the floorboards above. Twisting and worming her way toward the hole, she startled a field mouse that sought refuge from the afternoon sun and watched it scurry out from under the house into the dry grass. She realized at that moment that she should have turned off the compressor on the pest control truck before crawling under the house, but it was too late. She had already reached her objective. The petty officer, in protective equipment, hesitated briefly, trying to decide if the best way to go down the hole would be headfirst or feet first? She decided to go feet first. Gwen tied the rope to a cross beam overhead and dropped the other end into the hole. She stopped her downward movement halfway into the cavity with her elbows and forearms. Gwen switched on the LED headlamp on the cowl of her suit and activated the night vision display. Whatever the LED torch failed to illuminate; the night imaging system would hopefully enhance at a distance. The light revealed the rope, short of the crater's bottom side, dangling several feet above the ground. "Okay, Petty Officer Gilhooley, here we go," she said to herself.

The hole was at least fifteen feet deep. Gwen grasped the rope with upstretched arms and was able to slow her descent by sliding down it initially. She reached the rope's end and dropped the remaining distance. The soft soles on the Hazmat suit's boots helped to cushion the landing and kept her from falling over. Loose dirt rained down and around her. She was in a tunnel. Within seconds she recognized that it was the same five-sided configuration as the one they had discovered in the desert, where she had been earlier. What the hell, that is at least fifty miles from here, she judged.

To Gwen's left, the tunnel appeared to terminate a short distance beyond the street where she lived above ground. The tunnel's ceiling had pancaked down in that area, and she could make out the remains of a crushed storm sewer pipe that had once conveyed the drainage for her subdivision. On the rare occasions that they experience rain at the navy base, the storm drain would always back up. Now she knew why. To her right, a northerly direction she estimated, the tunnel seemed to stretch on forever. Forever, she knew, was an exaggeration because even with the headlamp and the night vision, her depth perception was limited to around thirty feet.

The odd-shaped tunnel became unbearably eerie when she

thought of it running under her house. It reminded her of "something lurked." The night vision displayed the underworld in green and made it all the more unnerving. The human eye, Gwen knew, was more sensitive to green than any other color, and the monochromatic green of the image display offered the most accurate view for the user. Even so, she felt like she had entered the sinister portion of a funhouse, and she wasn't laughing. There was a hissing sound that she heard over the soft puffing of her suit's oxygen regulator. To the left of her feet was the end of the hose. A trigger release valve on the back rested against a loose piece of tile from the tunnel's ceiling. It had become half-cocked and slowly releasing pesticide into the tunnel. Picking it up, Gwen fiddled momentarily with the mechanism shutting the valve off. The hissing ceased. She tossed it onto the tunnel floor. That was when she heard it. The audio amplifier in the suit was highly sensitive. The sound of movement directed her eyes towards the north.

It was a dark, inhuman thing with too many eyes and too many mouths, a shapeless entity composed of a viscous jelly. It filled the tunnel. The massive unending body glistened. It was smooth, pale, and slimy, like an oversized intestine. Within its flesh, something moved. It was as if someone was trying to erect a tent from the inside. It rippled and shifted.

Gwen retreated from the approaching mass but stopped abruptly, realizing that she was backing into a dead end. Time would probably be too short for her to climb back up the rope in the bulky suit. Her feet became rooted to the tunnel floor with fear. She became conscious of the colorless and translucent quality of the thing. It actually wasn't a dark consistency. It churned with the reflection of the tunnel's walls, floor, and ceiling as it moved. She cursed herself for not having the foresight to bring her Glock with her.

A light pulsed within the transparent flesh, and there was a movement within the jelly-like form. It was the slow flailing of arms and legs. Gwen could make out a person's writhing form in a white shirt and slacks as the grotesque bulk came closer. The white shirt had a red collar, red piping ran along the top pocket, and the slacks' pockets were also red. "She screamed inside her suit. It was the uniform the man from the pest control service wore. He had become an insect trapped in malleable amber. She was only a few feet away from him and it. The man appeared to be screaming, but no sound ensued. A fleshy tube dangled above and through it, Gwen could barely make out the garbled cries of a man in excruciating pain. From her vantage point, it looked as if his face was melting. A deafening screech, "Eeeeeeee! Eeeeeeee! Wawk Wawk Wawk Wawk!" emanated from the monstrous thing. The snorkel tube extended to twice its length and formed into a tentacle. It lashed out with lightning speed and wrapped around her waist.

Gwen saw her reflection in the greasy tissue just before the creature of the tunnels consumed her.

CHAPTER 19
UNEARTHING

Admiral Jack Hawkins snatched up the smartphone and pressed the "Home" button. He had meant to upgrade to one but hadn't gotten around to it. The admiral still used a flip phone. He wasn't entirely technology ignorant, though. His son had an iPhone, and he had used it on several occasions. And for this occasion, he had practiced extensively with his son's phone. This was Clayton Eastwater's phone, and time was of the essence.

He had challenged Eastwater to a game of racquetball, and relying on the Captain's over-inflated ego, he knew that he wouldn't turn down the contest. Eastwater beat him badly. The wiry Clayton found it easy to outmaneuver Hawkins's substantial frame, and with the twenty years' difference in their ages, the younger captain definitely had the advantage. Admiral Hawkins wasn't concerned about the results of the game. He had planned the encounter very well. He was sitting on a bench in the officer's club locker room. Eastwater was taking a steam, which Hawkins hoped would buy him enough time to complete his task. The captain's uniform and his cell phone were in locker number 37, and the admiral had the passkey.

Rank doth have its privileges; he waxed philosophically. He also had another advantage. Hawkins knew that the only places on the base where security cameras were not allowed were the men's and women's locker rooms.

Admiral Hawkins opted for the "Camera" icon on the phone's display. He chose the "All Photos" option and watched as a collection of pictures popped up. "Eureka!" He whispered to himself. What he hoped to find was glaring back at him in full color. There was a series of twelve photographs of old yellowed documents, all in crystal clear focus. The navy base transmitted 4G mobile broadband Internet access; he hoped it would be fast enough. Hawkins selected the photos, along with the email option, and entered his email address along with Ironwood's. Safety in numbers, he told himself. He pressed "Send" and waited. In what seemed like an eternity, the admiral anxiously watched the phone's readout. The agonizingly slow messaging system put him on edge. Maybe he had attached too many photos than the broadband could handle? A few seconds later, he received the "Delivered" notification. Only one more thing to do, he thought as he remembered what his son had taught him. He located the "Sent" selection in the phone's index and deleted the email record. Not taking any chances, the admiral wiped his fingerprints off the smartphone with his gym towel and returned it to Eastwater's belt holster before securing the locker door.

Less than a minute elapsed when Clayton Eastwater entered the locker room, drying his hair on a towel. "Admiral, this is no place to rest. You should take a steam," he announced. "It will do you a world of good."

"I'm good, Clayton, I'm good," he answered with a smile.

***

Jason Riggs's face was one big grin. If you asked him, "What makes life great?" His answer would have been simple, "Gwendolyn Gilhooley and how she could be devastating in jeans and a tee-shirt."

He drove his Ford F-150 up to her house fifteen minutes early. He was anxious about their date. He was off duty and out of uniform. Jason wore a neatly pressed pair of beige Dockers slacks, a brand new Polo shirt, and white Converse High Tops. He was going to take Gwen out to dinner. He had reservations at the Grape Vine in Ridgecrest. It was a four-star restaurant with an excellent wine list.

Jason walked up to her front steps. He was nervous. He had known Gwen for quite a while, but this was to be their first date. His anxiety lessened when he noticed that Gwen's house's front door stood open, and the screen door rested loosely against the frame, unlatched. "Gwen, are you there? Anybody home!" he repeatedly shouted, only to be followed by silence. Roused from his loving caprice, he noticed a small Toyota truck parked alongside the house for the first time. He also realized that Gwen's silly little car, the Dodge Neon, was also parked in front.

Leaving the porch and walking up to the truck, Jason spotted the hose leading away and into the crawlspace. The compressor on the back of the truck switched on, and he jumped with a start. Whatever the compressor's system was feeding, Jason assumed, it must have been triggered by a drop in pressure. He squatted down and observed that the hose continued under the house and disappeared into a large hole. Overhead a thick rope tied to a joist was suspended into the same opening in the earth. The crawlspace's dirt floor had been disturbed as if someone had left a trail while slithering across the ground towards the hole.

The thought of someone down in that dark hole made Lieutenant Riggs tremble. Two things made him feel uneasy: swimming in the ocean at night and dark enclosed spaces. This was his abnormal fear of not having enough room for him to feel comfortable. He ran back to the front porch of the house and up the steps. Opening the screen door wide, he yelled for Gwen once more. Still no answer. Feeling like a cat burglar, he slowly crept across the living room carpet. "Gwen, anybody home!" he offered again, louder than the other times. He was confident that nobody was at home, but he had to be certain. The kitchen was void of any personnel. There was a laundry basket on the Formica counter overflowing with wet clothes. The dining area was equally empty, and so was Gwen's bedroom. He felt uncomfortable about going in there and was glad when he saw that it too was empty. Jason lived in an apartment off base, but he was familiar with the post-war housing on Nimitz Avenue. All of them were two-bedroom Cape Cods, so he had one more room left to explore. The spare bedroom in Gwen's house was used as an office of sorts. A small desk was up against one wall with a laptop resting on its wooden surface and a mesh-back chair on castors under it.

A twin bed and nightstand were on the other side of the small room. What immediately caught Jason's eye was the aluminum case that was laid open on the bed. He was also acquainted with the Bio Hazzard Unit on the NWC. He was not part of that team, but he had observed the hazmat suits in use during training. The large aluminum case contained a hazmat suit when not in use, and this one was empty. Stuck to its lid was a Post-it note with writing on it. Printed in black felt marker were ten words that screamed at Jason's dreaded phobia, "**IF YOU CAN'T FIND ME, I AM UNDER THE HOUSE.**"

***

After reading the note five times and then breaking free from its spell, Jason dashed from the house and to his F-150. Light, a light, I need light; he kept telling himself. Light was the weapon that, at times, could help to dispel his fear of being trapped in narrow places. Light gave him courage. In the glove box of his pick-up truck, he kept a two million candlepower rechargeable spotlight. He turned it on momentarily, assured by the green indicator light that it contained a full charge. There was no time to think—thinking only stirred him into a panic. He ran to the crawl space with his lightsaber in hand. "So much for my Sunday go to meeting clothes," he said as he proceeded to crawl through the dirt calling the petty officer's name, "Gwen, Gwen."

Reaching the hole under Gwen's house, Jason switched on the spotlight and leaned into the opening as far as he could. Shouting her name again, he shone the powerful beam of light below. There was no reply. Hanging upside down in the cavity, he waited in the silence that followed. The torch of his light flung far, but beyond that was total blackness. The pitch dark caused the quiet to become unbearably eerie. There was no escape down there, he sensed. There is suffocation residing in that darkness. He felt the cold pressure of claustrophobia.

In the moments that followed, the dark pit filled with a shuffling. The sound resembled a heavy object dragging across gravel. Jason also imagined a faint sucking gurgle mixed up with the dragging. He shouted, "Gwen!" one more time. The mention of her name became a talisman. He realized that his need for her was greater than his claustrophobic panic. Placing the spotlight's wrist strap between his teeth, he grabbed the dangling rope in a sudden burst of courage and slid down it.

Dropping to the tunnel floor into a squat, all claustrophobia symptoms in Jason vanished as he stared at a jelly-like monstrosity. There was a sweet sickening smell. A shapeless mass of protoplasmic bubbles, faintly luminous with myriads of eyes forming and un-forming, filled the tunnel as a piston fills a cylinder. It was bearing down on him. As it came closer, he could make out the source of its luminescence. Inside the thing was a soft golden glow that seemed to grow stronger as it approached him. The transparent bubbly flesh glistened brightly under the two million candle-powered glare of his spotlight. It was slimy like an oil slick, and he could see through parts of it. Nearer by every second and knowing that his fear of "no escape" was not unfounded, he could not move from where he stood. He was both terrified and mesmerized by what was indeed about to crush him to death.

Then he saw her. At first, she looked like an astronaut clad in a yellow space suit floating within the thing. Initially, it wasn't there, and then, upon coming closer, it materialized, looking as if it suspended in a weightless state. Good God, he grasped what he was seeing. It was the yellow hazmat suit. It was Gwen.

A tentacle the diameter of a man's arm lashed out of the shifting contours of the creature and snatched the spotlight out of Jason's hand. Jason fell to his knees as he watched a mouth, which instantly formed within the putrid mass, swallow the electric torch. "Jesus, it wanted the light," he cried out. His instrument to dispel the dreaded darkness had been taken from him, and its radiance was slowly diminishing as the creature absorbed it. He had no weapon now. Jason backed away from the impending doom on his hands and knees and touched something with his left hand. It was a hose nozzle with a trigger release on the end. He picked it up and pointed it at the horror that hovered just above. Knowing that it would be like using a squirt gun against an M1 Abrams tank, he laughed out loud at his futile attempt as he pulled the trigger. The hose was under pressure and filled with insecticide. The walls of the tunnel filled with a deafening wail, "Eeeeeeee! Eeeeeeee! Wawk, Wawk, Wawk, Wawk!"

Expecting to be swallowed up like the flashlight, Jason looked towards the ceiling as though he was trying to see the blue sky above. In his mind's eye, he could see Gwen by candlelight. She reached across the dinner table and touched his hand. He squeezed his eyes shut and pulled the trigger again on the pest control sprayer. Slowly Jason opened his eyes, expecting to see the monster from a sailor's worst drunken nightmare begin to tear him apart. Instead, he was astonished to observe the giant organism retreating into the confines of the tunnel whence it came. Jason got to his feet. Keeping the pressure release valve pressed in the open position, he waved it back and forth, saturating every inch of the creature with the pesticide. The more Jason sprayed, the faster it retreated. At once, he observed that it was also retreating from around Gwen in her hazmat suit. If he kept at it, he might have her free from the jelly mass.

***

Gwendolyn Gilhooley had the wind to her back. The clear night sky was black velvet charged with a brilliant array of stars. A faint breeze ruffled her blond hair; she handled the wheel of the 37-foot Catalina with expertise. The sails were down, and the single diesel inboard kept them at a steady six knots. Her dad was in the galley below preparing dinner. They would eat after they docked. She could hear the rattling of pots and pans. It made her smile. It had been a while since she had last visited her parents. Mom would be at the dock waiting for them, but you couldn't keep her dad away from the water. Although retired, he was Navy through and through. It was a joyful homecoming.

Gwen and her dad were heading towards their yacht club. The lighted buoys clearly illuminated the channel—the green ones on her left and the red ones on the right. Red right returning, Gwen recited to herself. A loud crash of cutlery, pots, and pans erupted from the galley, followed by cursing. Leaning to one side of the wheel, she wanted to shout down to her dad to find out what had happened, but nothing came out of her mouth. No matter how hard she tried, no sound emanated from her lips. Endeavoring to draw in a lungful of air so she could attempt to call out again, Gwen could not breathe. She was gradually losing consciousness. The light from the galley below was dimming. She could no longer see the starlit sky. Losing her balance, she slid to the deck, barely holding on to the boat's wheel with one hand. Try as she may, she was unable to get up. The sailboat shifted to port and headed towards the green markers. She knew that the Catalina's draft was seven-foot, and outside the markers, it would surely run aground. At six knots, it would be a devastating crash. There was nothing she could do. She stared into a night sky comprised entirely of a bubbling mass.

***

Jason had removed the helmet from Gwen's hazmat suit. The only light in the tunnel now came from his cell phone. He had taken it out of his pocket after the protoplasmic horror had retreated. He was sitting on the dirt-strewn tunnel floor with Gwen's head cradled in his lap. The light from his phone made her look deathly pale. Parting her lips, he began applying mouth-to-mouth resuscitation. After a few seconds, Gwen gasped and gently pushed him away. She smiled. Then grabbing Jason by the back of his neck, she looked as if she changed her mind. Gwen pulled him down on her and kissed him hard on the mouth. "Hi," she said. "You found my note.

"You know," responded a smiling Jason. "I used to be afraid of being in small spaces."

***

Admiral Hawkins opened the laptop in his study and powered it up. He had emailed the images from Eastwater's phone to his personal account where it would be safe from prying eyes, he hoped. The NSA could secure information from any source it desired. He just prayed that Congressman Stream didn't have them in his back pocket, or at least they hadn't thought to hack his laptop—yet.

He looked around the room with the satisfaction of accomplishment. It was a beautiful house, and his wife, Katherine, was an expert at creating a homespun atmosphere. The mahogany bookshelves and desk that she had picked out in Ridgecrest, along with the subtle earth tones she had the walls painted, gave his study a welcoming warmth. A picture of the two of them fishing in the Adirondacks sat on his desk. It was his favorite. On the wall in front of him was a Thomas Kinkade painting of an old farmhouse. It was their dream picture—the kind of place where they would like to live when he retired.

Waiting for his Gmail account to boot up, Hawkins unlocked the bottom drawer of his desk. He removed a .50 caliber Desert Eagle. Initially designed by the Israel Military Industries, it is the most powerful semi-automatic handgun in the world. Even though the Desert Eagle had a huge triangular barrel and gaping muzzle, it looked just the right size for the admiral's ball-mitt-sized hands. He kept a loaded clip in its grip. He chambered a round and slipped it between the folds in his briefcase. The admiral spent over thirty years in the service. He had always done his duty with honor. If the bastards tried to take that away from him, they were going to have a helluva damn fight.

The email was in his Inbox. He stared at the first attachment. It was a photo like the others—the first page of an incredibly old document. Moments passed before he realized what he was looking at.

In the midst of World War II, adequate facilities were required for the test and evaluation of rockets. At the same time, the Navy wanted a proving ground for the analysis of aviation ordnances. The military needed a site that would meet both their needs. The Navy established China Lake as its testing station in 1943, which today is known as the Naval Weapons Center, the NWC. Its mission was to research, develop, and test weapons, with the additional function of furnishing training in the use of such weapons. Admiral Hawkins scrutinized the digital photo of a report written in 1942 by a Seabee surveying the area. His name was Lieutenant Hayward Phillips. It appeared written on a typewriter of the period.

Amphibious Force, Pacific Fleet,
Camp Elliot, San Diego, California

July 7, 1942

From: Lieutenant Hayward Phillips
To: The Commandant, U.S. Navy

Subject: (A) Discovery of China Lake Anomaly
(B) Action Taken with China Lake Anomaly
(C) Waiting Further Orders

Disclosure: Lieutenant Hayward Phillips reporting as ordered with only three remaining in my command. Initially seven in my Construction Battalion. Petty Officers Matthew Delaney and Albert Gedney were killed, and Seaman Joshua Neely is missing. Carroon, Reichenheim, and Green comprise the balance of my crew. Seaman Victor Carroon was my survey assistant; Reichenheim and Green are locals we hired as laborers. The original mission was to survey the million-plus acres of the area known as China Lake for the future establishment of the Naval Ordnance Test Station and to investigate an abnormal structure (anomaly) at northwest parcel #37-0073 previously discovered and photographed by a SO3C Navy reconnaissance plane on June 5th of this year.

Day 1: Outside temperature over 115 degrees and the humidity at a moisture sapping fifteen percent. Diesel Ford transport truck overheated the first day. Can only use it for two hours at a time and will be unable to maintain a large enough water supply to replenish its radiator if it keeps boiling over. We have hung a water bag over the truck's radiator in hopes of cooling its engine. Set up camp approximately 47 miles from parcel #37-0073. We will begin the initial surveying of the proposed boundary tomorrow. Heat is grueling. Men became dehydrated quickly. If there isn't a break in this intense desert climate, we will only be able to perform our duties during the cooler hours of the morning.

Day 2: Surveyed and charted 30 miles along the northwest perimeter. Heat is unbearable. Battalion and truck are overheated. No more work today. We have stretched a canvas from the truck's back to some spare tent poles to make shade. I made a severe miscalculation. I am from Providence, Rhode Island, and my experience in arid climates is minimal. My crew left our camp where we had pitched it on day one, believing that we would return before evening. The morning was briefly overcast, and taking advantage of the gray skies, I had my Seabees work longer than we should have. Within a few hours, the sky cleared and once again was greeted by the merciless desert sun. We had traveled too far. The diesel truck was unable to make the trip back without roasting. The radiator water bag sprung a leak emptying its contents. Each of us only had enough water that we could carry. Not enough to cool down the truck's engine. I planned to correct my error the following day by spending the next morning traveling back to camp and vowed that all of our supplies and tents would move with us, from then on, like wandering Nomads. Fortunately, we had a good supply of c-rations in the truck.

At sunset, Seaman Neely drew my attention for the first time to the anomaly. It was silhouetted on the horizon. The ground in China Lake is very flat for long expanses dotted occasionally with only a few outcroppings of sagebrush and rabbitbrush. Where we were, there was nothing to obstruct our view for miles. What we saw was a tall, dark form to the west. It was blackened by the setting sun but what we could make out was striking. It was a huge monolith that, from our perspective, it must have been several stories high and appeared to be very precise in its form. We all wondered if it was a manmade structure.

Day 3: Lost an entire day of work traveling back to our campsite. Too hot to return to our last surveyed point to the northwest. We would have wasted another day driving back the following morning, but Joshua Neely volunteered to drive us all back that evening. Neely has keen eyesight, and he assured me that he could easily find our way back by following the truck's tracks in the sand. At night the temperature drops down to the mid-sixties in the desert. The merciful cool evening temperature was a blessing for us all cooped up in the truck. I sat next to the seaman in the passenger seat, and the rest of the crew was holed up in the back under the truck's canopy.

The trip back was a lot longer at night than it would have been in the day because Neely very seldom exceeded twenty miles per hour and many times drove considerably slower. Trailing our tire tracks in the dark was a tiresome task. Joshua Neely navigated most of the way with his head and left arm hanging out the side window steering the truck with his right. The Ford's bright lights only illuminated our pathway for about fifty feet in front of us, eliminating any opportunity to go faster.

Around about 2 a.m., we heard a chilling sound. Neely straightened up in his seat with a start and slammed on the brakes. I had dozed off and banged my head against the passenger's side window upon being jolted awake. "Did you hear that!" he shouted.
"Hear what? I said.
"Roll down your window," he answered. Forgetting all protocol in regards to my navy rank, I did as ordered. I only heard the evening breeze, at first, playing amongst the scrub wood. Then a sound crept up out of the desert. It was faint, to begin with, rising to a definite screech.
"Oh my God," I cried out, neglecting to maintain my officer's composure. It was an animal sound, wide-ranging. Eeeeeeee! Eeeeeeee! It resonated in my brain, and the hairs stood up on the back of my neck. Initially, I was unable to discern what kind of creature could make such a noise nor what direction it came from. It was all mixed up in the wind. At first, you could scarcely tell them apart. It would begin again each time it would start low, competing with the barren region' s wind growing in intensity until you could hear nothing else. Eeeeeeee! Eeeeeeee! It continued to wail. "A seagull," I said out loud. It would utter its keening screech followed by the clucking or rattling familiar with the seabird, except we were within a million square miles of arid desert hundreds of miles from the Pacific Coast. "There shouldn't be any gulls out this far," I reasoned out loud, and besides, I had never heard any voice their call with such magnitude.

Our entire crew was awake by this time, and we got

out of our transport and stood dumbfounded, staring in all directions. Neely had turned off the truck's engine to save on fuel and to allow us all a clear listening field. The next interval, the screeching sound came forth several of us jumped. Except for Neely, we had all been sleeping, and the prospect of being roused from our slumbers by an alien scream would have made anyone jumpy.

Petty Officer Matthew Delaney observed that the wind was coming out of the northwest, and he believed that that was also the direction the sound emanated. He also thought that since the sound started out low and then raised in volume that it was not unlike a coyote's howl that could carry for miles. Therefore, whatever made, it was probably a reasonable distance away. We accepted his theory but still did not venture beyond the lights of the truck. After behaving like brave, stalwart companions through each succeeding screech after screech, the wind shifted from the south, and all unearthly sounds ceased. Subsequently, we all climbed back into the truck; I said a little prayer to myself that the rest of the evening would be uneventful.

Day 4: Only five miles from parcel #37-0073 and the anomaly. The stone megalith, or "monolith," as the men of our Construction Battalion preferred to call it, was now clearly visible at all times of the day. We had set up camp facing the south. Even in the insufferable heat, the men seemed to work harder and for longer hours than before. I chalked it up to a driving desire on their part to get the job done and back to a cooler climate. However, there appeared to be an underlying meaning for their motivation, but they never talked about it, at least not in my presence. Could it have been that the strange screeching wails of the mysterious night creature had put them so severely on edge that they yearned to return to civilization as soon as possible?

Joshua Neely's enthusiasm for work was of another sort. He confessed to me that he hoped to return to school after the war and get a degree in archeology. His longing to unlock the secrets of unsolved eons had appealed to him ever since he was in his early teens. Neely would be pursuing that dream even now if it hadn't been interrupted by the Japanese attack on Pearl Harbor. There was talk in Washington D.C. that to help out our servicemen, in the future, that they might craft a piece of legislation to be called the Servicemen's Readjustment Act, known as the G.I. Bill, that provided a range of benefits for war veterans that included cash payments for tuition and living expenses to attend a university. Neely hoped to take advantage of just such a benefit when the war was over if the bill ever passed. A lot of "ifs." So, as it unfolded, the seaman wanted to bridge the distance and explore the anomaly at parcel #37-0073, also as soon as possible.

Nighttime temperature down to 60 degrees. I didn't sleep. The Eeeeeeee, eeeeeeee, shrieking was intolerable. The wind was a light breeze out of the south, but the direction it came from didn't alter the sound level. We were only five miles from the anomaly, and it was evident that that was its source. Matthew Delaney was correct the night before when he observed that the animal screams were coming out of the northwest. To the northwest is where the so-called monolith is located. The volume of its cries was almost ear-splitting compared to the previous evening. There were only two weapons in our survey crew—a bolt action M1 with a 5-round magazine and my sidearm. I stood guard leaning against the front fender of the transport, smoking cigarette after cigarette. I had chambered a round in my sidearm, prepared for anything that may appear. I had each man take turns standing guard in three-hour shifts with the loaded M1; Petty Officer Albert Gedney was the first. The rest of the men had buttoned up their tents and stuffed cotton, from a first aid kit, in their ears in hopes of getting some rest.

Day 5: The rest of the evening was uneventful. At sunrise, the amplified seabird keening stopped. Petty Officer Albert Gedney and Seaman Neely were the first to rise. The two had hurriedly gobbled down their morning rations and headed towards the anomaly. Neely had instilled some excitement in Albert Gedney over the possibility of a great archeological find. Victor Carroon had already taken the surveyor's transit tripod along with the lenker rod out of the transport and set them up to begin our morning shoot. The transit is used to measure horizontal and vertical angles along the horizon and the earth to establish property lines. The five-foot-long lenker rod is the surveyor's measuring stick. We mark the lines with steel pins driven into the ground, which are numbered and entered into a logbook. These are called "benchmarks." The transit we use is equipped with an optical theodolite (a small telescope) for topographic surveying.

A quarter of an hour passed, and Carroon and I had set three benchmarks when I noticed something peculiar through the eyepiece of the optical theodolite. Gedney and Neely had set out on foot to cross the five miles between us and the anomaly. They were about halfway to their destination when I spied what appeared, in the lenses of the theodolite, as a large animal hunkered down in the sand. The hide of the thing shimmered with movement. It was directly in the path of the Petty Officer Third Class and the Seaman. Dropping my logbook, I ran to the transport and yelled for my crew to follow.

The diesel engine was warm from the morning sun, and it caught instantly the first time I laid on the starter. Slamming the truck into first and spewing sand behind us, we raced towards the Petty Officer 3rd Class and the Seaman Recruit. We bridged the distance between the two Seabees and us within a few minutes. "Get in!" I ordered, slowing to a stop. Gedney and Neely did as ordered. Speeding up again, I unholstered my sidearm and was ready for whatever lay ahead. Gedney snatched up the M1. Everyone in our battalion probably thought that I was suffering from heatstroke and was off my rocker. Everything had happened so fast that I didn't have time to brief the men. They were blindly following my lead. Two nights in a row, the unearthly screams of a wild animal had laid siege upon us, and now it was waiting out there in the sand. All of us were on edge and were suffering from a lack of sleep.

The sand encrusted brakes of the Ford diesel screeched when I forcefully engaged them. I kicked the driver's side door open and, with a two-handed grip on my semi-automatic pistol, slid off the seat and faced the creature. Gedney pulled up the rear with the M1 pointed at our prey, and I heard him chamber a round.

The thing was dark brown and hairy. There was a horrible stench in the air. It was like a thousand rotting corpses. Our adversary was a large oval. The poorly observed Gremory did not shift its position when we approached. A thick layer of flies bristled over its body. What I had witnessed through my surveyor's scope as a movement of a creature was simply the swarming of flies over a rotting corpse. The dead animal had once been a mule. It had become severely bloated as the gases of decomposition built up inside of it. Empty saddlebags nearby told us it had been used as a pack animal. Leading away from it were footprints in the sand, human footprints.

I ordered the men to spread out. We stepped around the body, trying not to think about the flies, some of which were probably already laying eggs in the savaged flesh of the Mule. Reichenheim and Green held shovels in a defensive posture. Matthew Delaney was on my right, and Joshua Neely remained close to Gedney; Carroon was still holding on to the lenker rod. Looming before us was the monolith. Seeing it up close, it resembled an obelisk, except the sides didn't taper to a point at the top. It was much taller than I had guessed the two evenings prior. It was a narrow square structure about fifteen feet by fifteen feet and at least six stories in height. The top, instead of being flat, terminated in a pyramid. It was no natural phenomenon; it was highly sophisticated in construction. It looked to have been carved from one solid piece of stone. The structure listed slightly to one side, probably due to the deterioration of its antique foundation. The sides were meticulously crafted with great precision and were undoubtedly as smooth as polished marble at one time but for the pitting caused by years of wind and sand erosion. Most likely thousands of years.

Closing in, we all stared at it in awe. Engraved into the sides of the structure were drawings, glyphs of a unique nature. We had witnessed the petroglyphs in a valley north of our current location, but prehistoric people had done them with crude stone tools. These were done with delicate execution. They looked machined as if done by a powerful router that had cut into the stone, creating multiple horizontal bands of various images. The technique was mature and doubtlessly done by a highly evolved civilization. Much of the art tradition was unfamiliar. There was minute detailing of elaborate vegetation that was rendered foreign by the representation of alien-looking animal life. Cone-shaped creatures with long thick tentacles were depicted with astonishing vividness. Neely ran his hand over one of the engravings.

"Pictoglyphs," he announced. "They're picture symbols. It's writing but in a series of images. You don't read them; you interpret it."

"What do they say?" I challenged.

"I'm sorry, lieutenant, that was the limit of my knowledge."

Turning from the stone edifice, we could see that our mysterious stranger's footprints led away from where we stood and to the west towards a large wash that had disrupted the ground. Washes are common in the desert. Some are small ditches, while others resemble miniature canyons carved into the earth by rushing water. These floodwaters occur when infrequent but heavy rains spill down mountainsides and run across the desert floor like a bulldozer obliterating everything in their path. The footprints disappeared into the wash. Walking away from the monolith, we followed the tracks.

The sides of the wash had been pushed up from the massive erosion creating a tall berm. Neely and I were the first to scale it, and as the rest of the crew followed from behind, we looked into the eroded area. It must have been a good twenty feet deep. We could see that it wouldn't be challenging to climb into the depression because the sides were gradually sloped, making it simple to walk down. When the rest of our crew joined us, we hesitated at the top of the berm because on the opposite bank was the opening to a cave. If it had been an old mine, it would not have deterred us. The hills in the area are dotted with old mine shafts and caves from the prospecting days. Gold and silver were once sought after and mined in this region during the nineteenth and early twentieth centuries. But this cave was not the results of some makeshift excavation. It was a five-sided tunnel that looked to be the outcome of modern engineering. No crude timbers were shoring up the opening synonymous with the bygone days of mining. The sun shone on it, allowing us to see several feet within the cavity. The walls were as smooth as poured concrete. The tracks that we had been following led into the tunnel.

"What should we do Lieutenant," asked Delaney.

"We've got to check this out, sir," interjected Neely before I had time to reply.

"We don't know if it's safe," replied Delaney.

"It looks like it might be okay," answered the

seaman. "We'll take it slow and easy."
"Proceed," I eventually said.
"Aye, aye, sir," shouted Neely as he raced down the bank.

Reluctantly we followed. I sent Reichenheim to get the two flashlights we kept in the truck. Examining the wash floor, it became apparent to me that the tunnel had probably extended in both directions (north and south) but had been cut in half and its southernmost end buried by the rushing water that at one time created the dry bottom gulch. We were heading towards the opened, north end.

It had already reached one hundred degrees by then, and the tunnel's cool interior was a welcome relief. We didn't venture in any farther than about ten feet waiting for Reichenheim's return so we could light our way. We paused and examined what we could see of the tunnel walls and ceiling by the ambient light; what I mistook as poured concrete was, in fact, five-sided notched tiles. Brushing away probably centuries of dust and sand with my hand, we noticed that the tiles interlocked with such exactness that the joints were hairline.

"Some engineering, Lieutenant?" whistled Neely.

Reichenheim came running up with a flashlight in each hand. I took one, and Neely wanted the other along with Delaney and Gedney, but when I noticed the look of fear on the laborer's face, I knew that it would be better if we didn't try to pry it from his two hands that he now held with an iron grip. Sweat ran down Reichenheim's face, and I could tell that it was more than the heat of the day that caused it. He looked terrified. Maybe it was claustrophobia; perhaps it was the uncomfortable evenings we spent listening to the chilling screeches that kept us from sleeping, followed by our discovery of the monolith and now the tunnel. I decided to let him keep the flashlight. It definitely gave him comfort.

The floor of the tunnel was covered with sand that had drifted in, and the footmarks of the person we were tracking led deeper into its interior. I took the lead, and Reichenheim pulled up the rear, searching for phantoms with his flashlight at every step. The tunnel curved to the west, and after several hundred feet in, we came across a squalid form. It was a man. Or what was left of a man. He was dead. The flies had made it in that far and circled his face and hands foraging for their morning meal. A crumpled fedora laid by his side. He appeared to be old because he wore a shaggy white beard that covered half his face. But the rest, the countenance, would have baffled any coroner. There was no fatty tissue left in the body. His skin was paper-thin and taught stretched over the skull and boney arms as if all the life had been sucked out of him. Reichenheim screamed, and Carroon and Green pushed him up against the opposite wall.

"He looks like a prospector," Neely offered, examining the dead man's clothes.

"Maybe he came in here looking for the motherlode and dropped dead of a heart attack. He looks like an old-timer," Matthew Delaney added.

"We will need to report this," I said. "They'll see that this fella gets a proper burial.

"Lieutenant, can we please go a little farther in.

There could be something valuable in there," Neely pleaded.

I looked around at everybody. Reichenheim had regained his composure but refused to look at the corpse. The rest didn't appear too badly shaken by our gruesome find. "All right," I finally said. "We will give it a look-see. Everyone stay close together."

The tunnel continued to curve to the west. The morning light no longer reached that far and without our two flashlights, we would have been engulfed in total darkness. I became aware of a sweet smell. Was it honeysuckle? The fragrance was pleasant and grew stronger as we progressed deeper into the tunnel. Delaney commented that it reminded him of the lilacs on his Aunt's farm in Iowa.

We halted our progress when we came across the entrance to a subterranean room. A ramp led downward, and we followed. We were entering a vast chamber, a cathedral-sized chamber. The best we could tell by the light of our battery-powered torches was that the room was circular. Around the cylindrical space, we followed the slope that spiraled down along its walls. Reaching the bottom, all of the men stayed close together as ordered. There were tall tables spread about the room. The tabletops reached head height and standing on our tiptoes; we could see sheets of a thin material that looked like metal but had paper flexibility. Neely grabbed one of them and, shaking the dust off of it, noticed that it contained some kind of foreign writing. After giving up on trying to read the thing, he tried to tear it in half and found it to be indestructible.

Delaney tried to light one up with his Zippo, but it wouldn't burn either. "Wow!" he said. "We could use this stuff as the skin on our fighter planes and bombers. I bet it weighs nothing."

All along the walls of the giant room were large metal drawers. They reminded me of the coffin-sized drawers that coroners use to store the remains of poor dead souls. Each drawer displayed more of the foreign writing. I didn't think that the place was an ancient mausoleum, but it did impress me as probably a library belonging to an ancient colossal race.

Several of the drawers had been pried open. Their fronts were ripped off and the contents removed. On one of the tall tables was an empty glass tube. It resembled a chemist's test tube, except it was approximately three inches in diameter and a good foot long. The top, along with its contents, was missing. I gingerly picked it up, and like the strange metallic paper, it felt weightless. I banged it against a tabletop, and it didn't shatter. Slamming it harder against the table, it still wouldn't break. Next, I tossed it straight up into the air and watched it bounce off the stone floor without breaking. Neely scooped it up on the second bounce and threw the tube with all his might at one of the metal drawers. It bounced off the drawer with a resounding "clang," and Neely caught it on the rebound. Turning to Delaney and waving the oversized test tube, he shouted, "How about this stuff for windshields in the cockpits of our fighters. The Jap Zeros have nothin' like this."

It was then that we heard the eeeeeee, eeeeeee,

which haunted our desert evenings. The screeching was much louder than we had previously heard. The rattling sound that always followed its wail was no longer faint. It must have been very close, I thought. Could the tunnel be its lair?

I took the large test tube from Neely, rolled up a sheet of the metallic paper, and shoved it inside. I stuck the tube and its contents in the side pocket of my slacks.

"Sir!" Neely exclaimed with a gulp.

"It is time for us to leave, gentlemen," I ordered. "Everybody close order, single file, now move!" We headed for the ramp double time. What seemed like a gradual sloping of the ramp upon descending became achingly tiresome on the way up. Reaching the top, I heard movement. It was a moist sucking sound. I leaned back from the five-sided archway to the tunnel and motioned for my men to do the same. Reichenheim started to whimper, but Carroon stopped him with an elbow to the gut. I failed to order the men to turn off their flashlights, but they didn't seem to attract the revolting organism that flowed through the tunnel at a frightening speed. I had a clearer view than anyone else, being at the head of the line and peering around the edge of the archway. The thing was colossal and repulsive. I almost threw up my breakfast. It was an enormous mucus ball that filled the tunnel from floor to ceiling, propelling itself with an array of tentacles and tendrils. Hundreds of human-sized eyes and mouths continually burst forth from bubbles that popped open in its slimy flesh and then quickly unformed. None, thank God, ever glanced in our direction. It was heading south, towards the wash and the open desert. What would happen, I thought, if this thing was free to roam the outdoors? If we were lucky enough to get out of the tunnel, would it be out there waiting for us?

Eeeeeeee! Eeeeeeee! The sound was deafening. Over and over, it repeated its hideous cry as it headed south. Then as quickly as the animal's shrieking began, it suddenly stopped. There was nothing, not even the usual rattle that followed. Several of the men, breathing heavily, were the only sounds within our subterranean prison.

Half of us, by then, had huddled on the left side of the archway with the rest on the right, peering out, not even trying to guess our next move. When I decided to give the order to "move," hoping that the creature from the tunnel was a safe distance away, the damn thing returned. It was screeching again. Maintaining our refuge within the archway to the cylindrical room, I ordered Reichenheim to turn off his light, and I did the same. The creature was bearing down, coming closer, uttering its earsplitting scream. It somehow seemed all the louder in the dark. If any of the men were like me, the impending horror played hell with their nightmarish imaginations. Just when I thought it would pass us again, this time, allowing us our gateway to freedom, I believed I detected several screams mixed up with the greasy thing's thunderous keening. Something wet sprayed the side of my face. Then all was quiet again. Several minutes passed when I gave the order to turn on the flashlights. Petty Officers Matthew Delaney and Albert Gedney were gone. Reichenheim screamed and pointed a shaky hand at me. The right side of my face was covered in blood.

Day 5, 6: p.m. It took me only seconds that morning to realize that the blood on my face was not mine. It was probably from Delaney or Gedney, or both. There were five left in my crew, including the civilian laborers we hired, and I was not about to risk them searching for the two that were missing and presumed dead. The body of the old prospector was evidence of the creature's deadly intentions. I ordered everyone to head south and out of the tunnel as fast as their legs would carry them. I pulled up the rear. Starting to run, I took a quick headcount and noticed that one was missing. It was Neely. He was still standing in the archway to the underground room. "Neely, get going, on the double," I ordered in a harsh whisper.

"Sorry, lieutenant, I'm gonna stay," he whispered back. "Gotta try and find Gedney and Delaney. It's my fault we all came here."

"Neely, that's an order now move," forgetting our situation, I had raised my voice. The seaman just shook his head and backed down the ramp into the dark cylindrical chamber. Still, with the flashlight in hand, I started to go after him, and then I heard the sucking sounds of that slimy thing. It was returning. I laid the light down at the entrance to the circular room for Neely and shouted, "Damn, you come on!"

I ran in total darkness towards the south and hopefully escape. Even though the tunnel was a good fifteen feet in width, I would occasionally collide with one of the side walls skinning my elbows and forearms. Eventually, I could make out a faint light. Escape was at hand. A tentacle lashed out of the nothingness and grabbed me by the leg. I fell face forward to the tunnel floor staring at the ambient light ahead. I heard a crack and felt a searing pain in my left thigh. My leg was broken, bone matter protruded through my trousers. The slimy tentacle was wrapped around my calf. The creature's substance soaked through my pant leg and nipped at me with a thousand bee stings. The tentacle stretched for several yards from the north, but the creature was not yet visible. Its reach must have been phenomenal. I screamed in pain and drew my sidearm from its holster. I aimed it at the enormous octopus appendage and fired all eight rounds with rapid succession. The .45 caliber slugs tore through it, severing its grasp. I observed with stomach-turning terror the severed tentacle moved on its own accord and began to rejoin with its other half.

Trying unsuccessfully to pull myself up, I became aware of Victor Carroon. He was, within seconds, at my side, pulling me to my feet. I yelled out in agony as he struggled to get me out and into the light. After great effort on Carroon's part, we made it to the wash, and he dragged me over to the opposite bank. Carroon collapsed to the sand, breathing heavily. He yelled for Reichenheim and Green to give him a hand.

It was then that I noticed with both astonishment and horror that the creature was at the mouth of the tunnel. The astonishing thing was that it did not come after us. It stayed at the tunnel opening for a few moments with its tentacles outstretched towards the afternoon sky and then abruptly retreated into its interior.

Green came running down the side of the bank, and together with Carroon, they pulled me topside. I thought all was safe when they got me above ground until I saw Reichenheim behind the transport wheel. He was crazy with fear. His teeth were clenched, and his eyes revealed nothing but pure madness. He must have backed the Ford truck up for a running start because it roared at full speed in third gear. In a brief second, we could all tell where he was headed. We all shouted for him to stop, but it was to no avail. The diesel transport slammed into the stone monolith with a loud boom. The mammoth structure's antique foundation snapped like a twig, falling with several tons of force and sealing off the tunnel. "No!" I screamed. "Neely is still in there." But it was too late.

Reichenheim had cracked his head on the steering wheel, but he would survive. As for the truck, it would never live again. The truck's fan had been crushed into the radiator, and water spewed forth, mixing with the desert sand. Carroon said that the engine block had been cracked from the collision as well.

Day 6: Carroon and Green tried to dig around the fallen monolith in hopes of getting to Neely, but it was hopeless. It would take several large earthmovers, many days, to complete the task, and it was time that we needed to concentrate on our survival. Green had bandaged Reichenheim's head, and although he was a bit dizzy at times, he appeared to be in good health. The common laborer from Ridgecrest was calmer now. I guess the stress had been too much for him. He even helped Carroon and Green with their digging around the monolith this morning. When he asked how the stone structure fell over, we realized that he had no memory of what he had done.

My condition is more severe. None of us are medics and the broken bone sticking out of my leg is beyond any of our skills. The only thing I can do is to try and dull the pain with the morphine supply in our first aid kit.

Day 7: We decided that Carroon, Reichenheim, and Green would try to make it on foot back to Ridgecrest to get help. We had a short-range field radio they would have been able to use when they traversed about half the distance to town, but it too was damaged beyond repair during the crash. I put Carroon in charge. They have adequate supplies to carry. It is a long way. I pray that they can make it. I did not go with them. Carroon insisted that they could jerry-rig a gurney out of one of the truck's doors and some canvas, but I refused. I would only have slowed them down, decreasing their chances for survival.

Day 8: It is the second day without my crew. I am typing this report on my portable. I decided to spend most of my time in the cab of the truck. I've been balancing my typewriter on my lap as I write the report. It was the most comfortable way I found, but now the pain in my leg is becoming unbearable. The morphine is running low.

Day 9: Leg has turned black and is beginning to smell.

Day 10:Can't type anymore. Everything is blurry. Will put glass tube and metal paper in glove compartment. Hope someone will come soon.

September 13, 1942
Hobart Winchell, Commandant, U.S. Navy Amphibious Force, Pacific Fleet

Lieutenant Hayward Phillips's remains were discovered in his Construction Battalion's transport at 0600 on September 7th. Carroon, Reichenheim, and Green have yet to be found as well as Petty Officers Matthew Delaney and Albert Gedney and Seaman Joshua Neely. We have recovered the glass tube and its contents and are having our scientists examine it. Massive precipitation in that area had caused considerable flooding, and our men have found no evidence of a tunnel or a monolith reported by Lieutenant Phillips. It is the opinion of this review board that the writings left behind by Lieutenant Hayward Phillips were the results of a feverish mind and not to be taken as factual. All contents of this report, until further notice, are classified TOP SECRET.

CHAPTER 20
SUBTERRANEAN

This was no simple hole in the ground; Ironwood told his credulous self. It was a vast network of caves leading deep into the impenetrable darkness. Ward and the professor walked out of a narrow stone artery into a wider passageway. Shining their mini LED flashlights in several directions, the two could see that the tunnel they were in was the same size and configuration as the one Gwen Gilhooley found herself in after falling through the earth.

"This is five-sided like the other tunnel," Ironwood opined.

"Yes," Alan replied in a low, hushed voice, momentarily distracted by an object on the tunnel's ceiling.

Ironwood fixed his gaze higher, pointing his light beam upward. The remains of a mechanical device hung from above. A twisted frame with brown wires dangling from it was all that was left of the mechanism. "A light fixture?" he conjectured. "A chandelier of some sort?"

"Could be," said Alan. "Look over here," he followed, pointing his light at one of the walls. Inscribed into the tiles with great precision were images. "Glyphs," he announced. There were two images skillfully carved, each image about three feet high, delineated above their heads. One was a cone-shaped creature with a bewildering array of tentacles, tendrils, and enormous claws akin to a lobster, attached to thick stalks protruding from the side of its body. The other was a rod or staff with a pointed end. Alan stopped talking, mesmerized by the outline of the conical being's profile.

"I wonder what it means," Ironwood put forward.

Alan snapped back to the moment and slowly answered, "I studied picture symbols like these in several ancient texts."

"You can read these?"

"Yes," he replied, still not taking his eyes off of the wall drawings.

"Well, what does it say?" prodded the professor.

Alan turned in Ironwood's direction with a faint smile on his face and pointed into the tunnel. "It says, 'this way.'"

The two proceeded to walk deeper into the five-sided conduit. "Did it say anything else?" implored Ironwood.

"Nope."

"Are you sure?"

"Yes."

"How did you know it was telling us to walk farther in?"

"It was an ancient form of a directional arrow. Like our one-way street signs."

"You are certain of this?"

"No," said the ex-English teacher from Miskatonic University, turned amateur archeologist. "But it is a good guess."

"I thought so," said the professor with a scowling grin.

"Given more time, I could probably draw out additional meanings. The best I can do right now is to offer a guesstimate, and beyond that, it would be heavier on the guessing part. Don't blame me if, later, I tell you it's about Lady Gaga on a unicycle."

Venturing further in, Ironwood stopped abruptly. He laid a hand on Alan Ward's shoulder, stopping him. "Alan, wait! Don't you notice something?"

"What?"

"The floor," he snapped back. "I get the sensation that it's slanted. I believe we are on a decline." Ironwood set his flashlight down on the tunnel floor and let go—it started to roll. The light cast eerie patterns on the floor and wall as it moved. The LED penlight picked up speed, made an arc to the right, and disappeared. It could have been a foolish action on my part, thought Ironwood; if Alan weren't carrying his light, we would be in total blackness.

"It seems to have chosen our direction for us," observed Alan.

The two moved on together. Alan and the professor walked by several passageways of equal size, branching off in opposite directions, ignoring them, for the time being, in pursuit of the mobile torch. It became increasingly apparent to them that they were treading deeper into a cavernous, eon dead honeycomb of ancient tunnels. Ironwood felt a touch of anxiety when thinking of the primal entities that may have dwelt in this subterranean place. They had already descended for what he thought must have been many stories below the earth, and the temperature grew cooler with every step. Was this a new-found gateway to secrets of inner Earth and vanished eons, he almost marveled out loud?

They rounded a bend in the tunnel and made out a pale blue-white light ahead. The torch had lodged itself up against the edge of an opening in the side of the passageway. The powerful lumens illuminated a portion of its interior.

"Come here, my little drone," said Ironwood. Ironwood walked quickly ahead, stooped, and retrieved his light off of the floor. He shined it into the adjacent room, standing frozen to the spot, and stared inside in utter amazement.

"Thomas, what's wrong!" shouted Alan, pulling up the rear.

Within a second, they were standing shoulder to shoulder, gazing inward. It was a room of considerable size. More of the ancient glyphs were carved into the walls, covered in some of the symbols they had seen in Alan's copy of the Necronomicon. Consistent with all of the foreign construction they had thus experienced, the room was approximately fifteen feet wide and fifteen feet high. Unlike the tunnels, it was cylindrical, and in place of wall tiles, the bulwarks consisted of large stone blocks. Incongruous to the alien architecture were the furnishings within its interior. Crudely fashioned bookshelves lined one side of the room jammed packed with papers, books, and what appeared to be scrolls, all dust-laden as if they had been resting there for an exceptionally long time, perhaps hundreds of years. In the chamber's center were two rough-hewn tables, several chairs, and a writing desk all piled high with papers and books also of varying antiquity. Next to the furnishings was a cot that had collapsed under its own weight, its cloth bedding rotting away.

Opposite the shelves, the size of Ironwood's Willys was a wooden barrel lying on its side, the end painted in red letters were the words, "Coal Oil."

Professor Ironwood was first to break the silence, "What on earth…"

Alan Ward ran into the chamber waving his flashlight around spasmodically and shouted, "Oh my God, I know what this is! It has got to be Isaac Morley's study."

***

Rummaging through the clutter spewed across the tables and desk, Ironwood came across several well-used candle stubs and eventually located a lantern. "Your Morley was a lousy housekeeper," he proclaimed, walking over to the wood barrel.

"What is coal oil?" asked Alan.

"It's an antiquated term for kerosene." After filling the lantern's reservoir from a spigot on the barrel, Ironwood raised its glass globe and lit the wick with a butane lighter.

"You don't smoke; why do you carry a lighter?" queried Alan Ward, a little befuddled.

"Living in the desert, I try to have all means of survival at my disposal. You should see inside my glove compartment."

"Better than rubbing two sticks together?"

"You've got it." Ironwood lowered the glass globe, and the lantern flashed a ring of light around the circular chamber with a warm glow. The room, lit by the old lamp's flame, the notion of architecture from a nameless geologic past grew stronger.

Ironwood brushed aside some papers on the writing desk and placed the kerosene lamp on its wooden surface. Some of the papers slid off the desktop exposing a thin leather-bound book.

Alan snatched up the slim book. Shaking the dust off of it, the letters I.M. appeared, engraved upon the cover. He quickly flipped through some of the pages. Crabbed archaic penmanship covered the leaves. "This is Isaac Morley's journal," Alan whispered, visibly shaken by the discovery. "It appears to cover all his studies in the region," raising his voice a little louder as he flipped through the pages. "Ironwood, do you realize what this means?" his voice echoing off the stone rotunda. "This is possibly one of the greatest historical and archeological finds of our era. Why there must be a myriad of secrets here waiting to be unlocked from the earth's past, these walls are a standing library going back, dare I say, thousands of years."

Ironwood had left Alan's side and was examining the glyphs carved into the wall. It is what archaeologists called a vanished language; he summarized images and symbols of a forgotten time. The stones of the enclosure were cut smoothly. They looked machined. The ancient writing wasn't chiseled into their surface by any crude method. Instead, they appeared to have been engraved possibly by an advanced cutting tool similar to a diamond-tipped dado or maybe even a laser. Who could have made such a thing for God's sake, and why? Ironwood shifted his attention from the wall and started to examine the clumsily built shelves. Although there were some books and papers, the majority of their contents consisted of scrolls. Each had been tied snugly with a strip of leather. Grabbing one at random, he attempted to untie the leather strip only to find it crumble to pieces at his touch. Ironwood unfurled it and was faced with more of the same alien script. He ran his fingertips along the writing surface and could instantly tell that the scroll was not comprised of any ancient parchment or papyrus; it was metal that had, after all this time, maintained the flexibility of a brand-new sheet of paper.

"Alan look at this," said the professor walking back to the desk and into better lighting. "It has more of the glyphs similar to what is on the walls of this place…"

"And the Necronomicon," offered Alan, finishing his sentence for him. Only glancing in his direction but keeping his nose in the journal, Alan shouted again, "This is amazing! Morley writes that he built his house over this spot shortly after discovering the entrance."

"It would take a team of archeologists to cover this place . . ."

"Your Captain Eastwater can keep his little section of the tunnel! We have got a hundred of them to explore," Alan declared triumphantly.

"Except for this room, everything we have seen so far has been void of all portable contents, a circumstance which leads me to believe that this was the result of deliberate desertion. The wall engravings and all these scrolls must be the remains of a vanished epoch. They contain a portion of its history."

"That must have been Isaac Morley's calling. From his journal and all of these notes, he undoubtedly spent years deciphering them."

"Definitely a man dedicated to his work," added Ironwood. "The answer or answers would probably have taken him years to unravel. All of the extraneous, unconnected, and redundant information he would have to sift through just to obtain one morsel of truth. Alan," he implored, "It would be similar to future archeologists endeavoring to learn relevant information about us by deciphering our train schedules."

Ironwood could tell that Alan was no longer listening. Lost within Isaac Morley's Journal and occasionally referring to one of the old scientist's notes on an arbitrarily selected sheet of paper, it would take artillery fire to bring him back to earth. Was Morley's obsession with a long-forgotten past also Alan's mania? Did Alan also believe that this preoccupation with lost eons would help him to find the lost years of his life? Ironwood was exceptionally tired. He no longer wanted to do any additional speculating. It was only three in the afternoon, and he shouldn't feel so sleepy. He was experiencing this weary feeling from time to time, he recollected, started after the day that he went spelunking through Gilhooley's tunnel with the top brass. Maybe he had picked up a flu bug of some sort. Hopefully, he smiled internally; he hadn't picked up a ten-thousand-year-old infectious disorder. As a matter of fact, he observed, Alan looked done in as well. Ironwood slammed his fist on the old desk and shouted, "Alan let's go."

Startled from his reverie, Alan shouted back, "What?"

"Time to go, Alan. We can come back tomorrow."

"I can't leave," he complained.

"It will take an hour to drive back to my place, and we will be just in time for dinner. I am hungry, and I need my rest."

"I have spent the last ten years of my life searching, and now I am here. This is everything to me, Thomas. I can't go."

"I am not going to leave you here!"

"Yes, you can," he answered in a calm but authoritative voice. It was an assertiveness that surprised Ironwood, coming from Alan. "I have an extra battery for my flashlight, and there is plenty of oil for the lamp. There are coffee and sandwiches in your car. If you fetch them for me, I'll be just fine. You can return for me in the morning."

"There's a blanket in the trunk of the Jeepster; I'll bring it as well," Ironwood muttered reluctantly.

"Very good," he replied serenely, returning his focus to the work at hand. "A blanket would be nice. Now all means of survival will be at my disposal."

***

Suddenly a sound from heaven like the howling of a fierce wind filled the entire house. Jason had just finished helping Gwen pack up her essentials. He was probably crazy to suggest that she move in with him, and he guessed that she was equally as crazy when she answered, "Yes." Was he in love? Were they in love? That was it; they were crazy in love. It was, of course, too soon to tell. Rescues can trigger the light fantastic. He did pull her out of that hole under the house, and she was responsible for him overcoming his claustrophobia. Good God, he hoped he was doing the right thing. After all, he couldn't let her stay here.

As if on cue, while stuffing the last article of clothing into one of Gwen's two suitcases, the house began to shake. The structure trembled and shook from its foundation to its rafters. Gwen let out a yelp. Jason grabbed the two suitcases and headed for the door. Following his lead, Gwen tossed a freshly pressed uniform on a hanger over her shoulder and sprinted alongside him.

Slightly winded and standing in the front yard, they could easily see what was causing the tremors. Gwen put her arm around Jason and squeezed him close to her. Dumbfounded for an instant, Jason watched as a series of tentacles the size of tree trunks burst up from the hole under the house, grappling the joist above and collapsing the floor they supported. He watched, feeling like a child experiencing a nightmare, as the cavity in the earth increased in size and Gwen's living room furniture slid downward, chasing the floorboards, and carpeting into the hole. Within seconds, the tentacles became a fountain of a primal force shooting straight up with the intensity of an element as destructive as a typhoon. Jason imagined its nightmarish appendages were slithering, exploring every room of the house. Was it searching for them? The creature beneath imbued with unearthly powers turned Gwendolyn Gilhooley's house inside out as if it was a piece of origami. Drywall, two-by-fours, roofing, everything that comprised the place she once called home was dragged below. Wires cracked, and circuits blew as it settled into the hole in the ground where the house once stood. A broken pipe expelled water like a severed artery releasing blood.

In a few minutes, quiet descended upon the property. Some of the remains of the post-war housing building materials protruded from the cavity. It appeared to be sealed tight. Nevertheless, thought Jason, he'd have the guys bring the dozer along tomorrow with several cubic yards of hard pack soil to finish the job. He'd make sure that the thing never got out of that hole in the ground again.

Some of the people that lived on Nimitz Boulevard had gathered behind them, asking questions. Jason ignored their inquiries. Tossing the two suitcases into the F-150's truck bed, he turned to Gwen and said, "Come on, we'll come back for the Neon later."

***

Ironwood felt the rush of warm air bathe his face when he came topside. It was still over 100 degrees outdoors, but it was a welcome relief after exploring that cold dark network of tunnels. To stretch his legs and work a little warmth into his tired limbs, he walked a short distance, his pointed boots leaving a string of meandering arrows in the sand. The sun was beginning to sink low on the opposite side of the vast sky. While ambling some, he read that an email had come through on his iPhone. When he came above ground, returning to the desert terrain surrounding the Morley property, his phone had chirped as it downloaded an email. It was from Captain Eastwater. What the hell did he want? There were several attachments. There was no message, just the attachments. Ironwood opened the first one, walked back to the house, sat down on the old house's wobbly front steps, and mulled over its contents. It was a photo of a top-secret document. It looked to be very old. Then he saw the date in the upper right-hand corner, typed in 1942. Why was he sending this to me?

Each attachment was a snapshot of another page. Within twenty minutes, he had finished reading the entire document. He was starting to sweat from the afternoon sun, but he still felt cold inside. Seventy some years ago, there was a thing living in a section of the tunnels. Something horrible unless the report was the result of a delusional mind. His phone played a few bars of the "Star-Spangled Banner." It was a text message from Vice Admiral Hawkins; "got capt e's phone, sent you his photos."

Things were falling into place. In the video that Hawkins had shown Alan and him, Captain Eastwater and Congressman Stream discussed photographing a top-secret document. The attachments must be what they wanted.

Before leaving Alan, Ironwood questioned him about the grant he received from the Nathaniel Derby Pickman Foundation. Even though the foundation had run out of capital years ago, Alan Ward insisted that that was where he got his funding. He added that he had received a cashier's check in the mail along with a brief note explaining that his request for funds had been granted; however, there was no conditional use agreement included in the post, which is standard procedure for all grants. The funds undoubtedly came from another source, but Alan's expertise in such matters was lacking, and his joy in receiving the money overcame any suspicions he might have entertained. Did Stream have anything to do with the phony grant? Was Alan a dupe in some master plan? He was starting to make sense out of the conundrum, but the picture was not clear yet.

Ironwood got the sandwiches and coffee from his Willys-Overland Jeepster's back seat and headed back into the Morley house. Stopping abruptly, he returned to the Jeepster. "Damn," he said. "I almost forgot my little friend's security blanket."

CHAPTER 21
ENCOUNTERS

Captain Clayton Eastwater strapped on a Heckler & Koch .45 caliber semi-automatic pistol. Along with the firearm dangling from his belt was a KA-BAR US Navy fighting knife and two fragmentation grenades. He walked over to a large metal ammunition case, inserted and turned a key in a lock, raised the lid, and removed two Colt M16A2 rifles. "Here," he said, handing the weapons over to two men wearing desert pattern camouflage uniforms and helmets of the Naval Mobile Construction Battalion. "I doubt we will need to use them, but it is always best to be prepared, gentlemen." Eastwater handed both of them three thirty-round clips and then closed and re-locked the metal container.

The rest of the Seabees in the tunnel looked on in amazement. It was beyond any protocol they had ever witnessed. After a grueling ten-hour day of digging and using every tool at their disposal to penetrate the stone barrier, they finally succeeded. A blast of frigid air accosted them the moment they broke through. There wasn't enough time to run additional electric cables into this new section of the tunnel because, from their point of view, the Captain was overly anxious to the point of being reckless to go exploring. The additional section of the tunnel had not yet been deemed "secured." At this late hour, there were no engineers available to inspect the disinterred passageway's structural integrity. They were also well aware of the commissioned officer's ill-temper. Offering the politest suggestion could have your head chewed off by Captain Eastwater and cause you to lose several weeks of shore leave, i.e., "liberty." No doubt about it, they were going to keep their mouths shut and just observe.

***

Alan Ward sat back in the rickety chair. His curiosity was high, and his mind was racing. Isaac Morley had painted an accurate albeit bleak picture of his years of research. He had also mapped out, in extreme detail, his areas of exploration. In his overly enthusiastic and naïve excitement, Alan had thought that the cylindrical room in which he sat was the remains of an ancient library. In reality, according to Morley's notes, this was just the tip of the iceberg. What he was witnessing were items that the old scientist had selected to examine in his makeshift study. Everything in this room initially came from a much grander library, and he was about to discover it firsthand.

Alan picked up his flashlight and inserted a fresh battery into it. He was determined to trace the route that Morley and his servants traversed many lifetimes ago. Out of the circular room and through a maze of connecting tunnels, he wondered how often they walked these passages throughout the years? The hardships must have been unbearable by today's standards, he decided. No central heat, obviously no air-conditioning to waylay each summer's grueling heat and the scarcity of clean water and decent food. To compound, the hardships were the crude scientific tools of that era the nineteenth-century scientist was cursed to use must have been analogous to a prehistoric man trying to construct a wheel using stone tools and sticks.

Alan used Isaac Morley's journal as a guide map and rounded a corner into an adjacent passageway. The tunnel abruptly terminated about thirty feet in, where a wooden door endured as a colossal guardian. In the journal, Alan had read that this tunnel, different from all the other arteries Isaac and his men had explored, opened into an immense cavern. That cavern was the library.

The English teacher from Miskatonic stood at the massively thick pine door listening through the latch hole. Overhead he observed a pair of wires attached to the tunnel's ceiling. By now, Alan had also learned that Morley had constructed a bomb. He called it his "safety device." He had recorded that there was a creature walled up behind the door. Morley had become uneasy about it escaping. Worried that someday the door may not hold, he planted an explosive charge above the door frame sufficient to bring the ceiling down, collapsing the artery with rocks and earth from the desert above. The bomb, made out of black gun powder, was placed in a tin, and tightly encased in a paraffin wax block. The detonator's wires were strung along the ceiling beyond the tunnel, opening to a small niche in the adjacent artery. From there, Morley had attached the two wires to the screw terminals of a static generator. Alan had observed the generator/detonator when entering the passageway. One thing that Alan knew for certain was that after one-hundred and thirty-plus years, Isaac Morley's monster, if indeed it had once existed, no longer walked the earth. With the air and confidence of a make-believe seasoned explorer, he lifted the latch and opened the door that had remained closed for nearly a century and a half. The wrought iron hinges protested through an epoch of rust.

***

Eastwater had his men spread out. Both were a couple of paces ahead of him. The two seamen in camo were spaced, one on his left and the other on his right. All were wearing Orion Helmet Lights with a battery life of thirteen-hours. They were prepared for anything. The force of three was there on the premise of locating and rescuing the absent Seabee. Seaman Rinaldi was still missing. Chief Petty Officer Domingo Mercado's body had been discovered two days earlier, and Seaman Jonathan Dexter was now a nut job. The seaman was in a psych ward, probably drooling all over himself, the Captain supposed. That left Rinaldi unaccounted for, at least for the time being. It made the perfect cover for his quest. Eastwater didn't believe the bull about a monster in the tunnel. It was crazy crap that Lieutenant Hayward Phillips wrote in his report back in '42. The guy was high on morphine, probably tripping 24/7. As for

Mingo, Rinaldi, and Dexter, they were most likely doing drugs as well. There had been a few meth heads in their outfit recently that they discharged. That stuff was wicked. It fried the brains. Every day there seemed to be a new deadly class of synthetic hallucinogens available to the right buyer. Whatever those three morons had been doing in the tunnel that night, it not only fried their brains, but it cooked them for good.

Eastwater didn't believe in monsters in his closet or under his bed. Even if there was one back during World War II, that was almost seventy-five years ago, and by now, the thing would be good and dead. If they did find Rinaldi, he would probably be dead as well, either that or a babbling idiot like Dexter. He could care less if they find him because Eastwater was there for the pot of gold at the end of the rainbow. The one thing he thought credible in that 1942 report was the existence of an underground lair full of valuable scientific gadgets that would reap a fortune on the black market. Congress Stream was certain of it as well, so much so that he had put his political career at stake to uncover it. The discovery of the toppled monolith that blocked the tunnel's passage was additional proof that it was worth the treasure hunt. The Seabees he had selected for the hunt were loyal to him. He would have to cut them in on the spoils unless—unless he could find a way to eliminate them.

The captain thought that it was dreadful that any place could be so silent. He found himself wishing that some sound would break in on the awful silence. They moved through the stygian darkness like phantoms threading their way through a dim labyrinth without the aid of a map or compass. Consistently five-meters across, the cave continued. Eastwater watched as the Seabee on the left cracked a glow stick, shook it to get maximum illumination, and then tossed it forward.

The two men ahead of him stopped and raised their right hands, gesturing to be quiet. The one on the right pointed into the darkness beyond. Captain Eastwater crept stealthily forward and stopped, standing between the both of them. He noticed that a trail had been wiped clean in the tunnel floor, leaving it polished, almost glistening. He wondered why his men had stopped. He was about to question their actions when he heard something. It was similar to the sound of an insect scuttling across paper, only louder, and it was growing in volume. It was coming closer. A bittersweet smell assailed his nostrils. The screeching of seagulls was unbearable.

***

Alan Ward left the wooden door wide open behind him. He crept inward on the balls of his feet. The tunnel appeared barren, empty. Feeling silly, he straightened up and walked flat-footed towards the opposite wall. Something clinked and rattled beneath his feet. He jumped back and shone his light on the floor. Bones, a pile of bones littered the area. Alan's knowledge of human physiology was limited.

Nonetheless, a rib cage and thigh bone of considerable size made it obvious it came from a large animal. Upon closer inspection, Alan observed, strewn amongst the slaughterhouse rubble were smaller, thinner frames possibly belonging to humans. He moved a little to one side, and his foot struck an object that rolled. He turned quickly to face an invisible intruder; Alan's light caught the reflection of a human skull looking up at him. It rocked backward and forward on the tunnel floor. The chin bone had dropped down, and he expected its oral cavity to burst forth with hideous laughter. He fought the bile that welled up in his throat. Alan shifted his light in the opposite direction, laying as if in wait were two complete human skeletons. He stepped back towards the door he entered through and could plainly make out the headless remains of another corpse stripped clean of its flesh and organs lying in the middle of the tunnel. It added to Alan's revulsion became clear that the rocking skull had been dislodged from its body by him when he came shuffling through the area. Could these be the remains of Isaac Morley and his servants? Morley did just up and disappeared! There are no records of his whereabouts since his trek to the Mojave. Alan tried to calm his jittery nerves. He took a deep breath and told himself to man up!

Something reflected Alan's light amidst the mound of bones. He bent over and reluctantly reached for the object. His hand momentarily brushed against the fingers of a skeletal hand. Alan felt the electrical charge of revulsion run up his arm. To his loathing, he had to sift through a few more bones before he could get hold of the artifact. It was a gun. A revolver. It was nearly a foot-and-a-half-long. It looked ancient. Even with all of the dust and grime that had accumulated on the weapon over the years, a portion of the nickel plating along its barrel still cast a reflection. Alan shined his light on it, and he could make out the maker's name engraved into the metal, "Colt Walker." Again, recalling Morley's notes in his journal, he was mindful that the old scientist was in the habit of toting a handgun. Evidence, if not conclusive, that this section of the tunnel had become Isaac Morley's resting place.

Remembering that the tremendous wooden door had been latched from the outside when he first opened it, Alan was overcome with dread. The door may have been the cause of Morley and his servants' demise. Upon close inspection, he could easily see that his suspicions were correct. When the door closed, there was no way of opening it from the inside. After all these years, the old gun was useless as a firearm, but it would make an excellent doorstop, he decided. He wedged the gun barrel between the door frame hinge side and the door forcing it to remain wide open.

Before leaving the area for other points unknown, Alan took notice of the walls in that portion of the tunnel for the first time. It was a polygonal artery like all the others they had seen, and the walls, ceiling, and floor were covered with the same five-sided notched tiles they had witnessed as well, but with one exception. Hanging from the ceiling and walls was a translucent material resembling a curtain of shredded flesh. Alan came closer and a piece of the substance broke off easily between his thumb and index finger. It was rubbery. It reminded him of tripe. The tips of his finger and thumb started to heat up. They became hot and burned as if dipped in acid. The fleshy material stuck fast to his skin. Alan produced a pocket-handkerchief with his other hand and clamped down on the mass ripping it free from his two fingers. He threw the kerchief aside and rubbed the offending appendages. Much of the burning subsided, spitting on the injured fingers, he rubbed them again. His saliva seemed to do the trick. It was time to press on.

A labyrinth of tunnels and colossal chambers unfolded before Alan. Seemingly endless corridors extended into the impenetrable darkness. Other tunnels branched off from the main artery in regular patterns forming extensive galleries. He would have easily gotten lost if, again, it wasn't for the journal. The nineteenth-century scientist and his two Narragansett Indians, back in their day, had marked their way by arrows painted with whitewash upon the tiled walls. In stark certainty, he was wandering amidst a death, which had reigned thousands of years ago, and in all probability even longer. Alan was confident that Morley had discovered its origin. But what it was and what purpose it served in the scheme of that ancient civilization had yet to be unraveled. Morley had written that he had established an unprecedented and almost blasphemous link with forgotten eons customarily closed to the human species. To most, those would appear as a madman's writings, but to Alan Ward, they made all the sense in the world.

***

Alan thought he was in a dream. He saw the tendrils at the end of a massive tentacle working furiously, penning long lines onto metallic pages, and turning them into script. The script was English. The tendrils didn't stop or rest for even a few seconds, and the stack of pages kept growing. Alan had halted his progress when he came upon the entrance to a subterranean room. The painted arrows left by his age-old predecessors had ceased. He was at his destination. A ramp led downward. He was at the entrance to an enormous circular chamber. The ramp spiraled along the interior of the curved wall. He knew where he was going. He had been here many times before. Memory-access to the events that had been lost to him years ago rushed in on him. Everything Alan could see was gigantic, towering, and colossal, insanely so. Portions of an alien city with spiraling towers in night-black masonry sprang into being. Narrow cylindrical structures shot up between the buildings into a steamy gray sky. In the past, these dream visions of his would shimmer briefly and then fold in on themselves, leaving only a faint memory of their existence. Now they were clear, noticeably clear. They were a memory. Repressed memories or retrograde amnesia no longer blocked his recollection.

Alan had often taken this same journey, and many times he tried with a great force of will to look down at his feet. Always when his eyes would slowly move the distance towards the floor and before afforded a view of his feet, he would wake up in a cold sweat. He recycled the past walking along the solid perceptible surface of the ramp. Alan was able, for the first time since he had regained consciousness in Arkham several years ago, to lift that veil. Instead of legs was a massive conical form. Sunken veins with elevated spaces between covered the lower portion of his body. The shock was almost overwhelming. He staggered down to the bottom of the ramp, barely keeping his footing. His feet! He did have feet and legs.

The memory vision gave way to the moment at hand. Alan now knew what he had expected all along but was always too afraid to confront. He was or was at one time, one of them—one of those monstrous and bizarre cone-shaped beings of eons past that he had seen many times in his dreams as well as carved into the tunnel walls. Morley had referred to them as Elder Beings. Creatures of immense intelligence that he believed inhabited our planet before the dawn of man. Things with vast intellects whose devices touched the entire solar system and whose life spans could ride out a thousand apocalypses. Alan knew, at that moment, that in all probability, Morley's theory was indeed fact.

Alan wondered if Morley's driving force was more than just an illuminating discovery, more than the insatiable thirst for knowledge, a quest to unlock the unknown? Maybe Isaac Morley was plagued by the same demons as he. Could that nineteenth-century scientist also have been inflicted by an out-of-body transference via the Elder Beings? Had Morley been searching for similar answers to his dreams?

Alan explored the room with his 300 lumen light becoming familiar with his surroundings. No longer was he riddled with only bits and pieces of faint, bizarre memories. He recognized the row upon row of coffin size charcoal metal boxes, each engraved with its curvilinear hieroglyphs. The metal boxes, or file drawers, were stacked at a great height, and each continuous row was separated by narrow tables running parallel to them. The tops of the tables were as high as a man is tall. It was at one of these tables where he once stood and wrote. The pain of solitude and loneliness he felt back then saddened his heart.

Not everything was as Alan remembered. The ancient library was deserted. A collection of bulbous eyes mounted on thick fleshy stalks attached to their colossal bodies no longer turned and looked at him. The nightmares out of time and space hadn't occupied the place for centuries. There was no hustle and bustle of alien seekers of cosmic knowledge. Alan's heart grew heavier when he noticed that several of the drawers had been pried open. Much of their contents were strewn across the room. Was this Morley's doing? Was this a clumsy attempt at archeology? Was this how the fool obtained his research? He felt violated. Somehow, through mysterious means or by way of an advanced form of science, he had become one of those Elder Beings, and he was, at present, sharing their racial memory, their anger for the vandalism they committed. His heartbeat heavily in his chest. Alan took a deep breath, told himself to calm down, and realized, as he forced himself to relax, that he had hands with fingers, not tentacles and tendrils.

Alan noticed several oversized, foot and a half long glass test tubes scattered amongst the litter left by the previous human intruders. All emptied of their contents. Were the contents at one-time chemical, biological? He had no way of knowing. Picking one up, he saw a light blue disc-like cap covering its mouth. It was completely flat; there was no securing rim to fasten it down and no threading around the glass tube's opening to facilitate the fastening. He touched the center of the disc and it flipped open on an unseen, invisible hinge. Consequently, swinging it shut, it became firmly attached to a seemingly invisible latch until the lid's center was touched once again.

Alan looked to his left and recognized the glyphs on one of the large file drawers. It was the identifying symbol given to him by the Elder Beings. As Alan's memory of events became more focused, it came to mind that he never had knowledge of their language or alphabet. Nonetheless, he was, over time, able to identify his mark. He stared at the symbol, the combination to unlock the drawer appeared in his mind. It wasn't a series of numbers or letters. Rather they were geometric shapes, three-dimensional images that warped and twisted, collapsing into one another so quickly that it was impossible to recognize one from another. As rapidly as the "combination" appeared in his consciousness, it disappeared. Were those images in his head placed there by the Elder Beings? Alan felt a sense of accomplishment. Something gurgled within the large drawer, followed by a loud metallic click. The face of the file cabinet swung open, and the drawer, with all its contents, slid out, floated across the vacant space, and landed softly on the table where Alan whence stood, in another form, ages ago.

Amazement, followed by a tremendous sense of purpose, filled every pore of Alan Parker Ward's body. He no longer questioned his sanity. His dreams, his amnesia was not the results of a deficiency on his part. It was the outcome of a grand scheme where he was just the pawn. A plot that he was about to discover the why's and wherefores. There was a problem, though. The large metal file drawer rested on the tall table, almost out of reach. Standing on his tiptoes and stretching every portion of his body upward, he took hold of the lower edge of the drawer. Alan inched it slowly off the table and was caught off guard by the container's tremendous weight. The metal box came crashing down, spilling its contents.

Alan clamored to sort through the clutter he had created and got down on his hands and knees trying to bring some order to the mess. In all the clutter were numerous sheets of the metallic paper plus an odd-looking device. It was a rod of some sort about an inch and a half in diameter and as long as a crowbar. Then it struck him. He was holding the writing instrument he used in his other, immense alien body. He shuffled through the pile of metal papers and came face to face with his handwriting. It was a looking glass moment. His heart raced again. There was no longer any doubt that he had been here in another time and another body. He was going to have to show all this to Ironwood. He had been a loyal comrade, but he also treated Alan as a sick person that needed constant supervision.

Alan spread the papers out and caught sight of passages about the elder race's history that once occupied these premises. A race of beings as old as time itself because they were able to traverse it. Not in a physical function but in an ethereal capacity. These beings of higher learning were capable of projecting their minds both into the past and the future. Maybe it wasn't their actual consciousness; Alan pondered; perhaps it was just a memory, he was never quite sure.

However, given the proper set of circumstances along with the equipment they used, one of them would ping off a solid slab of emptiness and shoot backward or forwards into another time, embedding itself in a brain where it could live, have meaning, and learn about the host's culture. The host's mind was propelled to the waiting Elder Being, where it was trapped in the sender's empty vessel until the two identities were returned to their bodies. Before the host's mind was sent back, all memory of its time with the Elder Beings, their cyclopean cities, and their alien science was erased.

As Alan read, his mind threw off the shackles of the black veil that had been forced on him by the Elder things. A story developed by his hand, written centuries previously. It flowed smoothly as a poem of beauty and horror, dictated to him by the beings that were long dead, or maybe never dead at all. The circular room, the ancient alien library, that he now occupied was once the base of a colossal tower in the center of a vast plaza. This maze of catacombs was all that was left of a vast metropolis that covered the entire planet both above and below ground. It was spawned by an intelligence far beyond human ken and scope. They inhabited the earth in its pre-human age traveling to our world from the galaxy's outer most reaches. They built the global city and called it Kadath. All this occurred during the early Cretaceous age. Alan was no geologist, but he knew that the Cretaceous period was over fifty million years ago. The numbers were staggering. He had surmised that the artifacts he had been examining were thousands, not millions of years old. The enormous amount of time was astounding, but there was something about it that he couldn't quite put his finger on, and it troubled him.

After eons of progress, the Elder Beings stopped erecting their structures out of metal and stone. They fell upon a new art of building. They were eventually able to produce a synthetic life form from a type of plastic protoplasm. At first, these were reared as slaves, beasts of burden to perform the heavy work of the community, and ultimately this living matter was willed by the powerful minds of their creators to be the buildings, the dwellings, the roadways, the entire infrastructure of their civilization. In due course, everything these creatures of the Cretaceous age touched, walked on, lived in, and slept on was alive in every sense of the word. They were surrounded, every day, by the living matter of their creation.

After untold millions of years away from his alien writing desk, Alan read on and reacquainted himself with the numerous achievements, secrets, and horrors of his long-ago captors. Some of it amazed him, some of it sickened him, and some made him depressed. It was when he came across a passage that contained the words “the coming of the meteor” that he grasped what had troubled him about the period of the Cretaceous age. Most archaeologists accepted the theory that a giant meteor fell on the Earth during that era, destroying most of the planet's life. Had the coming of the meteor been forecast, and had this outlandish extra-terrestrial population left en masse to seek a less doomed world? Or was he simply reading the results of their ability to look into the future and foresee their impending doom?

Without warning, a piercing bird-like cry screeched from somewhere within the tunnels. Alan froze momentarily as if a malevolent force had passed through his body, making its presence known. "Eeeeeeee! Eeeeeeee! Wawk Wawk Wawk Wawk!" echoed through the passageways.

A rattling noise trailed the shriek. Fright and panic overcame Alan. Isaac Morley's belief in his monster behind the door could be attributed to a lack of rationalism, compounded by superstition owing to his being cooped up in these tunnels for so many years. Could one of those synthetic life forms still be alive and roaming the subways of a forgotten time? His common sense told him that it couldn't be, but his alarm overcame Alan's reasoning faculties.

"Eeeeeeee! Eeeeeeee! Wawk Wawk Wawk Wawk!" it resonated, growing in volume.

Dread and anxiety permeated Alan's every fiber. "Run!" conquered all desire for further exploration. He gathered up a handful of his metallic papers, scooped up the large glass tube, rolled up the ancient essays, and slipped them inside, snapping the lid shut afterward. Now it was time to run.

Alan took long strides sprinting up the ramp that left him exceptionally winded when he reached the top. He was in lousy physical shape, and he knew it. He had to leave that behind him just now, mind over body. He was a long-distance runner when he was in high school. He would be again. The loud cry swelled in volume. "God help me," he prayed as he took flight like a teenager. He gripped the glass tube tightly as if a baton in a relay race. His breathing became heavily labored. He could hear it slithering at an insane speed, still screeching, "Eeeeeeee! Eeeeeeee! Wawk Wawk Wawk Wawk, coming closer. He knew he couldn't keep up this pace much longer. He didn't dare look over his shoulder. Just run, damn it! Run until you drop and then crawl.

The body of the creature filled the tunnel bearing down on him, slithering over the glistening floor that it had swept so free of debris. And still came the ancient mocking cry, "Eeeeeeee! Eeeeeeee! Wawk Wawk Wawk Wawk!"

Alan turned the corner mapped out by Morley and his men and found himself in the room with the pile of bones. He was amazed that he had made it this far. Gasping for breath, he crushed the rib cage of one of the skeletons with his right foot as he ran towards the exit. The large old wooden door was plainly in view. He dashed through the opened doorway and grabbed the iron handled on the outside moving hard against it to slam it shut. The door sprung back and slammed into his forehead. Blood ran down his face from a splinter that the age-old pine barrier had stuck in his brow. The gun, he remembered, as he stumbled backward. That damned old gun, I left it wedged in the jamb! Completely out of breath, he summoned what little inner strength was still inside of him and charged the door once more. The charge was more like a stagger, but he reached the old revolver and yanked it free. From inside the open doorway, he heard the rustle and clatter of dry bones. Alan threw his body weight against the wood door and pushed with every pound of his force. It sprang back again. For a fleeting instant, he questioned whether he had indeed removed the gun's barrel from between the door frame and the door or had he hallucinated. A truckload of gray-green tentacles exploded through the opening. The passageway burst with the ear-splitting cries of the creature, "Eeeeeeee! Eeeeeeee! Wawk Wawk Wawk Wawk!"

Alan was thrown back into the middle of the short tunnel section. A tentacle lashed around his chest, but he quickly tore himself free. He crawled in a mad frenzy and ripped the flesh on the palms of his hands over loose gravel. Another tentacle impacted his left leg's ankle and tightened; a hundred tiny hungry cups like tiny lampreys' bit down and sucked at his flesh, trying to draw him closer. Alan beat at it with the indestructible alien glass tube and momentarily freed himself. He regained his footing and dove for the niche located at the opening to the passageway. He set down the test tube and grabbed the tee-bar plunger on the static generator—Alan pushed it down. Nothing happened. There was no report. Frantically he lifted the generator friction bar up and again pushed down the plunger. Still no explosion. A mass of tentacles and tendrils shot out of the thirty-foot side tunnel. Alan saw everything in slow motion. One tentacle, the longest of the throng, was traveling towards his throat. In a split second, it would have him in its grasp, and he would end up helplessly dying a slow and painful death like one of Isaac Morley's animals fed to the thing so long ago.

He pressed the friction bar with his last ounce of strength. An enormous explosion rocked the tunnel.

***

Alan Parker Ward awoke from what felt like centuries later. Some of the five-sided tunnel wall tiles were scattered around him, sand and dirt coated his body. Slowly he rose to his feet. Every muscle in his body ached. His ears rang from the loud report. A million years of silt poured like a waterfall from his hair. His flashlight, half-buried in the rubble, gave off a friendly glow. He picked it up, shook it free of dirt, restoring its brilliance, and looked around. Not all the dust from the explosion had settled, leaving a foggy presence in the air. He repeatedly coughed, spitting up a blackish residue. The oversized glass test tube was where he had left it within the niche next to the static generator, that wonderful, fantastic, out of this ever-lovin' world static generator.

Alan shined his light at his feet. He saw something move. It was a piece of the shoggoth. He no longer withheld its name. Everything that Morley had written about in his journal was true. Nothing was delusional. The shoggoth was the given name that he had discovered in his research that belonged to the Elder Beings' synthetic lifeforms and written about in the Necronomicon. Outlined in the beam of his light was a severed tentacle. It was about six inches long, and it was still moving. Writhing was more like it as it tried to wriggle towards the toe of his shoe. It must have been sliced off by the falling rock when Isaac Morley's "safety device" exploded, he marveled. With a shudder, Alan remembered that the longest of the shoggoth's appendage was the one that was reaching for his throat. He removed the rolled-up metal papers in the glass tumbler and squatted down within arm's reach of the thing. With a swift move of his right hand, he scooped up the severed section of the creature's limb into the crystal receptacle and snapped the light blue lid shut. "Gotchya," he said with a smile.

Alan stood upright and was met with a pounding in his chest. It felt like someone hammered on the inside of his ribs.

***

Ironwood parked his Willys on the roof of his house. He was dead tired. The sun was setting. The horizon-grazing celestial body poured its reddish rays over the mountains. "Red sky at night, sailor's delight," he told himself. He walked the slant of the tar and gravel roof to the ground level and hesitated before taking the few steps downwards to his front door. There was a light on in his courtyard behind the house. The professor circumnavigated the left side of his home and strode across the flagstones of the back patio. The light came from the inside of his Airstream trailer at the end of the courtyard. As he approached the old travel trailer turned study, he heard the sound of muffled voices. Ironwood placed one foot on the lower rung of the aluminum steps; with a hand gripping the staircase railing, propelled himself into the trailer's interior, hoping to catch his intruders off guard.

"Hello professor," cheerfully hailed Congressman Neville Stream. The member of the U.S. House of Representatives was sitting behind

Ironwood's desk casually looking through a stack of papers. Two men in dark suits stood on either side. They were big, very muscular-looking, and infinitely menacing. Ironwood quickly surveyed the situation. He thought that in a fair fight, he might be able to take one of them out, but he would have little chance against the both of them.

"What the hell are you doing here? Those papers are mine. They're personal."

"I like to understand people. It puts motive into context, and then I am better to predict them."

Stream's mockery fell flat. The inside of the trailer was marked by an atmosphere lacking in cheer. "Tell us about the shoggoth, professor?" he said with a malicious smile.

Professor Thomas Ironwood was at a loss for words. He hadn't heard the name "shoggoth" since his days at Miskatonic. Many of the "new age" associates in the Mythos Department didn't subscribe to the belief that they actually existed. They would refer to the legends about them as Necronomicon fairy tales. A terrible, indescribable thing vaster than any subway train. A shapeless jumble of protoplasmic bubbles, with myriads of temporary eyes, bearing down on their victims, crushing, and devouring them. Most of the stories about them came from the imagination of a writer by the name of H.P. Lovecraft. Unless he conjectured, it had something to do with that old top-secret report. "I don't know what you are talking about."

"Oh, come now, prof. I know that you received that email

forwarded from my nephew's cell phone," he countered, getting angry. "He was clumsy and downright stupid to let it fall into the wrong hands. Be that as it may, I'm not sure who got a hold of his phone, probably Hawkins, but it doesn't matter because he wasn't so clever either. You see, he did delete it from the phone's 'Sent' file, but he failed to remove it from the 'Delete' file."

"Shoggoths are nothing but a mere legend." Ironwood was not about to acknowledge that he had received the email with the old top secret document's photos, let alone confess that Admiral Hawkins had sent them.

"Not so, prof; the evidence is overwhelming and has been backed up by some of your old colleagues from Miskatonic U."

Ironwood was aware of the 'Inner Circle' within the Mythos Department, a cabal of elites that kept the darker days of our planet secret. Although he was an associate member of the department, he was not part of that faction. What he did know, however, was that followers of this Inner Circle were sworn to absolute silence about its purpose and would never divulge its innermost secrets.

"Highly unlikely, congressman. They don't communicate with the outside world."

"Cthulhu fhtagn!" the congressman bellowed out. His face turned red and was overcome with laughter, a demonic, nearly hideous guffaw.

Astonished might have been the word that the professor would have chosen to speak if he hadn't been at a loss for words. Flabbergasted was even more appropriate because Congressman

Neville Stream had just uttered two words that are taken very seriously by not only the staff at Miskatonic University but his old colleagues within the Mythos Department. “Cthulhu” is a gigantic cosmic entity worshiped by cultists, and “fhtagn” is a shortened prayer of its worshippers' to awaken him.

Stream recovered from his merriment but still smiling and pointed out a chilling fact, “Oh, you’d be surprised how effective a little physical torment can be when extracting information. You see, prof; I know all about your little shoggoth. A long, long time ago, these elder things inhabited the earth, and they created these slaves to do their bidding. They were indestructible. Only they have now outlived their masters, and one of them, maybe more, I hope, live in the tunnels beneath the Mojave Desert. They are known to consume every living thing in their path, and they grow bigger with every gobble. We found Isaac Morley’s underground study over a year ago. His work is well known to a few colleagues and me. My goal, because I know you are interested. . . Oh, I can see that you are on pins and needles, professor . . . My goal is to set the shoggoth free. Hopefully, your pal Alan Parker Ward’s nosing around will do the job for me. Never attribute to a good plan what can be accomplished with incompetence. Even if Ward doesn’t release it, we have other means at our disposal, but we’ll still blame it on you and him.

“This is ludicrous. Shoggoths do not exist. This is all a sick joke.” Ironwood knew that logical reasoning with one who had chosen absurdity was never easy. He looked about his study, carefully searching for the right words to use next, convinced that the congressman was insane. At the far end of his book-lined wall, Ironwood noticed, for the first time, his housekeeper, Mrs. Murchison sitting in a chair. Her face betrayed nothing. She couldn't be part of this scheme?

"Truly, professor, they do exist. Believe me when I tell you that we know everything about these creatures and the ancient world that produced them."

"Oh, you have a systematic understanding of the world we live in, do you?" challenged Mrs. Murchison, her eyes becoming a steely glare. "Like, why is the sky blue? Where does the flame go when you blow out a candle?"

Stream casually looked over his shoulder in the housekeeper's direction. "That is enough out of you. If I want any information from you, Mrs. Murchison, I'll have my men beat it out of you." He returned his attention toward Ironwood and sighed with the aspect of heavy exasperation. The congressman removing a sizeable smartphone from the breast pocket of his suit jacket touched a few icons and turned it in the direction of Ironwood. "A picture is worth a thousand words."

What unfolded on the five-inch screen was a video that appeared to have been shot in one of the tunnels. A Hispanic man in the uniform of a Seabee was holding a thick electrical cable. Two wires, stripped bare at the leads, protruded from the end. Two other men similarly attired stood by observing. The man with the wire thrust the two exposed prongs into a cigar shape on the tunnel floor. Sparks flew, and within seconds, a horrible spectacle took place.

Thomas Ironwood looked on with both revulsion and amazement. The shape on the floor swelled, slithered up the cable, and engulfed the Seabee in a gelatinous mass as it grew. The whole thing occurred in only a few seconds. The man writhed in enormously noticeable pain. His mouth formed a hideous scream, but there was no sound to the video. He kept screaming until, shortly, the bulk of the thing covered his face and head. Numerous vile, pustule arms erupted from the consuming slime and lunged for the other two men.

Stream turned off the video. "I enjoy watching this, but I muted the sound. The screaming gives me a migraine."

Ironwood was slowly putting the pieces together. He realized that what he had just observed was a video of Chief Petty Officer Domingo Mercado and his men. There was no longer any mystery as to what happened to them. He was sickened with grief for them and the terror they must have felt. "How on earth?" he started to say.

"It's simple, I've got eyes everywhere," the congressman interrupted, his self-esteem bristling. "There is always the right man for the job at my beck and call; he conceals a small camera for me, and voila, it's movie night. We don't even need Netflix."

Stream sat casually with his hands folded and both of his elbows resting on the desk. Ironwood wanted to grab the smug bastard by his bald head and smash his face with all his might into the desktop, not once but a dozen times, reducing it to a bloody pulp. He knew, however, that he wouldn't be able to get within a few feet of the congressman before his two goons would be all over him, and then he'd be the one beaten to death. "Why in Heaven's name would you want to release a thing like that?"

"Because prof," he chortled. "It will create a lifestyle change, a political opportunity presented by chaos. Just think, a shoggoth, hopefully, an army of them, foul creatures the size of wooly mammoths consuming the locals like grains of rice."

"You're insane," he shot back.

"Unequivocally, no! It is political acumen. I need all the victims I can round up. Victims are great, professor! Victims need government. My poll numbers are remarkably high. There will be a presidential election in eleven months, and I will be Número Uno for my party."

"This is about money?" he challenged.

"When isn't it about money? More importantly, it is about power. What is money without power?" he sighed. "What is power without money? This economic malaise we are in is good for my career. Most people derive their self-worth from their work. Without such, an internal emptiness evolves and becomes a life without meaning. So, a shoggoth-infected world is a perfect act to follow in their already miserable existence. A separate menace is now growing and lurking in the corners. And I am the one to reveal the cause of this malaise of horrible death. I know the culprits, I will be the white knight, taking revenge for the people, and I will be the one to save humanity, i.e., my political platform."

Infuriated, Ironwood shouted, "Thousands of people could be killed."

"Perhaps millions."

"This is cruel and ruthless, all for your own personal gain," he answered back, fury rising in his voice.

"Only the cruel and ruthless are ever successful."

"Pure madness, no one will ever fall for your scheme. They will stop you, and you will spend the rest of your life in a padded cell!"

"Nibble sparingly at the mushrooms, professor, lest they turn out to be toadstools. It will not be considered the ravings of a few so-called clairvoyants or conspiracy theorists. It will, most assuredly, succeed because people will embrace the cynicism all due to the willingness on the part of the gullible because everybody is predestined to believe pessimism. Whether it is the acceptance of global warming, acid rain, or economic collapse orchestrated by a new world order, everybody is predefined to believe that something will be the end of all of us."

"So, this is where your blame game comes into play?" he challenged, understanding the psychosis of the plan.

"Oh yes, I am so glad that you are beginning to understand. You see, it is all the military's fault and, of course, you meddlesome scientists. Prying and snooping around to create the ultimate weapon. Uncovering things that humanity was not meant to know."

With both fists clenched tightly, Ironwood disputed the congressman again, "And if you release this scourge upon the earth, how do you propose to destroy the indestructible? You said you knew how."

"I don't know. At this point, it is just pure rhetoric. Part of the old platform, you know. Eventually, someone will figure it out, and my administration will, naturally, take the credit for it. In the meantime, we'll declare martial law across the country, and there will be no further need for elections."

"And you will be the first dictator of the United States. A cruel and ruthless one."

"Not so harsh professor, I like to think of it as ruling with a velvet glove over a steel fist."

"So, now comes the obvious question. Why are you telling me about your murderous plans?"

"To shut you up, prof."

"You intend to kill me?" he dared for the last time.

"Oh no, professor Ironwood," he laughed. "I reserve such actions for people higher up on the food chain than yourself. I would prefer not to leave a trail of bodies behind me, but, of course, if I have to, I will. You are simply a mild nuisance, a fly in my ointment. I knew that you were close to unraveling part of our plans, and I merely wanted to have the fun of filling you in on the whole picture. It is no secret that I dislike you immensely, and I was looking forward to seeing your face when I broke the news and warned you to stay away. I'm a busy man, professor, and I don't have the time or patience to deal with your pathetic attempts to stop me."

"I can go to the press and on the internet exposing your plot."

"You can try. We own the data flow. The sycophantic media will follow whatever lead I give them. It will just appear as a pathetic attempt, on your part, to shift the blame of the shoggoth scourge from yourself to me, a good and conscientious civil servant. I suggest that you find some deep hole of academia to crawl into, professor, before some angry mob rips you apart."

There was a .38 revolver in the glove compartment of Ironwood's Willys Jeep. At that moment, he wished he had it with him. A bullet through the head of congressman Neville Stream would be a blessing for an unsuspecting world. There is no death penalty in California, and he would end up spending the rest of his natural life behind bars if the congressman's two bodyguards didn't shoot him after the deed was done. The bulges caused by the shoulder holsters beneath their jackets spoke well of the men's concealed carry. "Since this is a tell-all," he said, trying to maintain his composure, "why the overt attempt of yours to construct a solar energy zone on the NWC base?"

"The acreage needed to accommodate it was just another thing to take away from the military as well as that space-based laser of yours. You know that thing might have ended up being an effective shoggoth killer. It also gave us the convenience of searching the area for additional tunnel sections."

"And that's where Captain Eastwater comes into play?"

"Ah yes, my nephew. As I told you, Ironwood, there is a plan 'B' to release our super-sized subterranean hobgoblin in case your Alan Ward's maladroit explorations don't do it for us."

"Where is Captain Eastwater now," he asked.

"Looking for the pot of gold at the end of the rainbow."

***

The sound of the two Colt M16A2 rifles and Eastwater's .45 caliber Heckler & Koch shattered their eardrums. It was upon them in seconds. The horror was swift. At first, they heard muffled musical piping that reminded Clayton Eastwater of the sound the wind in mountain caves can make. Then a twisted mass that slithered came abruptly into view. Its immense mucous-covered bulk undulated like a crawling leech, quickly stretching, and contracting as it moved. Over fifty-rounds were fired between the three men within a matter of seconds. Pieces, blown away from the creature by the gunfire, regrouped in an instant, leaving trails of dark fluid that rapidly coalesced back into its body. Speedily moving forward, hunger drove it onwards. There was no time for the Captain to feel fear, be repulsed, or even for his skin to crawl; they were consumed within a blink of an eye. Their screams became a constant obbligato to the keening cries of the shoggoth.

CHAPTER 22
MOONRISE

Ironwood drove the Willys across the desert floor pedal to the metal. It was midnight, and the moon was full. After Stream and his henchmen left, he spent a few minutes comforting Mrs. Murchison. She was a strong woman and didn't need much in the way of comforting; nonetheless, the professor's interest grew beyond that of an employer versus an employee. He appreciated strong women. She had been with him for over a year taking care of his household needs, and he realized that he didn't remember her first name until that moment when he asked.

"Amy," she answered with a smile.

All he knew about his housekeeper was that she had been widowed, like him, and that she had a daughter living somewhere in Oregon. If he came out of this with his skin intact, he would make it a point to learn more about "Amy."

The cloudless sky accompanied by the full moon and the Willys' headlamps illuminated the desert floor. Visibility was a little better than decent for a night drive. Ironwood knew he was reckless, driving so fast, but he had to get back to the Morley house and get Alan out of there. Stream's story of a mammoth shoggoth scarfing up humanity under any other circumstance would be rendered ridiculous if it hadn't been for that damn video. Ironwood couldn't get the images of the unsuspecting Seabee being consumed by a translucent greasy thing out of his mind.

As enchanted cities, distant mountains flew by while the professor tried to turn a one-hour drive into a forty-five-minute run. Chocolate brown bits of exposed basalt rock dotted the landscape adjacent to the limestone roadway. Flatland, occasionally interrupted by large pyramid-shaped knolls sprinkled with sagebrush, were visible in all directions. Some, also, were inverted cones, while others were rectangular. They looked almost architectural, shaped by centuries of wind, and shifting sand. It was times like these that Ironwood would entertain a fantasy that he had been blessed with x-ray vision so he could explore their interiors in hopes of finding the vestiges of a lost civilization. Now that fantasy felt more like a reality. Since Alan Ward's visit, he had been reacquainted with some of the Necronomicon legends because, within the course of one day, he explored the relics of an ancient sunken city and seen a man horribly killed by one of its inhabitants. If everything the crazy congressman said was correct, then there is a primal force in play here, an element as destructive and empty of thought as a tsunami.

Ironwood skidded the Jeepster to a stop in front of the old house. He kept the motor running and the headlights on in hopes of a quick getaway. He paused briefly removing the .38 from the car's glove box, slipped the gun into his waistband, and sprinted indoors.

The fifty-year-old professor dropped through the manhole

opening in the cellar floor and swiftly down the length of the cast iron ladder as agile as a man half his age. He clutched the revolver in one hand and the flashlight in the other retracing his steps back to Isaac Morley's underground study. He knew deep down inside his Smith & Wesson Police Special would be an ineffectual weapon against a shoggoth. Still, it gave him comfort to point it in front of him.

A light still burned in the circular room. Alan sat at one of the tables. His head leaned back, and even under the yellow glow of the kerosene lamp, he looked pale. "Alan," Ironwood called out.

Alan Ward stared at his professor friend with eyes that looked into another world. His threadbare sports jacket was now tattered and heavily soiled beyond recognition. His face was grimy, there were small clumps of dirt in his hair, and there was a bloodstain on his forehead. Ward's right leg was resting on a short wooden stool. The pant leg was torn up to the knee. Ironwood focused his light onto the exposed limb and made out a number of circular welts about an inch in diameter. Red scars inside the circles glistened with fresh blood. It reminded him of the suction marks giant squids leave on their prey. The bleeding looked as if there had been tiny teeth or minute curved claws within the suckers. Then he thought about the video and the tentacles that lashed out at the other two Seabees. The professor was dismayed. He felt useless. He didn't have anything to treat the wounds. Not even a handkerchief to wrap the leg. He was contemplating tearing the sleeves off his shirt to use as bandages when Alan spoke.

"It almost got me," he said, coming out of his daze.

"What almost got you."

"It was a shoggoth."

"My God, where is it now," Ironwood asked, holding his gun in a defensive posture.

"We are safe, Thomas, at least for the time being. Unless," he sighed, looking up at the ceiling. "Unless it finds another route out of this place. There was a cave-in; I caused it. Isaac Morley left a well-preserved explosive device in one of the tunnel sections, and I was able to use it. The thing is sealed up behind hundreds of tons of dirt and rock."

"And you, Alan, how are you doing?"

Alan clutched his chest with his left hand and winced slightly. Short of breath, he answered, "I've been better. I can't seem to move my right arm, though. There are some pills in my pocket."

Ironwood reached into the right side pocket of Alan's jacket and produced a small metal tin. Taking out a tablet, he placed it under his friend's tongue. "Nitro?" he asked.

Alan shook his head, "yes."

Thomas Ironwood was aware that nitroglycerin sublingual tablets are used to treat angina episodes in people who have coronary artery disease. He also recognized an emergency when he saw one. "Alan, we've got to get you out of here."

"No! Movement by me is the worst thing we could do right now."

"I'll get help."

"What are you going to do? Call road service? Does Triple-A come out this far? No, what I need is to rest and let the nitro take its effect."

"How long have you had this condition?"

"It was a gift left to me by my other-self. When I woke up after my five-year coma, I had a seizure, almost died then. They tell me that the only cure for my condition is a heart transplant, but that costs a million dollars. You don't have a million bucks on you, do you?" he laughed, followed by a harsh cough. "Go ahead and call 911, and maybe they'll send a chopper out here with some medical personnel if they don't get lost first, but you are not going to wrestle me up that ladder and out of that sewer. That would definitely kill me."

"I will go topside, get a cell signal, and call the base."

"Stay and listen," Alan Ward commanded as if lecturing one of his students back at the university. He pointed to another chair and motioned Ironwood to sit down. Taking a deep breath, Ward slumped further into his chair. "Everything you see here was once part of a great race of beings that occupied this planet millions of years ago. Although highly advanced, they became a civilization void of any instrumentalities. No machines. They synthesized life forms that became the structures that they lived in and the infrastructures that they traveled on. These tunnels were once alive as well. The five-sided notched tiles on the walls and floors were formerly a cell structure that held everything together. If it were damaged, in some way, it would simply grow replacement parts and repair itself because that is how it was programmed to perform. Remember the remains of what we thought were light fixtures hanging from the tunnel ceilings?"

"Yes, I remember."

"They were, in a sense, ancient chandeliers—conductors of light, not producers of it. At one time, they were part of giant trumpet-shaped organisms that sprouted through the tunnel ceilings at regular intervals towering hundreds of feet into the sky. They collected sunlight and transmitted it to those fixtures below. Why and what for, I am not sure; maybe they simply lit up the passageways. Maybe there was another purpose that is lost to us. I doubt we'll ever know."

Alan got animated acting a bit like his old self, the English teacher turned amateur archaeologist and continued, "Either way, after a period, everything died off. The Elder Being's living structures crumbled back into the earth, and the tunnels, in desert areas like the Mojave, became mummified. We are privileged to be in a part of our country, possibly the world, which still contains these relics."

"But some 'thing' did survive?" inquired the professor.

"Yes," Alan replied, his voice becoming almost a whisper. "These life forms were also shaped into beasts of burden so that even all physical labor by their race was eliminated."

"And the shoggoth?" Ironwood pressured.

"One of their slave labor force as far as I can tell."

"The one that tried to attack you, what did it look like?"

"I won't describe what I saw. It was only a glimpse that sent me rushing out of that place. That cave-in gave us a shoggoth sample that will probably produce years of scientific study and position papers in academia."

Ironwood looked befuddled.

"Over there," Alan said, pointing at the table next to him.

Ironwood realized that he had indicated a large glass tube lying amongst a stack of papers. Standing, he picked it up. There was something inside. Was it a salamander? It was the wrong color. Then it moved. Not a slow slither, rather it jumped as if it was trying to break through the glass. He dropped the tube and hollered, "Damn, it's a tentacle." Ironwood watched as the glass tube bounced off the table and onto the stone floor without breaking. It evoked the passages in Hayward Phillip's top-secret report about the unbreakable oversized test tubes.

"A piece of a tentacle," Alan said brusquely, applying humor, trying to salve his discomfort. "A severed tentacle, to be precise. Guillotined by the roof falling in just when the little bastard tried to grab me."

Alan started to laugh, "The boys at your Michelson Lab will have fun trying to reverse engineer that abortion. If they ever figure the thing out, it will mean to biology what Einstein meant to mathematics and physics. There is a good chance that Isaac Morley's meddling may have activated a once forgotten experiment in environmental science. He never mentioned how he came across it in his journal, only that it was small when they first found it. I discovered many opened and empty tubes like that one littering a tunnel chamber. Possibly that was the source of their discovery. Whenever Morley and his helpers fed it, and it grew, it became enormous, but surely, it must have atrophied, becoming dormant after their demise and when the feeding stopped. I haven't been able to figure out how it regained its bulk after so many years of stagnation."

Ironwood thought about the electrical voltage that the chief petty officer had plugged into the thing. Did the shoggoth also thrive on pure energy? Did it consume other organisms only for their life force energy? The idea was too fantastic. "Alan, how big was the creature you encountered?" he urged.

"The size of a freight train," he shot back, holding his chest again, momentarily gasping for air.

"Isn't the nitro taking effect yet?"

"I think so; strange, it feels like a cheap vodka hangover," retaking a deep breath, he smiled at his old friend. Calmly he said, "There is something else you should know. After the Elder Beings bred an adequate supply of shoggoths, they experimented with developing other cell groups. One of these was a shambling primitive sometimes used for food and at times as an amusing buffoon. You'll find its likeness carved into that wall over there," nodding towards an area opposite the entryway.

Ironwood walked in the direction Alan indicated and shined his light on a wall section to the left of the bookcase. Just a couple of feet above eye level was a picture symbol of a two-legged creature whose vaguely simian and human foreshadowing's were unmistakable, Man!

"Writings in the Necronomicon claim that certain elder things created all life on earth as a jest or a mistake. Perhaps those writings were not a myth." Alan coughed severely but continued to drive his point home. "I suppose beliefs about a supreme being who created us in his image are as much of a joke as our ancestral buffoons were to the Elder Beings."

Ironwood wasn't about to disturb his fellow academician, especially considering his condition. He felt sorry for him. Poor Alan, his pessimism was so deeply ingrained that, for him, every silver lining had a cloud in it. It was no wonder after all the life-altering and devastating events he had experienced. Losing five years of his life, his wife and child gone from him as a family unit and a serious health condition. Pitiable Alan not only had become a pawn in the power of those Elder Beings, but he had also become a victim to the scheme of Congressman Neville Stream.

Professor Thomas Ironwood had his convictions about creationism that he would remain mute until his friend's health recovered. He remained aware of the recent studies of the human genome and ancient DNA that have produced conclusive evidence that Neanderthals and Homo sapiens, modern man, were two completely different species. The pictoglyph, like the others they observed, was highly detailed, and it was apparent to him that it was depicting a hunched over Neanderthal man, not Homo erectus.

When it came to other fields of understanding, Alan must have trusted that his and Ironwood's beliefs were not so dissimilar. When

Alan shouted out, "I am certain that you can appreciate that it is essential, for the peace and safety of humanity, that some of Earth's dark, dead corners and unplumbed depths be left alone. That fool Eastwater is digging a tunnel several miles from here. The shoggoth may be heading that way now. He must be stopped."

"It was our job," answered Ironwood, pleased that they had found some common ground, "when I was with the Mythos Department, to keep arcane secrets out of the hands of those that would use it to their own selfish and destructive ends. I will leave you here and send detailed information as to your whereabouts while I go and stop the 'fool' as you say." Turning around to face Alan, he noticed that he was not moving.

Rushing over to his old friend, he placed two fingers against his neck. "Alan!" he shouted. There was no pulse.

***

Alan Ward couldn't hear his friend talking to him, the ticking of his watch, or even feel the soft beating of his own heart. It was as if he had stepped into a vacuum. He no longer felt any pain. Alan was certain that he had attained full use again of his right arm and the injuries on his leg no longer throbbed. The lighting in the circular room, for some reason, increased. He was standing, and every essence in his body experienced peace. There was no more internal turmoil.

Alan Parker Ward observed his death from a quiet place as every bit of himself expanded into the ether.

***

Grief-stricken, Ironwood stood over the body of his friend. The pain and angst he felt over the loss of his colleague were unbearable. He felt useless; he felt old and foolish, a decrepit old fool that should have been more cognizant of Alan's malady. Maybe he could have gotten him proper medical attention. He shouldn't have brought him out to this harsh desert environment. He shouldn't have left him alone in the tunnels. Anger overcame his grief and turned into rage. The real culprit was Congressman Neville Stream. He had lured Alan Ward to these bizarre burrows and ultimately lured him to his death. The Elder Being's rampaging shoggoths were not necessarily malevolent. They just rolled over and assimilated you. It was simply what they did. They were probably oblivious to the existence of puny creatures like us, he decided. We are just a source of food to them, the energy needed to drive their internal engine. They are indifferent, inimical. But the congressman was of a different ilk. He didn't think like a normal person. He didn't have the ingrained moral codes that define our species; likewise, our perceptions of "good" and "evil." Stream has an excessive, if not, erotic interest in himself, he thought, he is narcissistic, and a powerful narcissist can be more dangerous than a shoggoth. Was it hopeless to oppose Congressman Stream? His ego was so huge; his self-interest so overpowering that he was incapable of recognizing his machinations as evil.

Interestingly, Ironwood mused that the words "ego" and "evil" sounded so similar.

Intently conscious of his complete isolation within the catacombs, Ironwood stared at the ceiling contemplating his next move. What do I do now, he wondered? An idea tickled Ironwood's brain like the tiny scuttling legs of a spider; Alan's view of reverse engineering didn't seem so comical by comparison, he decided. He bent over he picked up the king-size test tube with its gruesome contents. The detached tentacle wriggled within its transparent prison. He stared at the grotesquerie and almost smiled. "Perhaps there is hope for mankind after all," he proclaimed. The tube fit snugly into the left pocket of his trousers. Moving the wooden table up against the large oak barrel containing kerosene, he picked up a circular tin used as a wastebasket. Ironwood looked at the body of Alan Ward and again at the simian carving on the curved wall. He scooped up all the notes of Isaac Morley's along with his journal and tossed them into the basket. Years ago, a colleague at Miskatonic University told him that "once a member of the Mythos Department, always a member of the Mythos Department." Grabbing the oil lamp and using both hands, he threw it forcefully into the wastebasket. The glass chimney broke; oil leaked out and became liquid fire consuming the papers.

"To keep secrets out of the hands of those damn fools that would use them for their egocentric means!" he roared to no one in the room. Ironwood no longer felt like a decrepit old man; he was an angry Jehovah. He kicked the waste bin with a swift and deliberate move, causing it to slide across the room and under the table. The flames ignited the brittle, dry wood almost instantly. The table burned rapidly. It would be only a matter of minutes before the barrel of kerosene would catch on fire. Ironwood took hold of his dead comrade and eased the frail lifeless body over his right shoulder. "Poor old Alan," he said to himself, "he couldn't weigh more than ninety pounds."

Balancing the load on his shoulder, Ironwood left the room, his shadow momentarily eclipsing the carved image of the Neanderthal that stood out orange amongst the reflected flames.

***

Getting out of that hell-hole and up the ladder to the cellar floor above was a cumbersome task for the fifty-year-old professor that made him grateful for all the years of weight training he underwent to slow down the onslaught of middle age. His energy level increased when he came outdoors and saw the warm, friendly glare of his Jeepster's headlights.

Gently setting Alan's body down in the backseat of the opened convertible, he removed his cowboy hat and wiped his brow with the back of his hand. He leaned against the rear fender to catch his breath. He wished at that moment that he had a cold beer at hand. A frosty brew would be just what the doctor ordered. He solemnly wished Alan alive and well and tipping a few with him.

Overhead he heard the whir of chopper blades. The Morley house and the surrounding area became floodlit. A voice boomed out of a megaphone, "Professor Ironwood, stand down. We are directed to escort you to the base." At that instant, the roof of the Morley house blew off. It wasn't proceeded by a thunderous roar or even a brief rumble. The entire rooftop suddenly went straight up, propelled by an ear-splitting explosion. Shingles and rafters flaming plummeted back to earth, fortunately landing behind the house. Ironwood was in front and out of harm's way. The helicopter was also at a safe distance.

It was a dust explosion. The kerosene barrel must have ignited, causing the rapid combustion of fine particles suspended in the air. Ironwood once read that dust explosions are a frequent hazard in underground coal mines. The detonations typically occur in enclosed locations. They happen where powdered combustible material is present in high enough concentrations mixed with oxygen and a suitable flame. Millions of years of filthy Elder Being dust just went up in smoke.

Mesmerized by the spectacle, the professor didn't take notice of the helicopter landing nearby. Zachary Taylor Harris set the SH-2G Super Seasprite down a good one-hundred yards away from the fire. He and Spuds Biddles ran towards the blaze just as the walls of the two-story structure collapse inward, an inferno filling the cellar.

Zach stared at the still corpse of Alan Ward in the backseat of the car. "What happened to your friend here?" he managed to spit out after a hard swallow.

Ironwood turned and looked at him, the fire delineating his stoic features, the flames reflecting in his eyes, "heart failure," he answered, his voice lacking any emotion.

CHAPTER 23
SUNRISE

Travis thought that he and Dorian looked positively erotic in their Navy uniforms. "Sexy," he proclaimed as they stood side by side, admiring their reflections in the full-length mirror that hung on the bathroom door. "We are lucky that we found these two boys in the nick of time," he added. "They are both the right size for us." Dorian giggled. The big lug was always doing that when he was nervous. Travis had done a lot of brainstorming. He always did the thinking for both of them. Travis was the brains, and Dorian was, of course, the brawn. The big sensual bodybuilder never ceased to excite Travis. I masterminded the whole thing; he prided himself, putting his lust aside. He thanked Ganymede, the god of homosexual love, for the military's policy of DADT, don't ask, don't tell. All he had to do was locate the gay bars in Ridgecrest; the internet supplied the info for him, and then searched for their doppelgangers.

Ganymede brought them good fortune last night because the first club they attended was fruitful. It wasn't even difficult to entice them to their motel room with the promise of a foursome. And it wasn't a game of golf they were going to play either. Travis and Dorian smiled at each other with intense satisfaction. In the king-sized bed laid the nude corpses of the two servicemen. Both were face down, bullet holes in the back of their heads made by 9mm's with silencers. They had timed the shootings to occur simultaneously. The smaller one was exactly Travis's size, while the other, although big like Dorian, was chunky and soft, not ripped like his sweetheart. Even so, his uniform fit Dorian well with only minor adjustments. Travis had removed his earring and filled the hole it made in his left earlobe with Clearasil. The uniforms were spot-on, and their doppelgangers IDs, which now belonged to them, were textbook.

Travis and Dorian had wiped the bathroom and bedroom clean of all their prints. They had rented the roadhouse room, on a stolen credit card, for three days beyond the time when they would have left town, and they put a DO NOT DISTURB sign on the door. There was no way that they could be traced. Everything was letter-perfect. Now it was time to go to work.

***

Lieutenant Jason Riggs' smartphone made the sound of Doctor Who's TARDIS. Snatching it off his bed table, he answered in a sleepy tone, "Riggs."

"Admiral Hawkins here," a voice on the other end announced.

Riggs quickly sat up in bed, "Yes, sir."

"Sorry to disturb your slumber, lieutenant, but you are to report to the Michelson Lab, Q-Section."

Jason always got a kick out of the name of the top-secret test center within the NWC Laboratory. "Q-Section" sounded like something out of a James Bond film. Whoever dreamed it up must have had a campy sense of humor. The bedsheets rustled, Gwen Gilhooley rolled over and hugged him. "When sir?" he asked back into the phone.

"On the double lieutenant," the admiral shot back.

Gwen kissed Jason on his neck, and his voice cracked, "Aye, aye sir!"

"And," Hawkins ordered, "bring Petty Officer Gilhooley with you."

"Aye, aye, sir," he said again, his ability to speak becoming a whisper. Lieutenant Jason Riggs knew that he wasn't in just hot water; he would be boiled in oil or made to walk the plank. He and Gwen had discussed it. They thought they could keep their newly formed relationship a secret for a short time while they decided which one of them would resign from the Navy. Gwen thought she could get a job with a local engineering firm. Construction was starting to boom again in and around Ridgecrest, and her chances of acquiring employment in her field would be promising. He knew now that he didn't want to lose her. He loved her blond hair that smelled of fresh green apples and the line of perspiration on her top lip after they had made love. And they both knew the U.S. Navy's policy on fraternization was strict and to the point. They had read and re-read the regulation together dozens of times:

REGULATIONS 1165: Prohibits personal relationships between officers and enlisted personnel that are unduly familiar and do not respect the differences in grade or rank. Such relationships are prejudicial to good order and discipline and violative of service tradition. Conduct is prejudicial to good order and discipline if it calls into question the senior's objectivity, results in actual or an appearance of preferential treatment, undermines the senior's authority and compromises the chain of command.

They had been cohabitating for less than twenty-four hours, and command already found out. Riggs hoped that when the admiral got through with him that it would be quick and painless. Maybe they would use the firing squad.

***

Admiral Jack Hawkins, who had seen things throughout his long and perilous career that would freeze a normal man's blood, was stunned to silence. He stood with hands clasped behind his back and stared through the four-inch-thick polymethyl acrylic barrier into the fifteen-foot square cubicle. The barrier was as clear as the windshield on his 65 Mustang, except nothing was appealing within its interior.

The tentacle was growing. It had devoured three lab rats, and now they were getting ready to feed it a guinea pig. Hawkins knew that the word "devour" was not appropriate for its feeding; hell, he didn't think that "feeding" was an appropriate term either for what it was doing. When the damn thing partook of its first live snack, a gobbet of gray-green flesh oozed out from one of its suction cups and encased the white rat morsel in goop. He could tell that the rodent was in pain by its squeaking and squealing until one of the techs turned off the sound system. After a while, the rat stopped moving and shriveled up to half its original size. Then they fed it another one. It grew with each successive feeding. The tentacle extended, and the goo expanded so that the creature was, now, the size of a coffee table.

There was a small acrylic door that swiveled. They used it to pass each lab animal into the containment chamber. It reminded Hawkins of the revolving doors they used to have on the old-style department stores. On the other hand, this one was no bigger than a breadbox and functioned similarly to an airlock. Dr. Marinus Bicknell Willett and several lab technicians retracted the solar shade screens from all the skylights in the Q-Section Laboratory and turned the incandescent lights dimmer on "Full." The amount of light created a showroom environment that made everything seem garish and movie-set-like. At first, Hawkins was grateful for the extra light as it dispelled the sensation of foreboding he felt. All lit up like stage actors. Willett removed a black and beige guinea pig from a cage and slipped it through the mini-airlock. The oversized rodent slid down a stainless steel chute and came to rest inches from the organism. The guinea pig ignored the living thing, and, surprisingly, the living thing ignored the guinea pig. Everyone's eyebrows raised behind the Plexiglas.

“It appears that Professor Ironwood’s theory that the creature sustains itself by absorbing solar energy is accurate,” announced Dr. Willett, wiping his hands on his white lab coat. It is also apparent that when that source becomes scarce, it resorts to the absorption of living carbon-based organisms. However, his premise that the thing drains energy from its hosts causing fatality is considered, for the moment, as speculation by the administration of Q-Section.”

"Everything that’s a ‘thing’ has some energy associated with it," said Ironwood as he approached Willett.

“That may very well be,” replied the doctor to the professor. It may also be that the ‘thing’ absorbs the proteins, carbohydrates, and fat in animals as fuel and converts it to energy. It will take further study; I am sorry to say. Only time will tell.”

“We don’t have time, Marinus, that ‘thing’ is a shoggoth. There is another one out there, somewhere, much larger, and it must be stopped. If it isn’t, it will gorge itself on the life force energy of all living creatures on this planet.”

“We agree on more things than you know, Thomas. Your shoggoth, as you call it, is not an indigenous biological.”

“What do you mean?” demanded Hawkins.

“Not of this earth, admiral,” answered Ironwood, looking like the weight of complacency was piling on his shoulders.

“That can’t be,” he shot from the hip.

“That is precisely what it is; I’m sorry to say, admiral,” rejoined Willett. "This alien life form you brought us has been bioengineered, made of complex hydrocarbons, more like basic tissue matter, with a simple cell structure that is almost protoplasmic. The lab boys are stumped because the proteins do not make sense. They are biological, but a biology straight out of a nightmare. It could be a mammal, could be a reptile, could even be jellyfish with all the mismatched DNA strands they've identified so far . . . And some don't match anything in the global genetic databases."

"This doesn't work for me, Doctor Willett!" Admiral Hawkins's fuse was burning short. He had been summoned out of bed at four in the morning with the news that Captain Eastwater and two of his Seabees had disappeared in the tunnel after the firing of several shots. Now all he was getting was scientific gobbledygook. "I sent for all of you!" he shouted, "To get answers, and so far, I've got nothing."

"Oh, but we have learned a lot about it," Willett answered, excitement rising in his voice. "For example, we know that it is a true primitive, but we have ascertained that it also has some level of intelligence."

"Intelligence?" interrupted Ironwood, also losing his patience.

"Yes, yes!" Willett answered enthusiastically. "It has a basic instinct to protect itself from harm, similar to the behavior of human beings and animals. When threatened with a destructive force, such as extreme heat, it retreats. We poked it with a red hot metal rod and observed the thing withdraw to the other side of the containment area. What is most remarkable is, if the damaging effect of the heat is continually applied, and a portion of the creature is destroyed, it will re-grow the missing segment once the destructive force is removed. Besides a primitive nature of self-preservation, it can regenerate body parts if we can consider, 'IT' has a body."

"We've heard this before," Hawkins fired back, his anger mounting. "Professor Ironwood told us what Alan Ward had said about the recuperative powers of shoggoths. If they were damaged, they would simply grow replacement parts and repair themselves."

"That is how they were designed to perform," the exasperated Ironwood interrupted. "The shoggoth's makers programmed it to repair itself when damaged. We are wasting time here. We need to mount a force to destroy this thing."

"That remains to be seen, Ironwood, and right now, my empirical evidence rivals your snap judgments," Willett parried. "Your contributions are priceless; it's your conclusions that I find faulty. Time, of course, is at the core of what we do here. I'd have more answers by now if it didn't take us a half-hour to figure out how to open the damn lid on that tube you brought. The samples of what you thought were brown wires and yellow silt that you so generously supplied, after careful scrutiny, turned out to be organic cousins of that thing in IT's plastic cage. All of this has taken time to analyze. But after this careful study, we can conclusively say that all, including my samples of the wall tiles, have the same recuperative powers!"

"Are you also telling us, doctor, that you know how to kill this thing or not?" barked the admiral, pressing for answers.

"In a sense, yes, admiral. That is if 'killing' is the correct term. With all prudence, I will say that we have a couple of theories on how to destroy it. Eradicate it. Lieutenant Riggs and MS Gilhooley's testimonies were most valuable in helping us to discover the creature's Achilles heel, so to speak. Which is the complete evisceration of every part of the thing, disintegration."

Admiral Hawkins had been watching Lieutenant Riggs and Petty Officer Gilhooley with intense scrutiny ever since they first walked into Q-Section. Riggs especially. The young officer looked like he was about to keel over with fright until asked to relate their encounter with Ironwood's 'shoggoth.' Hawkins more than sensed that the lieutenant and the petty officer were exceedingly delighted when confronted with a debriefing. It was as if they were expecting something else, something terrible to happen, and then relieved to discover otherwise. "Continue," he commanded, keeping one eye on the two.

"Well, the lieutenant here temporarily repelled the anomalous organism by spraying it with an insecticide."

Everyone in the room stared at Willett in anticipation of expecting more.

"Don't you see!" he hollered. "Insect-repellents have been known to use chemicals from the carboxymethyl group, the resulting core being pyrethric acid. Acid! The acid in the insecticide caused the larger version of itself to go into its self-preservation mode. The repellent probably wouldn't have had any damaging effects on it, but something inside of it told it that acid was 'bad' and retreat. Kind of like the Frankenstein monster running away from a flame bellowing, 'fire bad!'"

"Are you saying, doctor, that the only way to get rid of this thing is to bathe it in acid? If what Professor Ironwood has told us is accurate, the thing is bigger than a bus, and we'd need truckloads of the stuff to dissolve it out of existence, let alone a way to come up with an effective delivery system in time; to halt its trip topside."

"No, but complete incineration would probably do the trick."

Everyone jumped when they heard the scream. Gwendolyn Gilhooley had been leaning against the Plexiglas chamber, listening to the squabbles. Her back was to the containment area. Turning slightly, Gwen looked over her shoulder, and that is when she cried out. The shoggoth had increased in mass exponentially and sprouted several more tentacles. It was, at the moment, the size of a compact car.

"It's the radiation from the sun and the incandescent lights," shouted Ironwood.

"Kill the lights," Hawkins ordered.

Willett and the laboratory technicians scrambled to their wall switches hurriedly, shutting the solar screens and turning off the overhead lighting. The emergency LED lighting automatically kicked in.

"I've seen enough," announced the admiral, primed for red duty. Turning to face Ironwood, he instructed, "Professor, I want you, Willett, Lieutenant Riggs, and half the technicians here, at the tunnel site on the double. There will be two Sikorsky's on the helipad in twenty minutes. You will figure out a way to contain this creature's cousin until I send a company of Marines with heat. And I do mean heat. When bullets, shells, and explosives don't get the job done, we'll burn the bastard down! We have access to some M2

Flamethrowers. The majority of them were scrapped years ago when they were declared obsolete, but we saved a few for testing, and they work damn well! Lieutenant, until further notice, you are in charge."

Hawkins, Ironwood, and Willett peered once more into the containment area. In a lowered commanding tone, Hawkins directed, "Willett, I want your remaining techs to destroy this thing, incinerate every last drop of it. Even if you have to burn down the entire building to do it."

"Yes, admiral."

"How did you refer to it?"

"An anomaly?"

"Yes, that was it, and Ironwood here calls it a shoggoth. Perhaps abomination is a better term. You know when the sun goes down, will they just hang around streetlights, or will they go about gulping down everything that moves?"

"I'm afraid it will be the latter, admiral," answered Ironwood in a whisper.

The shoggoth behind the Plexiglas was a ghostly blue-white under the illumination of the LED emergency lights. Provoked by the lack of infrared radiation, it mounted the guinea pig draining the tiny mammal's life force.

***

It was a fifteen-minute flight from the heliport to the site of the original tunnel discovery. Ironwood was exhausted, and even if he could sleep, a quarter of an hour of rest would not have been sufficient. Power naps didn't work for him. Hopefully, there will be time later, but not now. There was a nagging sense of unease in the pit of his stomach. The thing was a massive amoebic creature made out of protoplasmic slime. The Elder Beings had also modeled their tough plasticity into various functional limbs and organs. Multiple eyes floated over its surface, popping open momentarily to stare before striking its prey. If it escaped to the surface, finding an ample source of solar radiation, what would happen then? Do shoggoths reproduce by fission? He wished that Alan Ward had imparted more information to him before passing. He felt selfish for wishing that, but expediency was vital. The chopper crew had taken Alan's body to the base sickbay where, later, it would be transported to the morgue in Ridgecrest. When this was over, if it were ever over, he would have a lot of questions to answer to the local authorities. He would make the funeral arrangements at that time.

Ironwood had been in the second helicopter. Lieutenant Riggs and several others had gone ahead in number one. He reached the site and went down the ladder. The professor quickly walked the mile or so toward the tunnel's end. Halfway to his destination, he spotted a considerable commotion amongst the people gathered there. He increased his gate and sprinted to what he believed to be the dead-end, based on the last time he had been down the passageway. Marinus Willett was standing off to his right, still wearing that damn lab coat, looking lost. Gwen Gilhooley was being held firmly in place by two Seabees. She struggled to get free and kept shouting over and over, "We've got to get him out of there! We've got to get him out of there!"

Quickly surveying the area, Ironwood saw several large pieces of fractured rock bearing etched symbols similar to the pictoglyphs he and Alan had discovered beneath the Morley house. They were probably the remains of the monolith that the greed-driven Eastwater had his men bust through. Another cave-in, another barrier, had terminated the tunnel's end. A small hole had been dug into the rubble big enough to allow a man to crawl through the obstruction. Most of the crew were in a panic mode. Before he could say anything, one of the Seabees piped in, "I should have checked the gas levels with a portable tester. I told Captain Eastwater that it wasn't safe. The engineers hadn't shored up the ceiling. Everything collapsed last night after all that gunfire. It must've been the vibrations. We hand dug that this morning," pointing toward the hole. "Lieutenant Riggs went in there looking for the Captain just minutes ago. There must be a volcanic vent leaking carbon dioxide. I should've checked the air in that hole."

"Do you have any breathing gear?" Ironwood demanded.

"I sent one of the guys topside to get a unit out of one of the trucks."

Ironwood was familiar with the deadly properties of CO2. Being heavier than air, it would displace adequate levels of oxygen. When it filled an enclosed space, CO2 will overcome anyone in contact with it in short order, no more than a minute or two. The unfortunate soul will simply pass out quietly and suffocate, not realizing anything was wrong. "There isn't enough time," he declared. He turned to Professor Willett spotting the AIS Audio Infrared Scanner on his portable specimen table. Ironwood picked up the headpiece and asked, "Does this thing really work?"

"Just push the red button," replied Willett.

Ironwood turned it on its side locating the "red" button and pushed it. A ready light winked. The professor removed his straw cowboy hat, plopped it onto Willett's noggin, and donned the extra-terrestrial style helmet. "Wish me luck," he said, his voice sounding tinny through the amplified mouthpiece, and then headed for the hole in the rubble.

Gwen broke loose from the two Seabees and rushed to Ironwood's side taking hold of his left arm. He smiled, patted her hand, and proceeded to crawl through the man-sized rat hole. Ironwood was halfway through to the other side before realizing that Gwen could not see him smile while wearing the helmet.

It was extremely dark in the blocked tunnel section, but the infrared scanner worked exceptionally well. Ironwood crawled on his hands and knees and made out a hunched-over outline a short distance in front of him. He rose to his feet and removed his penlight from his pocket. The miniature torch outlined the image of Lieutenant Jason Riggs's unconscious form. He was still breathing, thank God! Professor Ironwood grabbed the young officer by the arms dragging him to the hole he had just come through and hollered for help. Ironwood threaded the unconscious frame of Riggs through the hand-dug cavity. It was cumbersome and awkward until the welcomed relief of helping hands stretched out from the other end and pulled him through to safety.

Ironwood rested briefly for a moment against some of the rubble from the rockslide. Getting the Lieutenant out of there was an exhausting task. "Come on, professor!" cried the voice of Gilhooley on the other side. He heard a loud ripping sound from above as if a giant tore a granite slab in half. Seconds later, the roof fell in.

The tired but agile professor ran from the man-sized rat hole toward the darkened interior in the nick of time. He congratulated himself, at first, on escaping the falling debris, then the professor's heart sank when he noticed that his avenue of escape had been cut off by tons of dirt and rock.

***

At that moment, she realized that she loved Jason Riggs more than life. Gwen wanted to lose herself in his body. She hoped that if they became one that they would grow old together. She didn't want to lose him.

The Seabees formed a human stretcher joining their hands and arms together, cradling their Lieutenant out of the tunnel into the fresh air. Three men on each side of Riggs, in unison, jogged the length of the passageway. Gwendolyn Gilhooley's voice became loud, rising and falling in an unnatural cadence as she ran alongside, "Wake up, Jason…I mean lieutenant!" Some of the Seabees smiled; there were no secrets here.

Only a second or two after pulling Lieutenant Riggs from the hole in the earth did the tunnel on the other side collapse spewing dirt and debris out of the cavity like a cannon shot. The air turned chalky with desert dust and sand. That was when they took hold of Riggs and fled the mile-long stretch of the tunnel.

Before reaching the ladder, a man ran up with the oxygen tank. The human stretcher came to a halt, and the man placed a neoprene face mask over Jason's nose and mouth and turned a valve. There was a faint hiss, and the lieutenant began to breathe deeply. Pushing the mask away, the first thing that came into Jason's view was Gwen bending over, looking him in the eyes. "Hello darling," she beamed.

"Was it your turn now to pull me out of the earth?" he asked, smiling back.

"No. Professor Ironwood got you out. Only now, he's trapped. There was another cave-in."

"Get me up," he demanded." The men eased Riggs to his feet. Swaying slightly, he leaned, briefly, against the shoulder of a Seabee who looked like he pumped iron in his off time. "Dig him out of there!" he commanded.

"If we had a week, maybe, lieutenant. This old structure is pretty flimsy in this area. We'd have to shore as we go," answered one of the Seabees.

Jason Riggs wished that he had brought the Komatsu excavator when he originally wanted to, but Eastwater had rescinded his request. It could dig through a tunnel ceiling in a matter of minutes, but it would take a day to get the excavator out there. The big piece of equipment had to be partially disassembled and transported by two lowboy trucks and then reassembled on site. He had no idea how much air was in that tunnel section. He had no idea, as well, if Ironwood had survived the cave-in.

Dr. Marinus Bicknell Willett came running up brandishing what looked like a metal detector with a red lens on its sensor. “We can locate him with this,” he said out of breath. “He has the AIS. The scanner is synced to the isotope locator on the helmet.”

“You sure that thing works, doc?” he challenged.

“I’d stake my career on it,” the pony-tailed scientist fired back.

“Everyone topside, gentlemen, on the double!” ordered the lieutenant.

***

The swift action of the cave-in had cut off the world around him. The inhospitable atmosphere enveloped Ironwood like cold silk sheets lining a coffin. He didn’t choke on the dust that swirled around him for the reason that the AIS breathing apparatus fed him clean air. When he first entered the tunnel section, the CO2 readout on the faceplate triggered a warning icon, and the compressed tank responded by filling the helmet with life-saving oxygen. After the cave-in, the warning indicator turned off along with the supplemental air supply. The collapse of the tunnel ceiling must have plugged the gas leak, he decided. A stillness now surrounded him. It was quiet. Occasionally, the sound of a pebble feebly sliding down the debris landslide would echo softly through the underground labyrinth breaking the silence. There was slight dampness, but for the most part, it was dry.

Over seven decades' navy personnel had traveled across this section of the desert, unaware that a vast network of tunnels laid below their feet. The tunnel Ironwood walked along was no longer an entrance to a dead end, but it seemed to stretch forever. Many branching shafts terminated at the passageway he traveled. They appeared empty. Still, he had the impression that someone or something lurked in their darkness, in myriad dark chambers. What added to his entrapment's anxiety was the lost age that Alan had described so vividly that had been buried beneath the Mojave for more than fifty million years, if his and Isaac Morley's stories were to be believed. This would, most likely, indicate that these endless channels and all of their artifacts predated humanity; some intelligent life clearly made them. It was mind-boggling. The Age of Dinosaurs came to an end roughly sixty-five million years ago due to an impact by a giant rock from outer space. The whole lot that existed so long ago was now a little more than bones pinned together in museums. All of which were insignificant when compared to a living, breathing organism from the region's primordial history.

Professor Ironwood had researched shoggoths in the days when he worked at Miskatonic University. Legend had it that humans were considered less than fleas on the hides of the hapless monstrosities. He read that the nightmarish creatures weren't blind, that they had countless eyes, but they probably didn't need them. The scent of a blood trail was doubtless as wide and as clear as a well-lit highway. The professor's thoughts became increasingly gloomy. Most likely, shoggoths owned the darkness, he contemplated. In all probability, this one was waiting. The morbid expectation that its great mass could feel the light footsteps of little warm-blooded souls added to his chill through miles of stone. He, somehow, sensed that it didn't plot its attacks. Maybe it didn't think of an approaching man as an object of aggression. Not even as prey. It was just waiting to feed. It was hungry.

The professor walked on in silence through the dark for what seemed like an eternity until the cave abruptly widened. He had hiked several miles by then and was surprised to discover a deviation within the unvaried five-sided subterranean architecture. His flashlight illuminated a familiar breach on the right side of the tunnel. It was a raised area similar to a loading dock. It was recessed. It was identical to the large rectangular hole in the wall that was in the other tunnel section, except this one was in an excellent state of preservation. Excluding eons of dust, the thirty-foot-long, four-foot-high ledge was entirely free of the dirt and rock that had all but buried the other platform. The most striking thing about it was the chromium object on its brink. Unlike the other silver pedestal, this one was completely intact. This solitary post with a conical bottom was crowned with a large sphere that loomed a good five-feet above its base. The globe looked like a colossal steel bubble a few feet in diameter. Its dust-laden exterior still gleamed when he directed the beam of his flashlight at it. Wiping the surface clean with the palm of his hand revealed a slight protrusion, a lens of a greenish hue.

Ironwood crawled up the edge of the platform to get a better view of the alien object. The professor noted that every artifact he came across in the tunnels appeared to have been built for giants. The platform was equally deep as it was wide, about thirty-feet. At the back was an enormous five-sided door that stood the height of two men and had a grab bar nearly six-feet in length. Eager that the colossal door might lead to an exit, he ran up to it only to be disappointed when, through a circular pothole in its surface, he observed tons of rubble blocking the way. Discouraged, Ironwood approached the steel bubble again. Wiping more of its surface free of centuries of dust, he discovered a small opening in the device. It was the size of a nickel. It was smack dab in the middle of the orb facing the interior of the platform. When he shone his light directly on it, the small hole was revealed to be five-sided in shape.

Ironwood stared at the familiar configuration for several minutes. An idea struck him; it was a silly thought, he knew, nevertheless, it might be so. "It couldn't be," he said to himself. Reaching into his pocket, he removed one of the star-shaped stones he had appropriated when Captain Eastwater wasn't watching. It looked to be the same size. Curiosity overcame common sense; he placed the five-sided stone into the corresponding receptacle. It was a perfect fit.

The lens atop the device radiated green, and a buzzing sound filled the chamber.

***

A squad of Marines approached Lieutenant Riggs. The unit had been subdivided down to eight soldiers assigned to be a fire team. Two of the men carried the flame throwers Admiral Hawkins had described, and the rest toted Colt M16A2 Rifles. The NCO reported to Riggs. "Stand ready," the lieutenant ordered.

The long arm of the AIS detector swept the ground, and the sensor winked red. "Found him!" Dr. Willett howled.

Lieutenant Riggs ran to his side. "Are you sure this time?"

"Yes," he answered back. "He kept moving before, but now he is staying in one place."

Riggs was relieved when Willett, earlier, had picked up Ironwood's movements. If he was moving, it meant he was alive. "Everyone over here," he shouted. "Start digging."

Seabees and Marines alike joined in with picks and shovels. Jason Riggs stood watching as dirt and sand went flying. At this rate, he thought, we might be able to break through before sunset. The sound of a truck's motor diverted his attention. Riggs turned around and spotted Gwendolyn Gilhooley backing her single axle flatbed truck with its drill tower mounted on the rear up to the spot where the men were digging. Jason smiled. He knew what she was up to.

Gwen hollered out the opened window of her truck and demanded, "Out of the way, you guys are too damn slow."

The Seabees and Marines turned to their lieutenant for guidance. "Let the lady through gentlemen," he directed, still smiling.

The men parted, and Gwen backed the truck up to their digging spot. The drill tower tilted up and aligned vertically over the area. Gwen disengaged the driveshaft from the transmission while still inside the cab and connected it to the drilling rig using the shift levers on the truck's floor. She jumped to the ground and ran around to the back of her vehicle to supervise the drill bar's operation. "We'll punch a three-foot hole in the ground. A five-pound charge should do the trick."

***

It was sweet, like the fragrance after the rain. There was a brief flicker on the edge of nowhere. From the dark burrow, a coiling mass of tentacles shot out. A great mucous-covered bulk writhed and squirmed as it finally revealed itself. Ironwood hadn't seen a shoggoth in its entirety until now. It was a parasitic protozoan on steroids. It had no form and moved using pseudopods, temporary projections, or membranes of unicellular construction. It didn't crawl or slither; it moved in, starts, and stops as its membranes stretched forward and moved, not unlike a swimmer doing the breaststroke. The cry "Eeeeeeee! Eeeeeeee! Wawk Wawk Wawk Wawk!" followed by a rattling noise, assaulted his ears.

Coming closer, Ironwood was repulsed by what he saw. The infrared scanner in the helmet coupled with the powerful lumens of his flashlight defined the ghastly image. The shoggoth's feedings must have nurtured it to a mature state because it terminated at one end by a star-shaped cluster of tentacles. It was an eye-opener for Ironwood because he realized with a shock that the star stones replicated its countenance.

Embedded in the slime of the shoggoth were the outlines of three men. All dressed in camo. Their skin stood out extremely white in the prevailing light as the creature, undoubtedly, sucked the very life out of them, liquefying their flesh and bones. Their faces contorted into continual screams that became muffled entirely by the putrid flesh, in which each was encased.

Increasing its speed while riding on the slick tunnel floor, the shoggoth moved forward, closer, and closer towards Professor Thomas Ironwood.

***

Captain Eastwater was in excruciating pain. The shoggoth slime had penetrated every inch of his clothing. It was a cancer seeping into every single pore of his body. Through the thick veil of the creature's substance, he could just make out Ironwood standing on a raised loading dock. It was a dream image. He had been overbearing, cruel to the man for no other reason than he was successful. He had been jealous. Eastwater was overcome with remorse and regret. Ironwood should not suffer the same fate as I, he reasoned despite his torment. Move arm must move the arm; he told himself, focusing all his will on the task. He had been a fool for the better part of his adult life. The captain stepped all over others to gain wealth and recognition.

The pain was agonizingly terrible. Captain Eastwater's greed had brought him to this hell. His entire body felt aflame. Somehow, he had become empathic with the creature as it slowly absorbed him with a thousand knives. He knew that the unbearable existence would last a very long time until the mercy of death befell him. Move that arm. He struggled in the viscous mass. His boney emaciated hand moved closer to his belt. That's it, his brain screamed, now closer! The Captain reached his objective; his hand closed around the grenade suspended from his belt, pulling the pin, his last thought was, "penitence."

***

The explosion rocked Ironwood backward. The tentacle thing blasted back down the tunnel-like the wadding from a cannon shot. With his ears ringing from the loud report, he regained his balance, climbed off the platform, and peered down the length of the tunnel. It was gone. The confined space must have acted like a rifle barrel.

***

The diesel engine of Gwen's truck had masked the report. No one felt the vibrations of the explosion below. Gwen moved the truck with the drill rig to a safe distance and removed a five-pound charge from the containment trailer. The blasting gel was tightly encased in a heavy plastic wrap and formed into a tubular shape. Inserting a blasting cap through the plastic wrapper along with the two wires attached, she lowered the gel, cap, and wires into the hole she had drilled. She trailed the wires away from the explosive to a distance of two-hundred feet and hooked one of the wires to a twelve-volt battery's negative pole.

Familiar with the procedure, Jason backfilled the hole with a few shovels full of earth. It was a method used to add weight on top of the explosive material that helped to drive the detonation downward.

***

The shoggoth reassembled itself as it moved along. Ironwood's disbelief was overwhelmed by his fear and astonishment. Pieces of the giant thrashing blob were rejoining. The tentacles momentarily blended into a ball of tendrils and muscular trunks thrashing in the air, pounding on the passageway floor resembling misshapen elephant legs. All the time, new organs formed over its bloated body; eyes, ears, mouths, none of them human.

Ironwood drew his revolver from his belt and emptied all six rounds into the advancing greasy flesh. It was a useless effort, but it was all that he had left. Since the explosion only detained the creature for a short time, his .38 caliber slugs were no more than bothersome gnats to the thing. The only avenue left to him now was to run. How long and how far the tunnel continued before it came to a dead-end, he had no idea. He would only prolong the inevitable.

A second explosion rocked the subterranean corridor. A large piece of the ceiling over the platform collapsed from the concussion, followed by an outpouring of dirt and rock. A six-foot diameter hole chock-full of sunlight appeared to pierce the darkness. Seconds later, a rope unfurled from above and dangled onto the raised deck. Two helmeted soldiers with metal tanks on their backs, carrying peculiar-looking rifles, immediately slid down the rope. Six more followed in rapid descent, each wielding a service rifle.

One of the weaponized men jumped down off the platform and, taking Ironwood by the arm, hustled him back towards his rescuers. Two of the other men reached over the edge of the raised platform and helped him up.

A giant orifice forming on the side of the shoggoth opened stickily. In a sweep of one of its tentacles, it lashed out. An oily gray lasso flung up and wrapped around the neck of the soldier still standing below the platform. He screamed. The soldier, dragged from where he stood, was then stuffed inside. The hole closed over him.

The remaining M16A2 Rifles discharged in unison, bashing the eardrums, and filling the tunnel with the pungent smell of burnt nitroglycerin gunpowder. The two flame throwers immediately ignited. The weapons Ironwood thought were strange-looking rifles, spewed liquid fire. He backed away, the putting the soldiers between him and the shoggoth. Ironwood could feel the backwash of heat from the flamethrowers on his face. The creature no longer advanced. Like the experiment Willett had conducted within the containment area, the shoggoth did not stay and become a toasted marshmallow. It retreated quickly.

Behind him, an aluminum extension ladder slid down from the opening in the ceiling. Ironwood turned and hurried up the ladder. Out of the hole and topside, Willett, Riggs, and Gilhooley encircled him. Gwen gave him a big hug and cooed, "Oh professor, I'm so glad we got you out of that hole."

"You saved my skin, sir," Lieutenant Riggs added.

"Save it," he replied abruptly. "These men can't keep this up forever down there. Gunfire has, literally, no effect on it. The creature will return, re-grown, once they run out of fuel for the heat they're throwing at it, and it will head for that hole in the ground you just made. Remember it wants the sunlight, and that means 'escape' for the shoggoth."

"The Marine's NCO did bring additional tanks for their flamethrowers," recalled the lieutenant, "considering the thing's possible number of retreats and advances, we might be able to hold it off for a half an hour. I also don't have any heavy equipment on-site to fill in the pit. We could do it by hand, but that would take too long."

Professor Ironwood stared at Riggs and then turned his attention to Gilhooley. "How much explosive gel do you have in that containment trailer of yours, Gwen?"

"Over two-hundred-pounds, sir, but wait! I know what you're driving at! To set off a charge of that size, you'd need a long-distance remote detonator. All I have is a twelve-volt truck battery. I'd need two miles of wire to be at a safe distance."

"You have blasting caps?"

"Of course."

"Good, we'll put your two-hundred-plus pounds of explosives at the base of that ladder down there, and I'll supply your remote detonator."

Ironwood looked around and realized that he was standing a short distance from the flat basalt stone with the five-sided icon engraved upon its surface that he and Alan Ward had observed only two days before. In the distance, he could see the remains of the Morley House, its foundation still smoldering. Ironwood next aimed his point of view at Marinus Willett. He was still wearing Ironwood's cowboy hat. Ironwood handed him the AIS Helmet and announced with the utmost gratitude, "Doctor Willett, this is a great invention of yours. It saved my life on more than one occasion. Thank you very much."

The look on Willett's face was as if he had just handed him the stone tablets from Moses. "You're welcome, professor," he choked back. "Here's your hat, professor."

"Keep it," he answered.

***

More Seabees joined the fray, working as a human chain. They formed a bucket brigade. They started a line at the containment trailer and gingerly passing one plastic-wrapped parcel of dynamite gel to the next across one-hundred-feet of desert sand and down to the base of the ladder. Gwen climbed down the ladder when the last tubes of explosives were in place. She pierced the plastic of all their wrappers with every blasting cap in her inventory. The blasting caps were metal, the diameter of a pencil but only half the length. They protruded halfway out of the blasting gel, looking like so many silvery bristles. Gwen squinted into the sun shining through the hole in the earth. She recognized the professor looking down at her. His face was grim. He outstretched a hand to her. Both of them were within hailing distance of the Marines.

The soldiers maintained their fortification of fire and bullets. The NCO holding one of the flamethrowers in a defensive posture scorched the shoggoth back into its lair. Glancing over his shoulder, he shouted above the mayhem, "Down to our last tank of gas, sir. Only minutes left."

Gwen climbed the ladder and looked at Ironwood with fear in her eyes. "You better come up with that detonator soon, professor."

As she climbed out of the hole and past the professor, he answered, "I will, Gwen, I will." Then he reversed course, clambering halfway down the aluminum steps, and yelled, "Be prepared to get out of here damn quick when I give the word, chief. You'll have very little time to move you and your men to safety."

"Aye, aye, prof!" he hollered back.

Standing next to the pile of explosives and with three bars on his iPhone, he called Cac.

***

Cac was wearing a faded Superman tee-shirt that was unattractively tight on his obese frame. He answered his cell phone on the first ring. “Hey boss,” he said excitedly, “I got those Type One Fresnel lenses in today. They should increase the efficiency ratio by at least three-point-two-percent,” he rambled on.

“Stop talking, Cac, and listen,” commanded Ironwood. “I’ve got my GPS turned on. I want you to Geo-Locate my mobile phone's position and lock on to it with the Space Guard Transmitter.”

“Are you kidding, boss? After I lock the SGT on to your phone, then what do I do?”

“You transmit, of course.”

“What! I can’t do that; it would fry you as well as the phone!”

“I’ll be a safe distance away, Cac. There is no time to explain; it has to be done right away. Don’t ask any questions. Just do it and do it now, Cac!”

Charles Augustus Chase consulted the Norsat Satellite Locator App on his laptop. “Number two Lithium satellite won’t be in position for ten minutes.”

“Then ten minutes it will be,” he answered, disconnecting the call.

“Oh, Pokémon,” exclaimed Cac. “One of the top brass must be demanding a demo. Well, phasers on kill, Cac out.” He pulled up Ironwood's cell phone number on his laptop and activated the location app. Within a few minutes, it locked onto his boss’s current position. "That's it!" he cried, almost jumping up and down. His tech geek excitement abated when he recalled that hackers refer to the people they geo-locate as victims in situations such as this. When the SGT kicks in, he hoped that his boss didn't become one.

***

Ironwood tossed his iPhone onto the pile of explosives. The smartphone looked out of place, surrounded by a tiny forest of blasting caps. While starting up the ladder, he saw Ensign Turco peering down at him from above. When their eyes met, Turco jerked back from the opening and disappeared. "What the hell is he doing here?" he asked himself. Ironwood turned to the Marines and yelled, "All right, gentlemen, it is time to leave. We have ten-minutes before this place gets nuked!" As he scrambled up the ladder, Ironwood could hear the seven Marines falling in behind him.

Reaching the surface and in the hot rays of the afternoon sun, he saw that Lieutenant Riggs had followed his lead and was ordering everyone to "bug out" as fast as humanly possible. Already people were running; helicopters were firing up their engines, and Humvees were racing across the desert. Everyone was moving fast except for Ensign Turco. He was standing next to a troop transport frantically tapping the screen of his smartphone with both thumbs. Ironwood recalled what Congressman Neville Stream had told him about his network of informers. He said that he had "eyes and ears everywhere." Could Turco be a mole?

***

Congressman Stream looked out the side window as a tumbleweed danced across the gravel road. It had reached 110 degrees that afternoon, but it was a cool 72 in his limo. The car was parked with the engine running. He was alone in the back seat. His driver waited for his next instruction. Stream's burner phone chirped. It was a text message from Turco. After reading it, he almost threw the phone against the bullet-proof glass partition. That bastard Ironwood, he lamented internally, I should have had him and his geeky pal killed when I had the chance. Hesitating briefly, he smiled and pulled up Travis's number on the phone. "I'll just text a few additions to the plan, that's all," he boasted.

A few minutes later, Neville Stream exited the vehicle and placed the disposable cell phone under the limousine's right-front tire. He returned to the car's interior, slammed the door, and ordered his chauffeur to "drive on." Everything should go as planned now, he decided. But as a little insurance, he'd transfer some of his accounts offshore; the campaign season might get warm after all. He could feel the burner phone crunch under the tire of the limo.

***

Caught up in a frenzy, Ironwood was about to put one foot forward toward the Sikorsky helicopter he arrived in when, looking down, he caught sight of something that made his blood run cold.

The tiles on the tunnel walls glowed, dark lines appeared on their surface pulsing with capillary action, and the shoggoth had returned. It was peering up at him from the base of the ladder with a thousand unblinking eyes. They had run out of time. At that moment, he profoundly wished that one of Cac's Lithium satellite's orbit could have been in line to transmit sooner. He had witnessed the speed at which the thing stalked and fed beforehand; he was confident that his time was up. His woeful expectation met with delay. The shoggoth's star-faced visage projected a tendril from each of its five-points but did not reach out for the professor. Instead, it spread them wide to the sun's rays resembling a Joshua tree. Realizing that further scientific study of the phenomenon did not warrant the additional time, Ironwood ran like hell.

***

Travis loved to kill and torture and do it often. Never could a more suitable job be found for a psychopathic profile. He had just received a text from Mister Money Bags. He added another quarry to their list of targets. "It's double coupon day," he whispered in Dorian's ear. His life, after this, was going to be filled with sunny beaches and awesome recreational drugs. He could almost hear the pounding of the surf.

Getting past the Master at Arms at the Michelson Lab was easy for the two professional killers. They both approached the security officer's dais, pretending to ask for directions in their dress blues.

That was when Dorian sneezed in the officer's face, and Travis popped him on the side of the head with his automatic. The suppressor silencer barely made a noise. Perfectly choreographed moves.

***

"Hot dog!" Cac exclaimed to the empty laboratory, "satellite number two is within our hemisphere. Enterprise to Captain Cac, we are ready to deploy the Space Guard Transmitter," he fantasized. Charles Augustus Chase had set the app for the trigger mechanism to the "D" for drive position on the 65 Mustang shifter attached to the old-fashioned plywood control panel. The honors were initially reserved for the admiral, but now Captain Cac was at the helm.

The double doors to the lab swung in, and Cac watched as two naval officers pointed guns at him. Before he could say a word, they opened fire. The low decibel pops of their 9mm's delivered round after round into the unsuspecting tech's body.

***

A tech named Barkley at the Q-Section had adjusted all the propane jets in the containment cell to full pressure. The shoggoth, the size of a VW Beetle, jumped when engulfed in flames. For the protoplasmic monster, there was no up or down to escape the searing heat. It was cooked down to half its size within a matter of minutes.

A moment later, nothing remained but a golf ball portion of black slime. Q-Section smelled of burnt plastic.

***

Their rules of engagement were simple as usual, leave no one alive and leave no evidence. For Travis, there was one extra rule; Jack Hawkins was to be his. He hated authority figures, and next to assassinating the United States president, the admiral would do just nicely. Travis made Dorian holster his 9mm. He would holster his as well. Travis wanted to do it quick draw style just like they do in the westerns, mano e mano.

Their sugar daddy had sent them an excellent set of plans for the building. Travis had poured over it for hours, memorizing every detail. Walking to the admiral's office was like he had done it a hundred times before. Hawkins' name was displayed on his office door in brass letters. They didn't knock.

When Travis and Dorian opened the door, Hawkins was at his desk writing on some papers. He didn't look up. The jerk doesn't even notice us, probably filling out some stupid reports, Travis sneered. He came closer and couldn't believe it could be this easy. Then Travis realized the admiral was writing with his left hand. He had read his dossier. He wasn't left-handed. He noticed that the admiral's right arm was at his side with an uneasy feeling, and it was under the desk.

The front of Admiral Jack Hawkins's desk exploded, sending a .50

caliber hollow nose slug and coarse splinters of mahogany into Dorian's left knee. He screamed and fell to the carpet holding his leg.

Travis attempted the sought-after "quick draw," he reached for his gun. The large bulk of the admiral rose out of his seat impossibly fast. In the blur of an instant, he watched as the long barrel of a Desert Eagle automatic pistol pointed at his face. When the weapon discharged, the top of Travis's head was blown off.

***

There was blood everywhere. Cac knew it was his. Sinewy strips of fat dangled from his torso, shredded away from his belly and back by the multiple gunshot wounds. He should have been writhing in pain but guessed that one of the bullets probably damaged his spinal cord. Using his arms only, he crawled across the floor, made slippery by his bodily fluids, and reached upwards towards the gray plywood control panel. A bloodied hand took hold of the t-bar Mustang shift lever. Pushing the black thumb button on the top of the bar, he slid it down to the "D" position before collapsing face forward.

***

Just outside the Michelson Lab, a pair of giant steel doors in the pavement opened. The elevator below was activated, and the Space Guard Transmitter rose, unfolding its solar collector. The Fresnel lenses and the ingester juiced up by Cac's quantum processors beamed the energy skyward.

***

Vice Admiral Hawkins rushed around his desk. Travis's blood splatters and brain matter were all over the opposing wall and entry door. Dorian lay curled up on the floor cradling his injured leg to the left of the corpse, crying. Eying Hawkins's approach, he reached for the gun in his shoulder holster. Hawkins stepped a size-thirteen shoe onto the pulp that was once Dorian's knee and pressed down. Dorian screamed and dropped his 9mm. "Don't try it, son," implored the admiral.

Glancing over at his computer monitor, he could see that the hallway to his office was free of any more intruders. The hidden security cameras he installed had Wi-Fi images to his desktop PC.

***

The low orbit Lithium satellite number two was in the proper hemisphere. Its solar-pumped laser redirected the energy beam transmitting it to the predetermined target. A shaft of amplified light from outer space skewered the clouds heading towards its chosen spot on earth.

***

Ironwood started to rest easy as the Sikorsky lifted off. Jason Riggs and Gwen Gilhooley occupied the two seats in front of him. From his window, he could easily see that no one was left behind. He praised God that there had been enough aircraft and ground transportation to evacuate everyone safely away.

They reached an altitude of five-hundred-feet and climbing. Ironwood witnessed a vast cloud of debris eject from the earthen hole. Some of the ground fell in, and a split second later, a shockwave buffeted the helicopter, followed by a loud "thump." The force of the massive explosion was probably more extensive, by comparison than the tiny orifice in the tunnel's ceiling was able to discharge, he decided. No sooner had he completed the assessment when a jet of intense heat erupted from where the hole was, gushing lava over the area that, just a short while ago, they all had occupied.

"What on earth is that?" Gwen asked over the sound of the helicopter's rotors.

"An enormous volcanic vent must have been torn open by your dynamite explosion," he answered. "It is probably filling the tunnel right now with molten fire."

It was apparent that the shoggoth hadn't escaped. There were no sightings of it ever leaving its hole. It was still down there.

Ironwood knew that the fear he had experienced wandering lost through that series of catacomb-like tunnels would stay with him for the rest of his life. He would never forget the creature made from nothing but synthesized matter and putrid slime with multiple eyes that floated freely over its surface, forming limbs whenever it willed. The enormity of the memory wrought unpleasant chills just beneath his skin.

There was a dichotomy, however, because Ironwood also felt sorry for the creature. He was certain now of its origins and its purpose. Solar radiation is light energy from the Sun. Ninety-three million miles from the Earth, it just sits there with all sorts of nuclear reactions going on. Since the beginning of time, it has always been giving off huge amounts of energy and radiation. That was what fueled the shoggoths during the age of the Elder Beings. Pure solar radiation. And that was why this particular synthetic life form never left the tunnel. It couldn't. The tunnels were its home. It is where it worked. It only consumed other organics for fuel when its source, the sun, was cut off.

All the pieces of the puzzle fell into place for the professor. Alan Ward had disclosed that this civilization without any hardware or instruments had willed their artificial life forms into every shape and need. This specific shoggoth, he wanted to shout from the top of the world, had been programmed to be a conveyance, the core of an underground transportation system. If it had pulled any carriages made of conventional materials, they would have crumbled to dust and back into the earth leaving no traces after millions of years. Or maybe the shoggoth transport formed its organic compartments to shuttle its Elder passengers. Given enough time and energy from the sun, we might have witnessed it, he settled. Maybe its strange keening cry was simply the imitation of its master's voice calling out something similar to, "Now leaving on track nine!"

He watched as Gwen put her head on Jason's shoulder. There was a tenderness there that, for their sake, Professor Thomas Ironwood hoped would last a lifetime. Ironwood leaned back in his seat and wondered what Amy Murchison was doing?

***

The Sikorsky helicopter reached a comfortable altitude of two-thousand-feet, turned to the west, and soared towards the setting sun.

ACKNOWLEDGMENTS

Thanks also to my good friend, who wishes to remain anonymous, who spent forty-two years of his life in the service to our country. This gentleman aided with valuable info on U.S. Navy protocol, rankings, uniform code, etc., that greatly enhanced my story's realism.

Finally, I must acknowledge Craig Siefkas, our pro bono tour guide from the Maturango Museum to Little Petroglyph Canyon within the Naval Weapons Center in Ridgecrest, California. Mr. Siefkas supplied accurate data about volcanic vents in the area and CO2 emissions.

Writing this book has been a labor of love, and I hope that I have done some justice to its contributors.

ABOUT THE AUTHOR

Byron Craft started writing screenplays, moved on to authoring articles for several magazines, and finally evolved his writing style into exciting, sci-fi, fantasy, horror novels.

"SHOGGOTH" is Craft's second novel of a planned four novel mythos series that reflects H.P Lovecraft's influence. Byron Craft's first novel, "The CRY of CTHULHU," initially released under the title "The Alchemist's Notebook," was the reincarnation and expansion of one of his most memorable screenplays. Craft demonstrates he is as capable a novelist as a scriptwriter. Craft's novels have all the ingredients of a classic Lovecraft tale, with some imaginative additions.

If you would like to read more about Byron Craft, please visit his website: ByronCraftBooks.com or visit Amazon.com

More books by Byron Craft:

The Mythos Project Series

The CRY of CTHULHU

This novelization of The Cry of Cthulhu film project is about a shell-shocked Vietnam vet, and his wife. They inherit an old country estate in Germany around the time his company transfers him to the same area. The two soon discover that the coincidence is really too good to be true.

Their new home rests near a timeworn door into the earth that is poised to open, exposing all to a horde of four-dimensional beings. Soon the line between our reality and that other space-time will be blurred forever, leaving mankind to be consumed by shrill, shrieking terror. Only one man has the slimmest chance to save our planet and, even though he has no place to hide, he prefers to run. [*Book One*]

SHOGGOTH

An accepted theory exists that millions of years ago a celestial catastrophic occurrence wiped out every living thing on the planet. This theory may be flawed. Fast-forward to the 21st century. A handful of scientists, allied with the military, discover a massive network of tunnels beneath the Mojave Desert. Below, lies an ancient survivor, waiting...and it's hungry! [*Book Two*]

SHOGGOTH 2: RISE OF THE ELDERS

Who creates and controls the shoggoths? For Professor Thomas Ironwood and his heavily armed team, the answer is crucial. The fate of the free world hangs in the balance.

The solution? Return to the tunnels beneath the Mojave Desert, locate a gigantic subterranean vault and unlock the secrets it contains. Deadly primal secrets that lie in wait from a time before human life began!

Byron Craft once again takes us below the earth in this SHOGGOTH sequel enveloping us with tentacles, claws, and mucus glop. A talented fusion of Lovecraftian sci-fi, mystery, fantasy, and horror with a 21st-century twist. *[Book Three]*

R'LYEH: THE LOST REALM

Professor Thomas Ironwood is back! The six-month old child of a Tanist is abducted and taken to R'lyeh—Cthulhu's dimensional prison. When the child 'comes of age' it will open the gateway allowing the malevolent primordial god and its hordes to invade Earth.

Once again the professor musters his team of brave compatriots together in order to rescue the child, on Cthulhu's turf, and save the free world. *[Book Four]*

The Arkham Detective Series

Cthulhu's Minions

A Novelette introducing the Arkham Detective. Cthulhu's Minions are Pilot Demons. Nasty pint-sized legless creatures that crawl on their hands, with razor sharp claws and fangs. The diminutive beings must be stopped before they conduct one of Cthulhu's Old Ones to the back alleys and streets of Arkham, likewise the entire planet. The story takes place during the Great Depression, a spot in time where H. P. Lovecraft and Raymond Chandler could have collaborated. *[Book 1]*

The Innsmouth Look

The second story in the series that brings the detective back, investigating a murder and the kidnapping of a small child, which leads to Innsmouth by the sea, the frightful creatures that lurk there, and what they plan to call up from the depths. *[Book 2]*

The Devil Came to Arkham

Follow the Arkham Detective as he attempts to discover the source of a deadly epidemic. Is it the devil? Is it a Night Gaunt? Or both? Find out when you read about a soul sucking creature that is bent on turning Arkham, Massachusetts into a ghost town. *[Book 3]*

The Dunwich Dungeon

A seven-foot tall man in black has caused the Detective's good friend to go missing. A woman is brutally murdered in a museum, and mysterious artifacts lead us on a trail to inter-dimensional horrors. This time the Arkham Detective is armed to the teeth, and determined to avenge murder with mayhem. *[Book 4]*

Death on the Arkham Express

Ride the rails with this Cthulhu Mythos mystery! The Arkham Detective is back! A well-earned first-class ticket on the train from New York to Arkham, intended as a pleasurable trip, is sidetracked into a grotesque journey. Commuters' heads are bashed in by an invisible assailant and the only law on board is . . . You guessed it; our detective from Arkham. *[Book 5]*

Who Stole the Necronomicon

Wisdom flowers in Arkham—with blunt force trauma. The Arkham Detective, now a private investigator, shadows the biggest theft ever to hit Arkham, Massachusetts. Someone stole the Book of the Dead, and a series of gruesome murders leave a trail to the ruins of the old Witch House; a place known for its hauntings and an unsolved homicide.

Victims are left with fist-size gaping holes torn through their bodies. Our detective from Arkham is the only one capable of tracking down the culprits and the unearthly. Tasked with not only finding out the "who," he needs to find out the "why?". *[Book 6]*

ANTHOLOGY CONTRIBUTIONS:

Cthulhu Attacks! BOOK 2: THE FAITH

The final act! Cthulhu walks the land. It's killing everything on Earth; instant death for billions, trillions of life forms. An apocalyptic force of shoggoths is at the forefront of the Old One's advance. A ragtag group scrambles to fight back in a last-ditch effort to salvage the remnants of humanity. Read on, if you have the courage!

Time Loopers: Four Tales from a Time War

Get rich. Wield incredible power. Get revenge. But avoid paradox, or get erased from the time-stream so you never existed. Time travel offers endless possibilities and limitless dangers. What would you do if you could go back and relive your past? What if others could too? Who polices time? How do you win a time war?

Four tales from a time war by veteran science fiction authors: David Hambling, Byron Craft, Matt Davenport, and John DeLaughter.

Keep reading for an excerpt from Byron Craft's
The CRY of CTHULHU

The CRY of CTHULHU

Warning

The statute of limitations has run out. What I stole from Miskatonic University, they still want back. They want to hide the truth.

The theft of what the news media called the "Alchemist's Papers" was made public in January of 1984 but the cover-up that followed, and the failed attempt to retrieve them, left the story only half told. The truth is a fold in the soft and otherwise smooth surface of time. It is a harbinger of evil so destructive that the current state of the world, plagued by terrorism and economic chaos, would only be a footnote in history by comparison.

The tabloids had a heyday with the story, claiming apocalyptic doom, while the mainstream media labeled it as another crackpot interpretation of the "Book of Revelations." Neither were accurate. Miskatonic University of Arkham, Massachusetts had done an effective job of discrediting the papers and me, and until now, no one would publish them.

The one piece of information that they were unable to keep from the public was the existence of a covert organization within the university itself. We were a group of select scholars who investigated what appeared to be supernatural occurrences worldwide. It was alleged that during some of these investigations, the group had acted like vigilantes, taking the law into their own hands, passing out judgment where they saw fit.

My name is Thomas Ironwood. I was a resident professor at Miskatonic and head of the Physics Department. I was a group member, known then, to only a few, as the "Mythos Department." My confessions to the press were not out of remorse for any wrongdoing, rather as a revolt against my colleagues who were becoming dangerously lax in their retaliatory measures.

I believed then, and believe even more today, that Faren and Janet Church's individual stories, and Faren's great Uncle Heinrich Todesfall, constitute a warning to an already endangered world and should not be suppressed. The rampant ignorance in the world has left me no alternative but to come out of hiding and go public with the documents.

The plausibility of our planet being threatened by an ageless horror may automatically arouse suspicion to the authenticity of the following chronicles and possibly create a backlash from the more serious elites in the media. How Miskatonic acquired the papers may be questioned. Why hide them if they are only a hoax?

The chronicles are authentic. They required some editing to clarify the timelines. The account's original forms were a journal, a diary, and a series of tape recordings. They have been edited into separate narratives, subsequently breaking the work down into four parts.

With my publisher's help, we have struck out redundancies that often occur in personal journals and eliminated digressions that the elderly Todesfall was guilty of doing when his mind would stray from the story and wander unchecked into the intervening years. Faren Church's was the least polished of the narratives because his hasty account was left on tape and required more extensive editing.

For the remainder, we have left well enough alone. The chronicles accurately tell the whole story without additional enhancement.

***

PART ONE
THE SCHLOSS

From Janet Church's Diary

I am almost out of Valium, only one more pill left. The stress is beginning to get the best of me. The tranquilizer is the only thing that has made life bearable for me these last few days. I wonder now what will happen next, if they will come for me after the drug runs out, or if I will be allowed to numb my last few minutes.

They won't come close to the schloss now. I have the lights burning in every room. I even have the oil lamp I found going, and every candle I could lay my hands on is lit.

They won't come this minute. They won't come until the mist hides the stars and the moon.

Dear God! I am not even sure who they are!

***

This evening, the mist rolled up from the hollow and engulfed the schloss and beyond. It moved across the road, lingering in low spots and ditches until the milky vapor covered the entire countryside. It spreads throughout the thick woods for miles, and on humid nights, such as this, it has often reached as far as Valsbach.

The countryside surrounding the house, even on the brightest days, is desolate and foreboding. Now, at dusk, the twilight lends the field behind our house a strangeness that sets it apart from the rest of the area. It suggests a watchful malevolence to the ancient trees, to the descending marshes with their thousands of chirping insects and the incessant croaking of frogs, to the timeworn and vine-covered stone walls pressing in upon the perimeter of the old estate, closing in on our home as if intent upon holding me fast.

Thick vapors from the hollow swirl and eddy about the schloss and the room in which I sit fills with moisture. The fog ascends in spirals from beneath the door, and its long, wet fingers creep across the carpet with caressing strokes.

Crowning a grassy summit, whose sides are wooded near its base with gnarled trees of the black forest, stands the old home of my husband's ancestors. For centuries, its lofty tiled roofs and tower have looked down upon the rugged countryside. The exact age of the house is not known. I guess its roots must go back centuries before the beginnings of the Church family line. I know very little about the family lineage not being a Church by blood, only by marriage.

The villagers say the ancient house has always been here. They tend to be superstitious and sometimes given to fanciful tales. One teller of these stories is a homeless old woman who makes her living sifting through the back alleys and dumpsters in town. Her name is Ilsedore Hulse, and she is probably the oldest living resident of Valsbach.

Once when I was able to get her alone and ask about my husband's ancestry, she confided in me that the house had a blackened past and that "evil still prevailed there as sure as the trees of the Black Forest have leaves and the creatures that dwell there have eyes." She summed up our meeting by informing me in a dramatically lowered voice that the old house was there even when her great-great-grandmother was a child.

Superstition plays a vital role with these people, and their fears can be justified living in an isolated area far from anywhere you, and I would consider mainstream. I can excuse their actions; their attitude towards us, however, is less than tolerable. It did not take me long to accept the shunned indifference by the shopkeepers and townspeople.

What I did consider strange is the lack of visitors to the surrounding area of the schloss. Travelers seldom enter the woods that border our property, and none come within walking distance of the old house.

I have never seen any wild animals on our property. If there are any, the woodland creatures are probably wise because the overall aspect of the region would give anyone the impression of leering death. The ancient lightning-scarred trees seem unnaturally large and twisted, and the other vegetation abnormally thick and feverish, while curious mounds and hummocks in the weedy, pitted field behind our house remind me of snakes and burial plots.

The strain is critical now, by tonight, I am afraid that if my husband does not return home . . . I will be murdered.

The woods appear to close in tighter about this lonely house.

***

Damn it, where is Faren? He better get here soon.

I have to remain calm. I won't end up screaming into the night.

I'll start at the beginning. The record must be complete. I'll tell you about my husband. I'll tell you about Boston, Chicago, and New York before receiving the telegram, and I'll tell you about this place.

I met Faren while still living with my parents in Ipswich, which is in Essex County, Massachusetts. At the time, I was in the midst of making what I thought were two very important decisions. One, should I keep pursuing a major in art history and, two, how to clear up my complexion when an old Dodge van lumbered down the street and died in front of our house. "Bring our boys home" and "Impeach Johnson" was painted on its side in day-glow colors.

The sound of the ancient motor in its final death throes was followed by the driver's door slamming. A moment later, the hood was violently flung up, and amidst the fury of clanking tools and sharp cursing, a full head of tightly curled hair shot out.

"Have you got a piece of wire?" he shouted. Then he added impatiently, "A bobby pin, a shoelace, anything? Don't just stand there; I have to strap this distributor cap down; I've got to be in Chicago tomorrow."

I wore my hair down and with a headband in those days, and although I knew I didn't look like I had just come from a hardware store, I felt embarrassed that I hadn't and blurted, "I'm wearing sandals."

His blue eyes looked right inside of me, and then he cracked a smile on one side of his face and said, "Hey, what's your name?"

I was back in junior high again asked to go steady for the first time in my life. The sensation shot through me; I became flushed; I am sure he picked up on it because he relaxed some, and with a broader smile, stepped forward, wiping his hands on an oil-stained rag.

"I'm Faren. Faren Church. You still haven't told me yours."

It didn't take us long to get acquainted. I was able to get the required length of wire from my dad's garage, and in the time it took him to make the repairs on the van, he was off, and I went with him.

Made in the USA
Las Vegas, NV
08 July 2024

92036354R00197